Nicola Cornick became fascinated by history when she was a child and spent hours poring over historical novels and watching costume drama. She studied history at university and wrote her Master's thesis on heroes. When she isn't writing she works as a guide for the National Trust in a seventeenth-century house. Nicola loves to hear from readers and can be contacted by e-mail at ncornick@madasafish.com and via her website at www.nicolacornick.co.uk

NICOLA CORNICK

Kidnapped

M&B™ and M&B™ with the Rose Device
are trademarks of the publisher.

First published in Great Britain 2009
Harlequin Mills & Boon Limited, Eton House, 18-24 Paradise Road,
Richmond, Surrey, TW9 1SR

© Nicola Cornick 2009

ISBN: 978 0 263 87536 2

11-1009

Printed in Great Britain
by Clays Ltd, St Ives plc

AUTHOR NOTE

A few years ago my mother-in-law gave me an ancient copy of Robert Louis Stevenson's classic novel, *Kidnapped*, as a birthday present. I had read and enjoyed the book many years before and now I picked it up again and was plunged into a world of romance and intrigue and adventure. When I finished it I thought how exciting it would be to write my own version, inspired by the original, and so the idea of *Kidnapped* was born. My husband's family are Scots and we visit the Scottish Highlands every year so I used all the places I know and love as the setting for my book. Writing a book set in Scotland was such a thrill that I definitely plan to write a sequel!

I hope that you enjoy *Kidnapped,* which is a homage to both Robert Louis Stevenson's wonderful story and to Scotland, one of the most beautiful countries on earth.

To Elspeth and Sheila, the original Miss Bennies and so much nicer than their fictional counterparts!

Chapter One

In which I meet the hero, as all good heroines should.

My name is Catriona Balfour and this is the story of my adventures. I will begin on a certain afternoon early in the month of July in the year 1802, when I buried my father in the graveyard at Applecross, beside the sea. I was eighteen years old.

A melancholy beginning, perhaps. Truth is, it had been a melancholy year. My mother had been taken a bare two months before, carried off by a fever brought to the village by a travelling peddler who came selling ribbons and buckles, gloves and scarves. My mother had bought a length of muslin for a new summer gown. When she died the pattern was only half made.

I stood by my father's fresh-turned grave and thought that at the least he had a fine view. The curve of the bay was before us, in all its harebell-blue beauty. Beyond it, across the shining water, were the jagged tops of the mountains of Skye. The air was soft that summer morning, and smelled of salt and seaweed. The sun was warm on my back and my best black bombazine dress—dreadfully disfiguring—crackled when I moved, the material so stiff that the gown would have stood up on its own. I admit it—even as I stood there, hazy with grief, I was aware of the ugliness of that dress and I was ashamed of myself. Ashamed that on the day of my father's funeral I could be thinking of fashion and wishing for a silver gauze scarf from Edinburgh, perhaps, or a pair of soft kid slippers.

'The child is vain, madam,' Mrs Mansell, the housekeeper, had said to my mother all those years ago, when I was eight and she had found me standing before the

mirror trying my mother's Sunday best bonnet. 'Take
the rod to her before it is too late.'

But my mother liked pretty things herself and instead
of beating me she wrapped me in a scented hug and
whispered that I looked very fine. I remember smiling
triumphantly at Mrs Mansell over my mother's shoulder.
Her thin mouth turned down at the corners and she
muttered that I would come to a bad end. But perhaps
she was only envious because she had a face like a prune
and no one to love her since Mr Mansell had passed
away, and possibly he had not loved her anyway.

My mother *was* warm and loving, and my father too,
doting on her and on me, their only child. He was the
schoolmaster at Applecross and had taught me my
lessons from the age of three. As a result I was the only
young lady in the Highlands who could plot a mathematical course by the stars, or who knew the botanical
names of all the plants that grew thick by the burn. The
squire's daughters, Miss Bennie and Miss Henrietta
Bennie, giggled and said that such knowledge would
not help me catch a husband. They spent their days
playing the spinet or painting in watercolours, whilst I

grew sunburnt red helping Old Davie set his crab pots, or walking by the sea without my parasol.

The Miss Bennies were present at the funeral that morning, standing with the squire and his wife a little apart from the rest of us. Of the other mourners present, we were split into a group of villagers and a separate small enclave of my father's academic colleagues, who had travelled from Edinburgh to pay their respects. I was touched that they had held Papa in such high esteem as to make the journey. Sir Compton Bennie's face was grave as he looked down at the coffin. He and my father had shared the occasional glass of malt whisky and game of cards. That had been to the disapproval of his wife. Lady Bennie was a woman very conscious of rank and consequence, and she had not considered the poor schoolmaster worth cultivating. I once heard her refer to me as 'that fey, ill-favoured child' when I was about six years of age, and it was true that I had been thin as a rake then, with tangled red-golden hair and a challenging expression in my blue eyes that my father had always commented was fierce enough to scare the wolves away.

There had not been wolves at Applecross for more than a half century now, and I hoped that time had also filled out my figure a little, smoothed the wayward curl of my hair and softened the fierceness in my expression. I was no longer as ill favoured as I had been as a child, although there was nothing I could do about the firm, determined lines of my cheek and chin, the fairness of my eyelashes or the unfashionable freckles that were not only scattered across my face but also sprinkled over the rest of my body. My hair was as thick and springy as the heather, and grief had turned me gaunt. I knew I was no beauty. I did not need the pink and gold prettiness of the Miss Bennies to point it out to me.

I noticed that today Lady Bennie was wearing her second best black gown, thereby conferring on the event precisely the right degree of importance; as first lady of the district it was her duty to attend, but despite the fact that she dabbed her eyes most prettily with her black-edged kerchief I knew it was all for display. The Miss Bennies had not the skill of their mother. Their boredom was plain to see as they fretted and fidgeted and even whispered under cover of the minister's words.

'Ashes to ashes...'

I threw a handful of earth onto the coffin and it rattled on the top. Tears made my throat ache.

'Dust to dust...'

Poor Papa. There had been so many things that he had still wanted to do. I felt so angry that he had been denied the chance. Someone, somewhere in the congregation, stifled a sob. Applecross folk were not the sort to cry, but my father, David Balfour, had been well loved. I had not needed to pay way mourners to attend his funeral, as Sir Compton Bennie was rumoured to have done when *his* father had passed away. But then Sir Compton's father had sided with the English in the harrying of the Highlands fifty years before, and people here had long memories...

'Come, Catriona...' The service was over and Mr Campbell, the minister, took my arm to guide me down the path to the lych gate. I paused for a moment, gazing at the raw scar of the grave. Douglas, the gravedigger, was leaning on his spade, impatient to be finished there. I looked down on my father's coffin and for a moment felt a desolation so vast, so terrifying, that I had to push it away, because I was afraid my mind would disintegrate under the pain of it.

I was an orphan.

I had no money.

I had no home.

Mr and Mrs Campbell had broken this news to me the previous night, gently, over a beaker of milk laced with whisky to help me sleep. Since my father's death I had been staying at the manse because it had not been seemly for me, a young woman, to continue to live alone in the schoolmaster's house. What I had not realised, though, was that I was never to return there. The house belonged to the Charity of St Barnabas, which had employed my father. The trustees had already arranged for a new schoolmaster to come from Inverness to fill the vacancy. He and his wife and young family were expected any day soon. It seemed like unseemly haste to me, but then the charity were efficient, and did not wish the children of Applecross to have an unofficial holiday for longer than need be.

The trustees of St Barnabas had not been ungenerous. They had paid the funeral expenses, and had also sent Mr Campbell the sum of five pounds 'to provide for the daughter of the late schoolmaster.' I was bitter; I thought how fortunate it was for the trustees that my mother had died a few months before, thereby sparing them the necessity of paying a further ten pounds for his widow. Mr Campbell had reproved me when I had said this, but he had done it kindly, because he knew I was miserable. But to me it seemed that my father was a footnote: recorded in the charity's ledgers, then swept aside, dismissed, forgotten. *Deceased.* I could imagine them drawing a thick line in black ink under his name.

We were to go to the schoolmaster's house for the last time now, to attend the wake.

The old path down from the churchyard was uneven, the stone cobbles grown thick with moss. Out in the bay the seabirds wheeled and soared, calling their wild cry. The sun was hot and it made my head ache. I wanted to seek the cool darkness of the shadows and hide away, to think about my parents on my own. I did not want to have to share my memories of them, or stand in the stone-flagged parlour of my old home feeling that I was a stranger there now as I made polite conversation with the mourners.

We reached the garden gate. Mr Campbell and I were at the head of an untidy straggle. Immediately behind us were the Bennies. Lady Bennie was accustomed to going first into all the drawing rooms in the county. I reflected that it had taken the death of my father to get her to concede precedence to me. It was never likely to happen again.

A little muted conversation had broken out behind us as we walked, but suddenly it hushed so quickly that I was pulled out of my self-absorption. I felt Mr Campbell stiffen with surprise, and for a moment his step faltered. Then a man came forward from the shadow of the garden gate and stopped before us. He was in the uniform of the King's Royal Navy, and the austerity of the costume suited his tall figure well.

He knew it, too. He carried himself with an unhurried self-assurance, and there was an arrogant tilt to his head and a gleam in his eyes—eyes that were so dark that their expression was inscrutable.

I sensed rather than saw the Misses Bennie shift and

bob behind me, like the tall poppies that grew by the roadside in high summer. They were positively begging for his notice. I raised my chin and met the dark gaze of the stranger very directly.

The air was suddenly still between us. Somewhere far away, in the furthest recesses of my body, my heart skipped a beat, and then carried on as though nothing had happened.

'Mr Sinclair,' Mr Campbell said, and I heard a tiny shade of uncertainty in his voice. 'We did not expect—'

The stranger had not taken his eyes from me, and now he removed his hat and bowed. He was young— perhaps five or six and twenty. The sunlight fell on his thick, dark hair and burnished it the blue black of a magpie's wing.

'Magpies are dangerous thieves,' my father had once said when we were discussing the ornithology of the British Isles. 'They are clever and reckless and untrustworthy.'

It was strange to remember that now.

The man had taken my hand. I had definitely not offered it, and I wondered how on earth he had possessed himself of it. He wore no gloves, and I was conscious that the inexpert darning on mine would be all too evident to his touch. I tried to pull away.

He held me fast.

This was most improper. There was a glimmer of amusement in his eyes now that made me feel as though the sun beating down on my bonnet was far too hot.

'Miss Balfour,' he said, 'please permit me to introduce myself and to offer my deepest sympathy on your loss. My name is Neil Sinclair.'

His voice was very smooth and mellow, like a caress.

There was a gasp behind me. The Miss Bennies were not good at dissembling their feelings. I sensed that in that moment they would almost have been happy to be attending their *own* father's funeral if it had entailed an introduction to this man. But he was not looking at them. He was looking at me.

And that was how I met Neil Sinclair, Master of Ross and heir to the Earl of Strathconan.

Chapter Two

In which I hear of my long-lost family.

It was late. The funeral supper was eaten, the casks of ale had run dry and the schoolmaster's house was scoured clean, locked and barred once more against the arrival of its new owner. I had worked my fingers to the bone to tidy up after our guests; anything to block out the cold sense of loss that threatened to break me.

Now there was no more to do, and I stood in the gardens for the last time and breathed in the heady scent of the roses my mother had coaxed to grow against the sheltered southern wall. Across the village green the lamps were lit in the manse, and the moths were bumping against the windows, trying to get to the light. The sea was calm and its sighing was a muted *hush* on the sand. The evening was sapphire-blue, with a half moon rising, and very peaceful, though cooler now that the sun had gone.

I crossed the green and let myself into the manse by the back door. The house was very quiet, but from Mr Campbell's study came the sound of voices. I had no taste for company that night, and I was about to go past and seek the comfort of my room when Mrs Campbell came around the curve of the passageway. Her face warmed into a smile of relief to see me.

'There you are, Catriona! Mr Campbell was asking for you.'

I sighed inwardly. I knew that Neil Sinclair was with Mr Campbell, and I had no wish to seek his further acquaintance. After he had greeted me he had spent the rest of my father's wake talking with Sir Compton Bennie and with Mr Campbell, and I still had no notion as to what he was doing here. Occasionally I had felt him watching me across the room, and had glanced up to meet the same speculative interest in his dark eyes that I had seen when we first met. I had no experience with men but I sensed that his interest had little or nothing to do with me as a woman. Instead I suspected that he knew something about me and was measuring me in some way, assessing my character. For some reason this annoyed me.

I knocked on the study door and went in, Mrs Campbell following me. The minister was seated at his desk, with Mr Sinclair in a chair beside the fire with a glass of the finest malt whisky on the table beside him. He looked up when I came in. He had a thin, watchful face, tanned a dark brown from sea and sun—a face with character and resolution in the line of his jaw. I gave him a cool nod, which seemed to amuse him, and addressed myself to Mr Campbell.

'You wished to see me, sir?'

I spoke very politely but I saw the flash in Mr Sinclair's eyes that suggested he thought this obedience out of character. A faint smile curled the corner of his firm mouth. I turned a shoulder to him.

'Catriona…Yes…' Mr Campbell seemed flustered, which was unusual to see. He gestured me to the long sofa. This piece of furniture was the most uncomfortable in the house, and necessitated me to sit upright as though I were a bird perched on a twig. This did nothing to improve my temper, especially as Mr Sinclair seemed deliberately to lounge back indolently in his chair with a sigh of contentment as he sipped his whisky and watched me over the brim of the glass.

Mrs Campbell had followed me in, and now hastened to see to her visitor's comfort. 'You have had sufficient to eat and drink, Mr Sinclair? May I fetch you anything else?'

I watched the gentleman smile his thanks and put Mrs Campbell at her ease. He had a very easy charm. I could not deny it. When Mrs Campbell went out again her face was flushed peony-pink, like a young girl's.

'Well, now,' Mr Campbell said, shuffling the papers on his desk, 'there are matters to be settled, Catriona. Matters to do with your future. You know that Mrs Campbell and I love you as though you were our own daughter, but I have been thinking that now your parents have passed on the natural place for you is with your remaining relatives.'

I assumed that he meant my mother's family, who lived far, far away on the south coast of England. My mother had made a scandalous match twenty years before when, as a young debutante, she had visited Edinburgh, fallen in love with my father, a poor schoolmaster, and eloped with him. Her family had cast her out after that, and I had absolutely no intention of going to them cap in hand now, when they had ignored my existence for eighteen years.

'Can I not stay here, sir?' I asked. 'Here in Applecross, I mean,' I added, in case poor Mr Campbell had thought I was suggesting I should live on his charity indefinitely. I knew it must be a wrench for him to speak of my going, for it was true that not only was he my godfather but he and Mrs Campbell had cherished me like their own.

'I could work for a living,' I added. 'Perhaps I could help the new schoolmaster, or act as companion to old Miss Blois…'

Mr Sinclair smothered what sounded suspiciously like a snort. I looked at him.

'I beg your pardon, sir?' I said frigidly.

There was laughter in his eyes. 'Forgive me, Miss Balfour,' he said, 'but I cannot see you as companion to an elderly lady. Nor as a schoolmistress, for that matter.'

I set my lips in a thin line. I did not see what business it was of his. 'You do not know me very well, Mr Sinclair,' I said. 'My father taught me himself, having no prejudice against the education of females. I can teach reading, and I write a very fair hand, and I am learned in mathematics and astronomy and philosophy and...' I ran out of breath in my indignation.

'I do not quarrel with your father's abilities as a tutor,' Mr Sinclair said lazily, 'nor indeed with yours as a scholar, Miss Balfour. I am sure you are most accomplished. It is simply that I have seen no evidence that you have the temperament required to do the job of schoolteacher yourself. Would it not require patience and tolerance and composure, amongst other things?'

I was so angry at his presumption that I almost burst there and then. 'Well, I do not see it is any concern of yours—' I began crossly, but Mr Campbell made a slight movement and I subsided, holding fast to the fraying shreds of my temper.

'It would not serve, Catriona,' he said. 'Applecross is a small place and it is time for you to go out into the world—the sooner the better. I have already had three requests from gentlemen for your hand in marriage, and have no desire to be turning more away from my door.'

I was astonished. Not one single gentleman had approached *me* with a view to marriage, and I could not imagine who could have asked Mr Campbell for permission to pay their addresses to me. I stared at him in puzzlement.

'Who on earth…?'

Mr Campbell ticked them off on his fingers. 'McGough, who farms up beyond Loch Ailen, young Angus the shepherd and Mr Lefroy of Callanish.'

This time there was no doubt that Neil Sinclair was laughing. His shoulders were positively shaking. I tried to ignore him whilst inside me the anger seethed at his discourtesy.

'McGough has buried three wives already,' I said,

'young Angus is kind, but a mere lad, and Mr Lefroy wants a housekeeper he does not have to pay for.'

'A wife is more expensive than a housekeeper in the long run,' Mr Sinclair observed casually.

I swung around and glared at him. 'Do you know that for a fact, sir?'

His dark eyebrows went up. 'Not from personal experience, madam,' he drawled, 'but I do know on the strength of a few hours' acquaintance that you would no more make a biddable wife than you would a suitable lady's companion.'

We looked at one another for what seemed like a very long time, whilst the air fizzed between us and all the discourteous, unladylike and plain rude things that I wanted to say to Mr Sinclair jostled for space in my head. I could see a distinct spark of challenge in his eyes as though he was saying, *Do you wish to quarrel further, Miss Balfour? You need only say the word...*

Then Mr Campbell cleared his throat.

'Which is nothing to the purpose, Catriona, since your papa, when he knew he was dying, wrote to his relatives at Glen Clair to ask that they offer you a home.'

Mr Sinclair shifted in his chair. 'It is all arranged. I am here to escort you to Sheildaig on the morrow, Miss Balfour. Your uncle will send a carriage to collect you from the inn there.'

For the second time in the space of as many minutes I was silent with shock. How could Papa have arranged such a thing without telling me? Who was this uncle and his family of whom I had heard nothing until this moment, and why should they, who were strangers to me, wish to give me a home? Most importantly, how could it *all be arranged* when this was the first that I had heard of it?

I took a deep breath and, ignoring Mr Sinclair completely, addressed myself to the minister.

'I beg your pardon, sir,' I said carefully, 'but you find me completely amazed. I did not know my father had any relatives in the world, let alone that they would be prepared to give me a home.'

Mr Campbell was now looking even more uncomfortable, and Mr Sinclair positively bored. He sighed, toying with the whisky in his glass, swirling it around and around. One lock of dark hair had fallen across his brow, giving him an even more rakish air. No doubt my amazement at the discovery of my long-lost family was of little consequence to him, and any attempt at explanation would be terribly tedious for him to endure. He had graciously offered to escort me—for what reason I was still unsure—and his attitude implied that it was my duty to be grateful for his condescension. I reflected that I was fast coming to find Mr Sinclair one of the most objectionable men of my limited acquaintance.

Mr Campbell rubbed his head, setting the sparse strands of hair awry. 'Truth to tell, Catriona,' he confided, 'I scarcely know more myself. When your father was sick he gave me a certain letter and asked me to send it to Glen Clair. He said that it was to do with your inheritance. He asked that as soon as he was gone, the furniture disposed of and the house taken back by the charity trustees, I should send you to the Old House at Glen Clair and to your uncle, Ebeneezer Balfour.' Here Mr Campbell looked hopefully at Mr Sinclair. 'Perhaps you have something to add here, sir?'

Mr Sinclair shrugged his broad shoulders—carelessly, I thought. 'I fear I cannot help you, sir,' he said.

'I am come to escort Miss Balfour as a favour to her uncle. That is all I know.'

I looked from one to the other. 'My father never mentioned that he had a brother,' I said. 'All these years I never knew he had any family other than my mother and myself. I do not like to find such matters settled when I have had no say in them.'

Mr Sinclair looked at me. 'You are familiar with the expression that beggars cannot be choosers, Miss Balfour?'

I glared at him. 'Mr Sinclair, I do not believe you are contributing anything useful to this situation at all.'

'Only a means of transport,' Neil Sinclair agreed affably.

Mr Campbell settled his spectacles more firmly on his nose. 'Family is always to be cherished,' he murmured. 'I know of the Balfours of Glen Clair, of course, but had no notion that your father was related. The Balfours were a great family once. Before the forty-five rebellion.'

'You mean they were Jacobites?' I asked, and for a moment it seemed that the very word caused the lamplight to grow dim and the shadows to flicker with secrets.

'Aye.' Mr Campbell looked grave. 'They suffered reprisals for their loyalty.'

Mr Sinclair shifted, and I remembered that he was a Navy man in the service of King George III. The enemy was Napoleon and the French now, not the English, and the old days were long gone. Nevertheless, something in my Highland blood stirred at the old loyalties.

'These days,' Mr Sinclair said, 'the Balfours are as poor as church mice, mistress. There will be no inheritance waiting for you at Glen Clair.'

I smarted that he might think me so shallow that all I cared for was a fortune—although if I were being completely honest a few hundred pounds would not have gone amiss. But I sat up a little straighter and said, 'If I have found a family I did not know existed then that will be more than enough for me, Mr Sinclair.'

I thought the sentiment rather fine, and was annoyed that he smothered a grin in his whisky glass, as though to say that I was a foolish chit who knew nothing of what I was talking about.

'We shall see,' he said cryptically.

I stood up. I had had about enough of Mr Sinclair's

company for one evening. 'If you will excuse me, sir?' I said to Mr Campbell.

'Of course,' he murmured. His tired blue eyes sought mine and I realised then what an unlooked for responsibility I was to him. He had taken me in out of Christian kindness, love for me and friendship to my late father, but he and Mrs Campbell were getting old, and though they would never say it, they could not want the burden of a eighteen-year-old hoyden.

'I will go and pack my bags,' I said. 'And I do thank you, sir, for I know that you always have my well-being at heart.'

It would take me little enough time to pack, in all conscience. I had barely a change of clothes and the few books that my father had left me.

Mr Campbell looked relieved. 'Of course, child. I'll bid you goodnight. I think,' he added, and I wished there had not been such uncertainty in his tone, 'that you are doing the right thing, Catriona. Mrs Campbell will accompany you as far as the inn at Sheildaig, under Mr Sinclair's escort.'

Mr Sinclair said nothing at all, but there was a

sardonic gleam in his dark eyes that I disliked intensely. He stood up politely as I left the room, and I felt his gaze on me, but I refused to look at him.

I went up the curving stair of the manse to the little room Mrs Campbell had given me on the first floor. My belongings, scattered untidily about the place, looked suddenly meagre and a little pathetic. This was all I had in the world, and soon I was to turn away from all things familiar and go to a family I did not know I had at a tumbledown house in Glen Clair. For a moment I felt a mixture of terror and loneliness, and then my common sense reasserted itself. Glen Clair was only two days away—which was fortunate, since I had no wish to be in company with Neil Sinclair any longer than I must—and I could always return to Applecross if matters did not work out for me. It was not the end of the world.

Nevertheless it felt close to the end of everything as I packed away my spare petticoat and my embroidered shawl, a few books and some sheet music, and the blue and white striped tooth mug that had been my father's. I sat down rather abruptly on the narrow bed and had to take several deep breaths to calm myself when once again grief grabbed my throat and squeezed like a vice.

I slept badly that night, which was no great surprise, and in the morning awoke to find the house abuzz. A quick breakfast of milk and wheat cakes awaited me in the kitchen, and Mr Sinclair's carriage was already at the door. I had barely time to snatch a mouthful of food and to hug Mr Campbell in thanks and farewell before it was time to go out to where Mr Sinclair awaited to escort me to my new life.

Chapter Three

In which I set out upon my journey to the house of Glen Clair, and Mr Sinclair behaves as no gentleman should.

It was uncomfortable being in an enclosed carriage with Mr Sinclair. The carriage itself was not uncomfortable, of course, being from the stables of the Earl of Strathconan himself. It had dark blue velvet seats with fat cushions, and was well sprung to protect us from the jolts and ruts of the road. No, it was only Mr Sinclair's company that felt so unwelcome on that bright summer day.

I was acutely aware of his physical presence within the enclosed space. It felt as though he was too close to me in some mysterious way I had not experienced with anyone before. Strange, because he was sitting at a perfectly respectable distance from me, and Mrs Campbell was there as well, as the most irreproachable chaperon. Occasionally, when the coach would lurch over a particularly bad hole in the road, his leg would brush against mine and I would move the skirts of my second best gown away, much to his apparent amusement. On one occasion the carriage pitched so hard that I was almost unseated, and Mr Sinclair reached out to grab me before I tumbled onto the floor. His hands were hard on my upper arms as he caught me, and for a dizzy moment he was so close to me that I could smell the scent of his skin and the lime cologne he wore. My head spun in a very peculiar way. I know I turned very pink and I know that he observed it. He placed me back on the seat with absolute propriety, and then ruined it by giving me a look that was not remotely proper and made my blood burn. I knew that he was only doing it to disconcert me, and not because he had the least admiration for me, and this annoyed me all the more.

Mrs Campbell certainly did not seem to share my dislike of Mr Sinclair. Indeed, as the journey progressed it seemed to me that Mr Sinclair's company was the only thing that made the whole thing tolerable from her point of view, for she hated to travel and had never been further than Inverness in her life. The two of them chatted away easily, about the weather and the state of the roads and the journey time between Applecross and Glen Clair, whilst I sat in my corner and wondered how a man like Mr Sinclair could get away with charming the chaperons into thinking he was not remotely dangerous.

It was another beautiful day. As the carriage climbed the track out of the village I watched the turquoise sea tumbling on the rocks far below and the black silhouette of the Cuillins of Skye against the sun. The air was full of the scent of gorse and hot summer grass. Presently I realised that Neil Sinclair was addressing me and withdrew my attention from the scenery with reluctance.

'I beg your pardon, sir?'

'I was asking, Miss Balfour, whether you had travelled much in the past?'

'I have been to Edinburgh with my father on several occasions, sir,' I said, 'and I have sailed to Skye and the other islands more times than I can recall.'

'And are you a good sailor?'

I saw Mrs Campbell nod a chaperon's encouragement at this blameless conversation.

'No, sir,' I said. 'I was sick in a bucket on all but one occasion, when the sea was as flat as a mirror.'

Mrs Campbell frowned.

'Are you a good sailor, Mr Sinclair?' I enquired. 'One would hope so, since you are in the Royal Navy.'

Neil Sinclair smiled without mockery for the first time—a real smile that reached his eyes and made my heart jump, and almost made me forget that I disliked him.

'No, Miss Balfour, I am not,' he said. 'I, too, was sick as a dog on my first few voyages, but unfortunately there was no bucket to hand.'

I smiled, too. 'You said that you know my uncle, sir,' I said, on impulse. 'What manner of man is he?'

Mr Sinclair was silent for so long that I started to feel nervous. 'Your uncle is a dour man,' he said at last. 'You'll have little conversation out of him, mistress.'

That was not encouraging. 'And my aunt?' I asked, wondering if I wanted to know the answer.

'Mrs Balfour suffers from her nerves,' Mr Sinclair said.

I did not really understand such a complaint, having not a sensitive nerve in my body, or so I had been told. Lady Bennie, who suffered from nerves herself, mostly when Sir Compton spent time with his mistress in Inverness, had commented sourly on my lack of sensibility on more than one occasion.

'Oh dear,' I said. 'And my cousin Ellen?'

Mr Sinclair smiled. 'Miss Balfour is delightful,' he said.

I felt an unexpected rush of jealousy and wished I had not asked.

The conversation waned. Mr Sinclair seemed disinclined to speak any further of my relatives, and I was sufficiently discouraged to think of my dour uncle and delicate aunt that I did not persist in my questioning. It did not sound as though a very warm welcome awaited me at Glen Clair, and I wondered once again why they had offered to take me in.

That night we stopped at the inn in Sheildaig, a building of whitewashed stone on the harbour. The bed-chambers were clean and the linen fresh, if threadbare. I wanted to open the window, because the room felt stuffy and unaired, but when I pushed the creaking casement open the smell of gutted fish blew in and over-whelmed me. It takes a great deal to put me off my food—grief had certainly increased rather than dimin-ished my appetite—but the rotten fish smell almost robbed me of any. I washed and went down to the parlour, where I took a little bread and cheese for supper and then retired for the evening. Mrs Campbell seemed relieved to see me go, for I think she was exhausted from a day's travel on poor roads. Mr Sinclair got politely to his feet and came to the bottom of the stairs with me to light my candle, then wished me a goodnight.

A thunderstorm was brewing as I prepared for bed, the wind rising from the west battering the eaves and whistling through the cracks in the windowframe. When I was undressed to my shift and petticoats I did not immediately get into the bed, but sat on the window seat with my elbows on the sill. The stinking harbour was in darkness now, and the view was a deal more appealing than the smell had been. Half the sky was clouded over with the gathering storm, and the rain was sweeping in over the islands out to sea, but to the north the moon rode high on ragged clouds, attended by a scattering of stars and laying its silver path across the black waters. I stared, enchanted.

The noise from the taproom downstairs was growing now as the fishermen came in. I was tired from the jolting of the coach and my head ached. I took my tincture of lavender from my bag and rubbed my temples, breathing in the sweet, strong scent. Tomorrow a carriage would come to meet me and take me to Glen Clair and my father's family. Mrs Campbell would return to Applecross on the drover's cart. And Mr Sinclair…Well, from the conversation I had overheard between him and Mrs Campbell earlier, I understood that he was posted to a naval station some way up the coast at Lochinver, but since the signing of the Treaty of Amiens the previous month he had been granted some leave.

I wondered idly where he would be spending it, and with whom. Perhaps he would choose to spend the time with his family at Strathconan? Or perhaps he might go to Edinburgh to enjoy the entertainments of the city? Inexperienced as I was, I did not for a minute doubt that Neil Sinclair lacked for female companionship when he had the opportunity.

There was the scrape of a step in the inn doorway beneath my window. The lantern swung in the rising wind. A movement caught my eye and I looked down. Neil Sinclair himself was in the street directly below my window. He was looking up at me. And in that moment I realised what I must look like, with the candlelight from my chamber window no doubt turning the thin linen of my shift quite transparent and my unruly red hair loose about my face.

Neil Sinclair did not look away. He held my gaze for what seemed for ever, as the hot colour flamed to my face and my traitorous limbs turned to water. I could not move. Then he smiled, his teeth showing very white in his dark face, and raised a hand in deliberate greeting.

Suddenly freed from the captivity of his gaze, I stumbled back from the window and closed the shutters with such a sharp snap that I almost pulled them from their hinges. I realised I was shaking. Of all the foolish, immodest and downright dangerous things to do—leaning from my window like a wanton Juliet! I should have realised that someone might see me. I should have thought how abandoned I would look. But the trouble with me, as I already knew, was that I almost always acted first and thought later.

There was a knock at the door. Assuming that it was Mrs Campbell, come to help me with my laces, I went across and opened it.

Neil Sinclair stood there. I realised that he had come directly up to my chamber. Though I had been thinking of him only a moment before, I could not have been more shocked had it been Mrs Campbell herself running down the inn corridor in her shift.

Before I could prevent it, he stepped inside the room and closed the door.

I found my voice—and grabbed my gown to my chest to cover my near nakedness.

'What do you think you are doing, sir? Leave this room at once!'

He smiled again, that lazy, intimate smile that had such a distressing effect on my equilibrium. I felt my legs tremble a little.

'Do not be afraid, Miss Balfour,' he said. 'I merely wish to speak to you.'

'This,' I said, 'is not the time nor the place to talk, sir. You are no gentleman to stand there staring at a lady in a state of undress!'

He gave me a comprehensively assessing glance that started on my heated face and ended with my bare feet, and he made no attempt whatsoever to disguise the fact that he was enjoying looking.

'No gentleman, perhaps,' he murmured, 'but a man nonetheless.'

My hands clenched on my gown. I would have slapped his face to emphasise my point except that that would have necessitated dropping the garment and revealing even more of myself to his gaze. I was not exactly over-endowed with a bosom, but there was enough of it that I did not wish to expose it to him. Whilst I hesitated with this ridiculous dilemma of to slap or not to slap, he spoke again.

'And I am beginning to think that you are no true lady, Miss Balfour.'

I froze, astounded. 'I *beg* your pardon, Sir?'

'No lady would see fit to undress and then lean from the window of a tavern in her shift, like the veriest wanton.'

I blushed hotly, the pink colour flooding not only my face but prickling the skin of my chest and shoulders as well. Having so pale a complexion can be such a curse.

'That was a mistake!' I said furiously. 'I did not realise—'

His dark brows rose in quizzical amusement. 'Indeed. You are wild, Miss Balfour, whether you realise it or not.'

We stared at one another, whilst the air between us seemed to sing and hum with something I did not understand. I was woefully inexperienced in the ways of men, but I could see desire darkening his eyes and I could feel an answering warmth in the pit of my stomach. I was shivering as though I had an ague, the goose pimples rising on my bare skin, but at the same time I felt hotter that I had ever felt before in my life. The fire hissed in the grate and the wind battered at the window, and I seemed sensitive to every sound and every sensation and most particularly to the turbulent heat in Neil Sinclair's eyes.

'You need not travel on to Glen Clair tomorrow,' Neil said softly. 'There is nothing for you there. Come with me to Edinburgh instead. You will have a house, with servants to attend you and fine clothes and jewellery. I would come to you often.'

I drew a deep breath. My heart was hammering. 'Are you by any chance asking me to be your mistress, Mr Sinclair?'

No doubt the Miss Bennies would have collapsed with the vapours by now to be so treated, but even though I had no practical experience I was not a sheltered lady who did not know what went on between a man and a woman. Living in a small village one became aware of such matters. Besides, I was as blunt spoken as any man.

A disturbingly sensuous smile curled Neil Sinclair's

lips. 'Would that be so very bad, Miss Balfour? I am offering you a comfortable home, instead of a ruin in the back of beyond with relatives who do not want you.'

'You are not offering it for nothing!' I snapped.

His smile deepened. He put out a hand and touched my cheek gently. I was so shocked at the physical contact that I jumped.

'All I ask in return,' he said, 'is something that should be intensely pleasurable for both of us.'

Once again I felt that jolt deep inside me—the tug of desire that had me thinking all kinds of wanton thoughts. I swallowed hard and pushed away the heated images of lust and loving.

'I thought,' I said, 'that you did not even like me very much.'

I saw something primitive and strong flare in his eyes, scorching me.

'Then you know little of men, Miss Balfour,' he said. His tone had roughened. 'I wanted you from the first moment I saw you.'

'Which was only yesterday,' I said.

'Sometimes it does not take very long to know.'

I spoke slowly. 'You think me wild?'

His eyes were very dark. His hand fell to my bare shoulder, his touch light as feathers brushing the skin, and I shivered all the harder. He traced a line down my arm from the hollow of my collarbone to the sensitive skin of my wrist where the pulse hammered hard.

'You are as fierce as a Highland cat, and with me you could always be as wild as your nature leads you to be.'

His words, so softly spoken and so intimate—so perilously tempting—made my stomach clench tight. But even so I knew that I had to stop this. Already, in my naivety and accursed curiosity, I had let it go on far too long. I should have thrown him out of my chamber within a minute, instead of allowing myself to be drawn in. The difficulty, the danger, was that Neil Sinclair was right. I *was* wild. I always had been. He had had my measure from the start.

My wayward mind whispered that it would be exciting, deliciously enjoyable, to be Neil's mistress. My knees threatened to give way completely at the mere thought of him seducing me. I realised with a shock that I wanted him as much as he wanted me.

But I was not stupid. I would not trade my good name to be a rich man's mistress, with my body entirely at his disposal. I would not do it even for those mysterious and seductive pleasures he promised. Yes, I concede I was tempted. Very well, I was *greatly* tempted—to within an inch of accepting. But…

'So,' I said, 'you know I am alone and unprotected. You know I am penniless and dependent on the charity of relatives you say have none. So you make your dishonourable offer. You are a scoundrel, Mr Sinclair.'

He took a step back. He looked rueful now, and a little chagrined. I knew that he had sensed the struggle in me and realised that this time my honour had won out.

'I am sorry that you see it that way, madam,' he said.

'How else is there to see it?' I demanded.

He shrugged. 'If you put it like that—'

'I do!'

He raised his hands in a gesture of reconciliation. 'Very well. I apologise. I made a mistake.' He gaze went to my whitened knuckles, still clasped tight about the gown at my breast. 'Have no fear, Miss Balfour. I am not a man who would force a woman against her will.' He laughed. 'It has never been necessary.'

Well! The arrogance of the man!

'Good,' I said. 'Because I am not a woman to shout for help and bring the whole inn down about our ears— but I will if I have to.'

He smiled, and for a moment I felt my all too precarious determination falter. 'But you were tempted by my offer,' he said. 'Admit it, Catriona.'

'I was not.' I turned my face away to hide my betraying blush and he laughed.

'Liar,' he said softly.

My chin came up. 'I like Edinburgh,' I said. 'I like the shops and the galleries and the exhibitions and the lectures. I would like to visit again. But not at the price you offer, Mr Sinclair. I am not for sale.'

'You have more resolution than I gave you credit for,' Neil said. The smile was in his eyes again, admiration mixed with regret. 'I should have remembered that you are a Balfour of Glen Clair. They can be damnably obstinate.' He sighed. 'I do not suppose,' he added, 'that you trust me now.' There was an odd tone in his voice, as though he sincerely regretted it.

'If I do not it is your own fault,' I said. I smiled a little, being unable to help myself. 'I never did trust you, Mr Sinclair. Not really. I always suspected you were a dangerous scoundrel.'

That made him laugh. 'Just as I always knew you were wild—even when you pretended otherwise.'

'The door is behind you,' I said. 'Goodnight.'

When Mrs Campbell came in a bare two minutes later, to help me with my laces, she found me sitting on the edge of the hard little bed with my gown still clutched to my breast, and she was forced to point out that it would be quite ruined to wear in the morning.

Chapter Four

*In which I meet with strange travellers on the road
and see Mr Sinclair again sooner than I expect.*

The rainstorm blew itself out in the night. The clouds
scattered on a fresh wind from the sea. Dawn crept in
at about five-thirty in the morning, the light spilling
over the mountains to the east.

I had been awake on and off all the night, my dreams,
when I had them, broken with memories of my parents
and fears about the new day, as well as with strange
desires and longings that seemed to feature Neil

Sinclair rather more than was wise. I heard the first of the fishermen drag his nets across the cobbles, and the splash of the boat putting to sea before it was properly light. I was ready, with my bags packed, by seven thirty.

Mr Sinclair greeted me at the bottom of the stair when Mrs Campbell and I went down together. I had wondered how I would feel to see him in the daylight, but his manner was so impersonal that I had the strangest feeling that the scene between us had been just another of my broken dreams. We took bread and honey and ale for breakfast, and then I went out onto the quay for a walk.

The carriage from Glen Clair did not come. The clock crept around to nine, then nine-thirty, and then ten. I walked the length of the quay in one direction and then back again, and then around for a second time. As I passed the inn I could see Mrs Campbell sitting in the parlour, her face starting to tighten into nervous lines. The drover's cart was due to leave for Applecross immediately after midday and I knew she did not want to be left behind.

I sat on a bench, looking out to sea, and thought of

my new relatives—who did not appear to have sent their carriage for me and had not sent a messenger to explain why. It scarcely argued an eagerness to see me. Even though the sun was warm again I drew my shawl a little closer about me. The seabirds were soaring and calling out in the bay. From here my road turned eastwards, away from the coast and into the mountains to Torridon and Kinlochewe and on to Glen Clair. I had lived by the sea all my life. It was in my blood. And though Glen Clair was only a day's drive inland, it felt as though I would be leaving a part of me behind.

I stood up, stiff and a little cold from the sea breeze, and made my way back towards the inn parlour. I could hear the chink of harness where the drover's cart stood waiting in the yard. Mrs Campbell would be starting to fuss.

She was. The maidservant had brought in plates of crab soup and crusty rolls for our luncheon, and just the smell was making me hungry, but Mrs Campbell was too nervous to eat. She sat fidgeting with her soup spoon.

'There is not another cart back to Applecross for nigh

on a week,' she was saying, 'and my cook and maid cannot manage a Sunday dinner alone. What am I to do?'

I laid a hand over hers. 'Dear ma'am, please do not concern yourself. I can await the carriage here on my own. I am sure the landlady will stand chaperon for a short while.'

Mrs Campbell's anxious face eased a little. 'Well, if you think that would serve—'

'There is no landlady,' Mr Sinclair said helpfully. 'The landlord is a widower.' He had come in from the stable yard with his dark hair ruffled by the breeze, and he smelled of fresh air and horses and leather. It was not unpleasant. In fact it was rather attractive, and I was annoyed with myself for thinking so.

I frowned at him to compensate. 'I am sure there must be someone who could help me?'

'I could help,' Mr Sinclair said. 'I could escort you on to Glen Clair.'

I looked at him. 'That would not be appropriate,' I said. 'Given that…' I paused. *Given that you are a scoundrel who tried to seduce me last night.* I did not say the words aloud, but I could see from the bright light in his eyes that he was reading my mind. He waited, head tilted enquiringly.

'Given that we would not be chaperoned,' I said.

He smiled. 'But we are cousins of a kind,' he said, 'so it would be entirely proper.'

Mr Sinclair had a habit of silencing me.

'So we are cousins now, are we?' I said, when I had recovered my breath. 'How very convenient.'

His smile deepened. 'I swear it is true,' he said. 'I am third cousin twice removed to Mrs Ebeneezer Balfour on my mother's side. You may check the family bible if you do not believe me.'

'Oh, well,' I said sarcastically, 'that is quite acceptable, then.'

Mrs Campbell frowned. 'I am sorry, Catriona,' she said, 'but I do not think that so distant a connection is entirely reliable.'

'No,' I said, trying not to look at Mr Sinclair, who looked the absolute antithesis of reliable. 'Perhaps you are correct, ma'am.'

We were saved from further dispute by the arrival of the carriage from Glen Clair. With a cry of relief, Mrs

Campbell swept me up, carried me out into the yard and installed me in the coach without even permitting me to finish my crab soup.

'All will be quite well now, my love,' she said, ignoring the fact that the coachman was the most villainous-looking fellow that one could imagine. 'You will be safely in Glen Clair by nightfall, and I know your family will be delighted to see you.' She kissed me enthusiastically on both cheeks. 'Pray write to me often.'

Mr Sinclair was handing my bags up to the groom, and suddenly I felt very alone. Neither the coachman nor the groom seemed inclined to speak to me, and neither had vouchsafed anything beyond a surly greeting.

Mr Sinclair came alongside the window to bid me farewell, and for once the impudent light was gone from his eyes. He looked sombre and very serious.

'I wish you good fortune, Miss Balfour,' he said, quite as though we might never meet again.

'Do you ever go to Glen Clair to call upon your third cousin twice removed, Mr Sinclair?' I asked impulsively.

He smiled then. 'Very rarely, Miss Balfour,' he

said. 'But you will see me in Glen Clair before the month is out.'

I felt relief and a strange sense of pleasure to hear it, but naturally I was also rather annoyed with myself for making it appear that I actually *wanted* to see him again. I tilted my chin haughtily and gave him my hand in what I hoped was a dignified manner. But he simply turned it over, kissed my palm, and gave it back to me with quizzically lifted brows. The colour flamed into my face and I wished Mr Sinclair at the bottom of the loch.

'Thank you,' I said frostily, 'for the service that you have rendered me, Mr Sinclair.'

'A pleasure, Miss Balfour,' he said. He smiled straight into my eyes. 'Should you reconsider my offer, you need only send to me.'

'A refusal so often offends, Mr Sinclair,' I said. 'You must be a brave man indeed to risk a second rebuff.'

He laughed. 'You have not seen Glen Clair yet,' he said cryptically.

'So you are the lesser of two evils?' I enquired. 'I shall bear that in mind.'

His laughter was still in my ears as the carriage

lurched out of the inn yard and away along the cobbled street that fronted the quay. I craned my neck for a last view of the sea, until the road turned inland towards the high mountains and the last shimmer of sparkling blue was lost from my sight. And though I tried not to think of Mr Sinclair paying court to the ladies of Edinburgh, the thought of him stayed in my mind for most of the long journey to my new home.

Now, it may appear to readers of my narrative that I am much concerned with modes of transport, but it could not escape my notice that the carriage sent from Glen Clair was much inferior to that of Lord Strathconan. As I sat down on the straw-stuffed seat a thick cloud of dust arose and settled on my skirts in a clinging grey film. I was sure that I saw a flea jump out of the cushions.

It seemed that with every rut in the track the coach threatened to shake to bits. I began to feel a little travel sore, so to take my mind from the journey I tried to concentrate on the view as we lurched along the road. Afternoon was well advanced by now, for our progress was slow, and the sun was dipping behind the high mountains. The heather on the slopes merged with the bracken into a purple and amber mist. Above the rocky peaks soared a single eagle, the sun bright on the gold of its head. The road wound its narrow way along the valley bottom beside a trickling burn fringed by pines. It was very beautiful, but to me, accustomed to the friendly scatter of the homesteads at Applecross, it seemed an empty landscape and a deserted one. I imagined that the jagged peaks and the bare hillsides might drive some men mad with loneliness.

The sun had long vanished behind the mountains, the purple shadows were fading to shades of grey and I was very hungry when we turned down an even narrower lane, rattled over a wooden bridge across the stream and drew alongside a broad loch that I realised must be Loch Clair at last. I sat forward, searching the dusk for my first glimpse of the house, but there was nothing ahead—no lights, no sign of life but the last flickering silver of the light on the water.

I sat back again, feeling slightly disappointed. As I did so the carriage lurched to a stop and there was a silence. I waited a few moments for one of the servants to come and tell me the reason for the delay. No one appeared, so I tried to open the carriage window to see what was going on. But the frame was splintered and the window stubbornly refused to move. I opened the door and stuck my head out.

We had stopped halfway along the edge of the loch. To one side of the carriage there was the water, and on the other side the rocky wall of the hillside rose straight and sheer from the edge of the road. It was only with the greatest difficulty that I was able to open the door wide enough to jump down.

Gathering up my skirts, I hurried around to the front of the coach. The horse—a tired old beast with a white star on its head and manners far more pleasant than that of its driver—whickered in greeting and nuzzled my pockets for a treat. I patted his nose.

The road unrolled before me, stretching away to a small wood at the end of the loch. There was no sound but for the whisper of the wind in the reeds by the water. The same wind brought the scent of woodsmoke faintly on the air. It was cold air, and it breathed goose-flesh along my skin, for the coachman and groom had completely vanished.

A second later instinct made me aware that I was no longer alone on the road. I spun around, but I was a moment too late. Strong arms had caught me from behind, pulling me backwards against a hard male body. A hand came down over my mouth. Through my struggles—for I wriggled and kicked and strained to be free, of course—I had a confused impression of movement about me, and I heard the scrape of steel on stone.

I never scream. I have never been able to. When I was a child and the village boys teased me and pulled my hair, my cries of anger always came out as frustrated squawks. It was most vexatious to lack this accomplishment at a moment when it would have been useful to scream loud enough to make the mountains ring. It would also have been useful to be built along more generous lines, for I was slight and thin, and no match for my captor's strength. In less than a moment he had both my hands held behind my back in just one of his. His grip was tight, and he held me hard against his own body so I had no chance to escape nor even to see his face.

'I never scream,' I said, when I had ceased my struggles and caught my breath. Since he still had his hand over my mouth, this came out something like, 'Mmmmmfffff.'

Surprisingly, he took his hand away.

'I never scream,' I repeated.

'No one would hear you if you did,' he said. He spoke with a remarkably strong Highland burr, so *his* words came out something like, 'Nae oon wuid hear ye an ye did.'

I have always liked the Highland brogue, and his voice was low and melodious and oddly attractive. I had to remind myself that he was a felon and up to no good. His words were all too obviously true. There was not a soul in sight. No one would come to save me even if I had a scream like a banshee.

I sighed instead. 'What have you done with the coachman and the groom?'

'They ran away.' The laconic answer held a hint of amusement.

I made a sound of disgust. 'Cowards!'

He moved slightly, though his grip on me did not slacken. 'I cannot disagree with you there.'

'So what do you want?' I demanded. 'Are you a footpad? If so, I can tell you that I have no money.'

This was not precisely the case. I had the five pounds that the trustees of St Barnabas had sent, plus a further five pounds donated most generously by my father's scholarly colleagues, and yet another pound confided to me by Mr Campbell—who had probably taken it, most improperly, from the Sunday collection plate. This grand total of eleven Scottish pounds would be riches indeed for a thief on the road.

I thought that I felt my captor shake with silent laughter. 'I do not believe you,' he said. 'You are a lady. You must be rich.' He slid his free hand caressingly down the length of my body and I stiffened with outrage beneath his touch. 'Shall I search you,' he continued, 'to see if you tell the truth?'

'Do so and I shall see you hanging on the end of a rope for your pains,' I said, between my teeth. It was strange, but I had a feeling that robbery was not his aim at all—nor the ravishment of innocent young ladies. Even as we spoke I sensed that his mind was working with some other urgent preoccupation.

'So you think me a highwayman?' he said.

Something clicked in my mind then—the smell of the smoke, the other men who had passed, the scrape of metal on the stone. I realised that they must have been moving a whisky still. The Highlands were rife with illicit whisky distilleries, tucked away in every mountain glen. It was the curse of the excise men, because all the local populace would be part of the conspiracy—even to the point of local ministers hiding bottles of malt in coffins in the church.

'No,' I said, 'I don't think you are a highwayman. I think you are a whisky smuggler.'

I felt the surprise go through him like a lightning strike, and in that moment his grip on me loosened and I pulled free and ran.

On reflection it was not a sensible thing to have done. The light was fading fast now, and I could barely see to put one foot before the other. I did not know where I was and I had nowhere to run to. Besides, my captor was a lot quicker and stronger than I was.

He caught me within six paces, as I dived into a copse of pine trees in a vain attempt to hide. If I had thought him rough before, it was nothing to how he treated me now. He grabbed my arm, knocking me to the ground and pinning me there with the weight of his body on mine. All the breath was crushed out of me.

The ground beneath me was dry and soft with last year's pine needles. I lay still, inhaling the sharp, fresh scent and trying to catch my breath. It was too dark to see his face, but I was aware of every tense line of his body against my own. My hands were trapped against his chest, and beneath the coarse material of his coat I could feel the hardness of muscle and his heart beating steadily. In that moment all my senses seemed acutely sharp, so much so that I could smell the scent of him: leather, horses, fresh air and an echo of citrus that mingled with the smell of pine. His cheek brushed mine, and I felt the warmth and roughness of his skin against my own. A shiver seemed to echo its way through my entire body. And in that moment, although I could see nothing of his face in the darkness beneath the trees, I recognised him and knew who he was.

'Mr Sinclair!'

I heard him swear, and he clapped a hand over my mouth again. 'Quiet!'

I ignored him, trying ineffectually to struggle free from beneath his weight.

'When you said I would see you within the month,' I said, 'I had no notion you meant it to be so soon.' I took a deep breath. 'And what the *devil*,' I added, 'do you think you are doing, smuggling whisky and accosting young ladies on the road?'

His grip relaxed a little, though he still held me pinioned beneath him. It was, in truth, disturbingly pleasant to be held thus, so hard against him. My body, which seemed to have developed a will of its own from the first moment I had met Mr Neil Sinclair, was busy telling me just how pleasurable the whole business was. I tried to ignore the stirring of desire deep inside me, but Neil would not let me up, trapping me with one leg across my skirts and thus keeping me trussed up beneath him.

'Stop struggling,' he said, and his voice sounded lazily amused. 'I rather like you like this, Miss Balfour.'

I gave an angry sigh. 'You have not answered my

question,' I said. I relaxed for a moment, staring at the spiky pattern of the pine needles against the dark blue of the night sky. 'Why smuggle whisky?'

'Why not?' He sounded maddeningly reasonable. 'The King's taxes are criminally high.'

'But you are an officer in the Navy and heir to an earldom!'

'Which has nothing to do with the exorbitant state of the taxes.' He moved slightly, his hand coming up gently to brush the tumbled hair away from my face in what was almost a lover's touch.

'I cannot have a conversation about tax with you in this situation,' I said, resisting the urge to turn my cheek against the caress of his fingers. 'It is ridiculous.'

'As you say.' His voice had dropped. 'Taxes are not the matter uppermost in my mind, either.' He leaned closer. And at that point, when every fibre of my being was aching for him to kiss me, we heard the sound of horses on the road.

We both froze absolutely still.

'Excise men?' I whispered.

'Maybe.' In the darkness his face was set in taut lines.

'I could call out for help—'

His gaze came away from the road and focussed hard and fast on mine in the moonlight. 'Then why do you not?'

For a long, long moment of silence I looked up into his face, and then I took a deep and deliberate breath.

Throw down the gauntlet...

His mouth came down on mine so swiftly that I never had a chance to call out, and after the first second I completely forgot that that was what I had been intending to do. The sensuality flared within me in a scalding tide, drowning out thought. He kissed me again, fiercely, hungrily, and I instinctively understood somewhere at the back of my mind that this was something that been going to happen between us from the very first moment that we had set eyes on one another.

No one had ever kissed me before. My being the schoolmaster's daughter, the village lads had thought me above their touch, whilst the gentlemen who had visited the Manor had thought me beneath their notice. So, although I understood the theory of love from my reading and from observation, I was quite an innocent. But Neil Sinclair did not kiss like a gentleman, and he made no concessions to my inexperience, so I had no time to worry about what to do, or how to go about the whole business of kissing. In fact, I do not believe that I spared it one thought, but simply responded to the ruthless, insistent demand of his mouth on mine.

When he let me go, the pine needles and the stars pricking the skies above them were spinning like a top. I saw the flash of his smile in the darkness.

'Thank you,' he said. And then he was gone.

I lay still for another long moment, thinking of the arrogance of the man in thanking me for something he had not had the courtesy to request in the first place but had simply taken, like the thief he was. Then I struggled to sit up, and from there, by degrees, to stand on legs that felt all too unsteady. I could still feel the imprint of Neil Sinclair's lips on mine, a sensation that threatened to rob me of any remaining strength. Then I told myself that I was acting like a silly little miss—and that Mr Sinclair had behaved like the scoundrel he undoubtedly was, and deserved everything that was coming to him. I took that long-delayed deep breath and found that I could scream after all.

'Help! Smugglers!'

I stumbled out of the woods and onto the road—right in front of two English Army redcoats. Their horses shied and almost set the poor old coach horse off at a gallop—except that it was long past such excitement. One of the soldiers was so startled that he already had his musket raised and wavering in my direction.

'What the hell—'

Indeed. What I can have looked like, tumbling out of the trees with pine needles in my hair and my clothing askew, can only be wondered at. He was a short, stocky man, and from what I could see of his expression in the rising moonlight I would have said he looked of nervous disposition. Not the kind of temperament to suit hunting smugglers through the Scottish glens.

His companion was a very different matter. Tall, fair and languid, he put out a hand to soothe the other man and stop him shooting me in a fit of anxious overexcitement.

'Put away your gun, Langley,' he murmured. 'Can you not see this is a lady? You will frighten her.'

He dismounted with one fluid movement and was bowing before me. 'Madam,' he said, 'Lieutenant Arlo Graham, at your service. Smugglers, you say?'

'Whisky smugglers in the woods,' I said. 'What are you waiting for?' I looked from one to the other. 'They are getting away.'

Lieutenant Graham sighed. He seemed utterly disinclined to plunge off up the wooded mountainside in hot pursuit. Perhaps it would have disarranged his uniform.

'Too late,' he said. 'They will be well away by now.' He turned to the carriage. 'Is this your conveyance, madam?'

'Yes,' I said. 'I am Miss Balfour, niece to Mr Ebeneezer Balfour of Glen Clair.'

'But where is your coachman?'

'I have no notion,' I said truthfully. 'I believe the wretch ran off when the smugglers stopped the coach.'

'And why should they do that?' Langley interposed. Rudely, I thought. 'If they were smuggling whisky why draw attention to themselves by stopping the coach?'

'I have no notion,' I said again, rather less patiently this time. 'I am not in their confidence, sir.'

Lieutenant Graham smiled. 'Of course not, Miss Balfour.'

Langley frowned suspiciously. 'And what were you doing in the woods yourself?'

I looked at him. 'Hiding, of course. What else would I do with such ruffians about?'

'What else indeed?' Lieutenant Graham said. 'That blackguard of a coachman, running off and leaving a lady unprotected! I am sure your uncle will turn him off on the spot. Now, pray let me escort you to Glen Clair before you take a chill, Miss Balfour. Langley, you can drive the coach and lead your horse. I will take Miss Balfour up with me.'

Before I could protest, he had remounted the very showy chestnut and reached down to swing me up before him. His arm was strong for such a deceptively indolent fellow. The horse, clearly objecting to the excess weight, sidestepped and threatened to decant me on the verge. I grabbed its mane and reflected that it was only in stories that the heroine was so featherlight that the poor horse did not suffer.

'Unchivalrous fellow,' Graham said, bringing it ruthlessly under control. 'I beg your pardon, Miss Balfour.'

'When you are quite ready, Graham,' Langley said crossly. He had already mounted the box and efficiently tied his own horse's reins to those of the poor old nag.

Graham pulled an expressive face. 'I apologise for Langley,' he whispered in my ear. 'I fear the climate in the north suits him ill. He is in a permanent bad mood.'

'He is lucky it is not raining,' I said. 'This is fine weather for these parts.'

'But cold,' Graham drawled. 'Always so cold, Miss Balfour. And on the rare occasions that it is warm the mosquitoes bite. Langley, poor fellow, is fatally attractive to the mosquito.'

It seemed to me that if Neil Sinclair was a handsome knave, then Arlo Graham was the smoothest gentleman this side of the Tweed. But both had one thing in common. They were well aware of their own attractions. Lieutenant Graham certainly did not require *me* to join the ranks of his followers, being his own greatest admirer.

We set off at a decorous trot. After we had covered but a few yards, Langley enquired irritably whether

Lieutenant Graham could not hurry it up a little, for the coach was in danger of running us over. Arlo Graham sighed, but speeded up slightly. It also meant that he had to tighten his arms about me as I sat in front of him, to ensure that I did not lose my balance. This was by no means an unpleasant experience, but I found that rather than dwelling on Lieutenant Graham's most respectful embrace, I was thinking of Neil Sinclair's rather less deferential one. Not that I needed to worry that either of these two were likely to catch him, for the one would end up shooting at shadows and the other would do nothing so strenuous as chasing criminals. So it seemed it was left to me to have a few severe words with Mr Sinclair when I next saw him.

After about ten minutes we clattered across another wooden bridge, passed a dark and silent lodge house, and found ourselves on a wide sweep of drive before the Old House at Glen Clair. I was home.

Chapter Five

In which I meet my family and receive a less than warm welcome from my uncle.

Although it could only have been nine o'clock, there were no lights. The house crouched silent like a pouncing cat. I shivered.

Lieutenant Graham dismounted and helped me down. He strolled across to the door and tugged on the iron bell-pull. It came away in his hand, so he knocked. I heard the sound echo through the house like a distant roll of thunder.

'Are they not expecting you?' he enquired.

I was saved the complicated explanations as the door sighed open with a shuddering creak. A tiny pool of light fell on the step.

'Who is it?'

Lieutenant Graham checked at the sound of so sweet a female voice. Then the lady holding the candle stepped forward, and we all saw her for the first time.

Quite simply, she was beautiful. She was perhaps a year or two older than I, and she had corn-gold hair curling about her face, and deep blue eyes. I heard Arlo Graham catch his breath and saw him draw himself up very straight. Lieutenant Langley, who had presumably abandoned the poor old horse in the stables, came scrambling up the drive with my portmanteau in his hand, and practically pushed Graham out of the way in order to make a handsome leg.

No doubt my cousin Ellen always had such an effect on all men. I was seeing her for the first time too, of course, but I was not a man. My feelings were vastly different, consisting of envy and admiration in almost equal measure.

'Madam! I...' Graham cleared his throat. 'I have escorted Miss Balfour to you. There has been an accident on the road...' His voice trailed away. Had he been knocked on the head by one of the ceiling beams— a distinct possibility, given the dilapidation of the entrance hall—he could not have looked more stunned.

'There were smugglers on the road,' I said, seeing that Lieutenant Graham had lost the power of speech. 'How do you do? You must be my cousin Ellen. I am Catriona Balfour.'

She smiled at me, the sweetest smile I had ever seen. I remembered Neil Sinclair saying that Ellen was delightful, and I felt a fierce rush of jealousy and an even fiercer one of shame a second later—for how could I hold such a sweet creature in dislike?

'Catriona!' She could not have seemed more pleased to see me had we already been the best of friends. To my surprise, she came forward and hugged me warmly. 'I am so glad that you are safe here! We were afraid that you were lost.'

'The carriage was late arriving at Sheildaig,' I said. 'And as I mentioned, there were smugglers on the road.'

I saw her glance quickly over her shoulder and draw the gauzy spencer more closely about her throat.

'Smugglers! How terrifying!'

'Nothing to fear, ma'am.' Langley stepped forward. 'They are considerably less terrifying with a musket ball through their throats.'

Ellen gave a little scream of horror.

'Pray, stop frightening the ladies, Langley,' Arlo Graham said. 'Madam, there is nothing to fear. We will protect you to the death.'

'Well,' I said, 'let us hope it does not come to that.' I waited for them both to take the hint and leave now that all was safe, but neither gentleman moved. Both were staring at Ellen, who was standing, head bent shyly, looking at nothing in particular. I realised that I would have to be plainer or we should be there all night.

'You must excuse me, gentlemen,' I said pointedly. 'It is late, and I have some hunger after the journey. Thank you for your aid, and I will bid you goodnight.'

Lieutenant Graham woke up at that. 'Of course, Miss Balfour.' He looked at Ellen. 'But which of you *is* Miss Balfour?'

'My cousin,' I said irritably, 'is Miss Balfour of Glen Clair, being from the senior branch of the family, Lieutenant. I am Miss Catriona Balfour of Applecross.'

Graham bowed—first to Ellen, then to me—as precedence demanded. 'Then I shall hope to call on you both tomorrow,' he murmured, 'to enquire after your health.'

'Please do,' Ellen said, smiling with luscious warmth.

'I shall call, too,' Langley piped up.

'Oh, good,' I said. I shut the door in their faces and turned to my cousin. 'I am sorry to disturb you so late in the evening—' I began, but she shook her head, smiling.

'Oh, Catriona, pray do not apologise! We keep early hours here at Glen Clair, for Mama is an invalid and Papa…' Her voice trailed away. 'Well, you shall meet him presently. Now, you said that you were hungry.' She slipped her hand through my arm and drew me along the stone-flagged corridor.

We passed two doorways, the oaken doors firmly closed. With each step the house seemed to get darker and more and more cold. I felt as though I was being sucked into the very depths, and shivered.

'There is no money for candles nor fuel for a fire

anywhere but in Mama's bedroom,' Ellen said apologetically.

She opened a door and I found myself in a cavernous kitchen with a scrubbed wooden table in the centre. Ellen put the candle down on this and scurried off into the pantry. She returned a moment later with half a loaf of bread, a slab of butter and a thin sliver of unappealing cheese. She looked as though she were about to cry.

'I am sorry,' she said, staring at the cheese as though she expected something to creep out of it—which it might well have done. 'It is all we have. Mrs Grant, our housekeeper, brings food from Kinlochewe on a Tuesday, and she will be with us on the morrow, but until then…'

'This will do me fine,' I said heartily, reaching for the rusty old knife I had seen on the dresser. I managed to hack a bit of stale bread off the loaf and smeared some butter on it. After a moment's hesitation I also decided to risk the cheese. It was strong, but surprisingly tasty, and not, as far as I could see, too rancid.

Ellen sat down on the bench opposite me. She looked the picture of misery. 'I am sorry!' she burst out again.

'I know this is a poor welcome to Glen Clair for you, Catriona. I have so looked forward to meeting you—my own cousin, and so close in age. It will be lovely to have a friend at last, for Papa allows so few people to call.'

She stopped. In the flickering light of the tallow candle she looked like a drooping flower. It was fortunate that Lieutenant Graham was not there to see it, for he would probably have carried her off on the spot, so desperate would he have been to make her smile again.

'I am very happy to have found you, too,' I said sincerely. 'I have no brothers or sisters, and did not even know of my uncle and his family until my father died. I had no home, so—' I swallowed the lump that had risen unbidden in my throat. 'It was splendid to hear of Glen Clair and to know that I had someone to take me in.'

Ellen smiled, her blue eyes luminous in the candle-light. 'Then we shall be the best of friends,' she said, clasping my hand, 'and it will be delightful.'

On such sweet sentiment there was an almighty crash at the back door, and a moment later it swung inwards, bouncing off the lintel. Several scraps of plaster fell from the ceiling onto my bread and cheese.

Ellen went white before my eyes. 'Papa!'

A man was standing in the doorway—or, more accurately, was leaning against the doorpost in the manner of one completely drunk. He had a blunderbuss in one hand and a bottle of whisky in the other, and was drinking straight from the bottle, splashing a vast quantity of malt down his stained shirt. He was a big man, powerfully built but run to seed, with thinning grey hair and grey eyes narrowed against the candle flame. How he could possibly have fathered the adorable Ellen was a mystery that I could not fathom.

'Papa,' Ellen said again, 'this is your niece Catriona, come from Applecross.'

Ebeneezer Balfour stared at me from beneath lowered brows. 'Davie's girl,' he slurred. 'Your father's dead, and that's all that brings you to my door.'

I heard Ellen catch her breath at the harshness of his words. 'Aye, sir,' I said. 'That would be right.'

I saw a glimmer of amusement in his eyes. 'Proud,' he said, 'just like your sire.' He leaned heavily against the wooden table for support and it creaked beneath his weight. 'We quarrelled,' he said, slumping down in the big carver chair at the table's head. 'Did he tell you that, girl?'

'He told me nothing, sir,' I said coldly. I could quite see how that had happened. Uncle Ebeneezer would, I was sure, pick a quarrel with a saint. 'But I am grateful to have family to take me in,' I added. 'Thank you, sir.'

The words seemed to stick in my throat, but I felt I had to force them out. Despite the coldness of Uncle Ebeneezer's greeting, I did not want it ever said that I was ungrateful to be offered a home at Glen Clair.

'There's nothing for you here,' he said, his eyes hooded. He nodded towards Ellen. 'Did she tell you? I drink what profits this estate provides.' He raised the whisky bottle in drunken salute.

'The smugglers are out,' Ellen said quickly. 'Catriona met them on the road.'

Uncle Ebeneezer lowered the bottle again, frowning. 'I know.'

Ellen started to shred breadcrumbs between her nervous fingers. 'There were two excise men on their tail. They said that they would call again tomorrow.'

Uncle Ebeneezer gave her a look of contempt. 'Then

you had better distract them, hadn't you, girl? We want no nose-poker-inners here.'

Unhappy colour flushed Ellen's cheeks. She did not reply, and a moment later Uncle Ebeneezer took another long slurp of the drink.

'Ye'll have had hopes of us, I daresay, Catriona Balfour?'

I looked at Ellen, but she avoided my gaze. Her face looked pinched and cold. "I confess, sir,' I said, 'that when I heard I had kinsfolk well-to-do I thought they might help me in my life.' My tone hardened. 'But I am no beggar. I look for nothing that is not freely given. I can always return to Applecross and work for my living.'

Ellen looked up, a spark of amazement in her blue eyes. 'Work?'

'Aye,' Uncle Ebeneezer said rudely, ''tis what you would have had to do, girl, had your mother not filled your head with foolish notions of gentility and seen that you were good for nothing.'

He reached across me for the bread, tore off a hunk and thrust it into his mouth. 'We shall see,' he said. 'We want no more mouths to feed here.'

I stood up. In that moment I was so angry that I would have walked all the way back to Applecross there and then had it been in the least possible. Then I caught Ellen's eye. She was looking at me beseechingly and I remembered what she had said about longing for a friend.

'I will show you to your chamber,' she said quickly, grabbing the candle. 'Excuse us, Papa.'

Uncle Ebeneezer snorted. 'Chamber! A broom cupboard amongst the rats is the place for Davie's girl.'

We left him sitting in the dark, gnawing on the remains of the cheese.

'I am so sorry,' Ellen whispered, as she dragged me back along the corridor to the foot of the stairs. 'Papa is always like this when he is in his cups.'

'What is he like when he is sober?' I whispered back.

She smiled. 'Not much better.' Her face fell. 'Oh Catriona, you will not leave, will you? Not when I have only just found you.' She grabbed my hand. 'Please?'

I felt terribly torn. Already I liked Ellen such a lot, and it was clear she was lonely here in the big, crumbling mansion whose future her father was drinking away.

'I will have to see,' I said. 'I cannot stay here if Uncle Ebeneezer does not wish it.'

She let go of my hand and started up the stairs. 'I suppose not,' she said. Her tone brightened a little. 'You said that you could work?'

'As a teacher or a companion, perhaps,' I said, trying not to think about what Neil Sinclair had said about my potential. Suddenly I wanted to ask Ellen about Neil— but that was probably a bad idea. He had said she was delightful. Perhaps she thought the same of him.

'A teacher?' Ellen said, as though such an idea were somehow miraculous. 'Only fancy.'

She threw the door open onto a small bedchamber on the first landing. It was clean and bare, empty of all furnishing but for a table with a jug of water and a bowl and a big tester bed that looked as though it were at least a hundred years old.

Ellen was looking anxious. 'I cleaned it myself,' she said. 'The linen is fresh.'

'It is lovely,' I lied. I kissed her goodnight. 'Forgive me,' I said. 'I am tired.'

Even so, it was a while before I slept. The linen was

indeed fresh, but the mattress was damp, and as lumpy as poorly made porridge. Mice scratched in the wall and the old house creaked and groaned around me like a foundering galleon. There was no peace to be found at Glen Clair.

I wondered about my father and the quarrel he had had with Uncle Ebeneezer. I wondered about my Aunt Madeline, whom Neil had said suffered from her nerves and Ellen had said was an invalid. And I wondered about Ellen herself, and the gentlemen who must surely be queuing up to take her away from all this squalor. Finally I thought about Neil Sinclair, and that I would have something to say to him when we next met. Smuggler or free trader, rogue or hero, he would have no more kisses from me. Or so I vowed.

Chapter Six

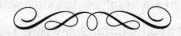

In which a great many visitors come to the Old House at Glen Clair.

When I awoke the sun was creeping across the bare boards of the floor and the old house was rattling with activity. I rolled over in bed and my back protested. After a night lying on the damp and lumpy mattress I felt stiff.

There were footsteps and voices outside my door, one raised above the others in querulous protest.

'Where is Ellen? I told you to send her to me. No, I do not require any medicine. It is too cold in this room.

Pull up the covers for me. No, not like that, woman. You are practically smothering me!'

A door closed, cutting off the voice abruptly.

I opened my eyes and stared at the frayed cover of the tester bed above me. That, I imagined, had been my Aunt Madeline, the invalid. There appeared to be nothing wrong with her lungs, at any rate.

I swung my bare feet to the floor and reached for my petticoat. Five minutes later I had dressed and was dragging a comb through my hair. Throwing open the curtains, I gazed out at the view and was immediately entranced.

The Old House stood on a promontory between Loch Clair and the smaller Loch Torran, and my room looked out at the back of the house, across a rough meadow that had once been a lawn, where peacocks pecked and prowled. Beyond the little loch the valley opened up in a wide bowl with the mountains, clad in amber and purple, reaching to the sky. I stared—and fell in love with Glen Clair in that moment.

Opening my bedroom door, I could hear my aunt's voice rising and falling like the peal of bells, even through the thick oak door opposite. No doubt Ellen would bring me to meet her later. But for now I was sharp set, and looking forward to my breakfast.

I did not have high expectations of what might be on offer, but even those were dashed. When I reached the kitchen it was to find Ellen herself stirring a pan of porridge upon the hob. The kettle was whistling. Ellen's face lit up when she saw me.

'I did not like to wake you,' she confided, 'knowing that you had had so tiring a day yesterday. Here—' she scooped a ladle full of porridge from the pan '—pass a plate.'

The porridge was a stewed grey, and slopped down into the plate in one fat blob. I tried not to blench and picked up my spoon, digging in whilst she poured me a mug of tea.

The porridge was almost cold. My stomach rumbled. Ellen was watching me anxiously.

'Is it all right?'

'Delicious,' I mumbled, chewing on a big lump of oats. At least the tea washed it down.

She smiled. 'Mama is out of spirits today,' she said,

sliding onto the kitchen bench beside me. 'She has taken a chill. Mrs Grant is sitting with her. But she is anxious to meet you, Catriona. I promised to take you up directly after you had eaten.'

I had done my best with the porridge, and, remembering that Mrs Grant was supposed to have brought food with her that morning from Kinlochewe, looked around hopefully for something else to eat.

'Did you wish for oat cakes?' Ellen asked. 'There is some homemade marmalade.'

There was a smidgeon of butter to cover the cake, and some whisky marmalade which, once I had scraped the mould from the top of it, proved surprisingly tasty. I wondered how Mrs Grant had taken the whisky bottle away from my Uncle Ebeneezer for long enough to put some into the marmalade.

'It's good, isn't it?' Ellen said, and I nodded, mouth full.

'We take luncheon at eleven and dinner at four,' she continued. 'As I said yesterday, we keep early hours.'

'Shall I wash the pots?' I asked, gesturing to the sink.

Ellen looked horrified. 'Gracious, no! Mrs Grant

does the pots. No, no…Mama is waiting, and she becomes a little impatient.'

I left the pots for poor Mrs Grant, who it appeared had no maid to help her about the place, and we hurried upstairs. I had the impression that my aunt must be a tyrant, ruling the house from her bed. Ellen was certainly anxious that she should not be kept waiting any longer.

Aunt Madeline occupied the room opposite mine, and when the door swung open it was like stepping into a fairy tale boudoir frozen in time. The bed, the delicate cherrywood wardrobe, the linen chest, the dressing table crowded with beautifying pots and potions… They were all tiny, fragile pieces of furniture. A collection of china dolls with pretty painted faces sat crowded together in a rocking chair. The drapes that kept out the sunlight were thin and fraying, their bright colours faded. And Aunt Madeline was faded, too—a golden beauty whose colour had drained to grey. At last I could see from where Ellen had inherited her glowing prettiness. Aunt Madeline must have been an accredited beauty in her day.

The room was stiflingly hot, for a fire burned in the

grate even though it was high summer. All the windows were closed, sealed shut with cobwebs.

Aunt Madeline was sitting propped against lace-trimmed pillows, and when we knocked at the door she turned her plump, fallen face in our direction and bade us come close. She had been crooning softly to one of the china dolls, which she held in the crook of her arm. Everything about her drooped, from the lacy nightcap on her curls to her mouth, which had a discontented curve. She did not smile to see me.

'So,' she said, 'you are Davie Balfour's daughter. Come closer, child, so that I can look at you.'

Her blue eyes had no doubt once been as vivid as Ellen's, but now they were pale. Nevertheless, they scanned me with shrewd thoroughness.

'Well,' she said, after a moment, 'you are no beauty, that's to be sure. Whatever happened? Your mother was such a pretty lass.'

'I am told, madam,' I said, 'that I take after my father.'

'That would explain it,' Aunt Madeline said. 'She plucked at the lace edging on her sheet. 'I heard tell he was a clever man. Are *you* clever, Catriona Balfour?'

'Tolerably so, I believe, madam,' I said.

'Enough to hide it, I hope?' Aunt Madeline said. 'It ill becomes a girl to appear too clever. Men do not care for it.'

It was on the tip of my tongue to say that any man who disliked me because of my wit was not a man whose good opinion I craved, but I did not wish to fall out with my aunt when I had only known her a few minutes.

'I have heard that said,' I agreed blandly.

Papa had once told me it was better to be ugly but clever than pretty but stupid, and I had always believed him. Now, looking at Ellen sitting there, with the firelight turning her golden hair amber and shadowing the curve of her cheek, I thought that he had perhaps lied to make me feel better. Not that Ellen was stupid, precisely, but you may perhaps imagine how I felt. When I thought of Papa, I felt more lonely and miserable still. This was his family home, and yet he had made no mention of it to me, and the only reason that I was here was because he had died and left me alone. In that moment I was so angry with him for leaving me that I could have shouted aloud.

Aunt Madeline gave me a thin smile. 'I hope you will be happy at Glen Clair,' she said, her expression suggesting that she thought it most unlikely. 'There is nothing to do, and no one calls, but you may come and read to me sometimes.'

'Thank you, ma'am,' I said.

She inclined her head like a queen. We were dismissed. As we left I saw Mrs Grant stoking the roaring fire, and felt the sweat slip down my spine as the heat of the room almost overpowered me.

'What is it that ails your mother?' I asked Ellen as we went down the stairs. I thought that the answer was probably frustration and disappointed hopes, for I could imagine such to be the fate of anyone who had married Ebeneezer Balfour. But to my surprise my cousin bit her lip and looked as though she were about to cry.

'It was all my fault,' she said.

I stopped and stared at her. 'How could that possibly be so?'

'Mama was the toast of the season—a diamond of the first water,' Ellen said, in a rush. 'She and Papa were the most handsome couple. All Edinburgh spoke of the match.' She sighed. 'For years they wanted a son, of course, but no child was born. And then, when mama was nearing forty, she became *enceinte*. It was a hard pregnancy and a difficult birth, and it ruined her looks and her health. And I was only a girl.'

It was a common enough story, I suppose. I had been right about disappointed hopes. The long-awaited son and heir had been an unwanted girl, and her coming had ruined the thing that her mother prized the most—her beauty. I thought of my own parents, and how they had had no son but had never made me suffer for the lack of it, and I felt such love for them and again such grief on losing them. Poor Ellen. I felt for her too, for I suspected that Aunt Madeline repeated the story of her loss over and over again, blaming Ellen to her face and making her believe it was her fault.

'I am sorry,' I said. 'But you cannot blame yourself. You did not ask to be born, nor choose to be a girl— nor, indeed, did you wantonly ruin your mother's health. *You* cannot be held responsible.'

She stared at me, her pansy-blue eyes drenched in

tears in a particularly fetching way. Clearly this was a point of view she had never thought about before.

'Well,' she said, after a moment, 'you have some quaint notions, Catriona Balfour.'

'I am sorry,' I said again, worried that I might have upset her with my implicit criticism of her mother. 'I do tend to speak without thinking. I did not mean to offend you.'

She laughed. 'You did not. I like your plain speaking. You make me see things differently.'

We clattered down into the hall, where the sun speckled the ancient stone flags with bright colour.

'Are you wondering, perhaps, at the thought that my father was once a fine figure of a man?' Ellen said.

'Well,' I said, 'I confess it is hard to imagine.'

'Papa was a handsome man before the whisky got him,' Ellen said. 'He had great prospects, but he always had a weakness for the drink, so I'm told.'

I wondered whether Aunt Madeline had told her that as well, in her disappointment and frustration. But thinking of Uncle Ebeneezer made me think of something else that I had wanted to ask her.

'Was your father out with the smugglers last night?' I asked.

She shot me a frightened look, as though the very walls of the old house might have ears.

'Oh, hush! I do not know—'

'You know that there is a whisky still on Balfour land,' I said. 'There must be! I smelled the smoke last night.'

'It is up by the tea house,' she said. She pulled on my arm. 'Come outside. We cannot talk here.'

We went out of the back door and into the wild-flower meadow. One of the peacocks scuttled away with a harsh cry. Ellen shivered.

'They are unlucky omens,' she said, 'but Papa likes having them about the place.'

It was warm in the sun, but there was a breeze off the water that prompted us to draw our shawls a little closer as we walked through the long grass down to the edge of the loch. A boat was tied up to a branch.

'Do you row?' I asked, but Ellen shook her head.

'It is unladylike.'

'Then you will not swim either?' I looked out longingly across the loch, where the sunlight danced on the water. 'At Applecross I learned to swim so that I could help with the crab pots.'

'Did you?' She looked intrigued rather than disapproving. 'That sounds fun! Mama brought me up to observe the conventions, even though she said I would never enter society nor marry.'

'I cannot believe it,' I said, 'and you so pretty. You will meet someone to marry, I am sure.'

She smiled, pulling a stem of grass between her fingers. 'Thank you. But no one comes to Glen Clair and we never travel. Papa does not permit it.'

Despite my best intentions I was beginning to hold my Uncle Ebeneezer in strong dislike. If Aunt Madeline ruled the house from her bed, then my uncle surely ruled their lives, denying them the pleasures of travel and good company as well as drinking away any money there might have been for small treats and indulgences.

'I am sure,' I said, 'that if only the young men knew there was such a pretty lass at Glen Clair they would be beating a path to your door.'

She laughed. 'And then Papa would see them off with his shotgun.'

There was a silence. Far up above the crags an eagle soared, the sunlight catching the gold of its head.

'So what do you do all day, Ellen?' I asked curiously.

Ellen shrugged. 'I do my needlework and play upon the pianoforte sometimes, though Mama dislikes the sound—she says it gives her the megrims, and it is true that it is sadly out of tune these days.'

'Do you read?'

'There are not many books at Glen Clair,' Ellen said. 'I read sometimes to Mama, but Papa burned most of the library on a bonfire a few years back.'

I felt shocked. No books! I had grown up with the profusion of my father's collection all about me. It had stimulated my interest in subjects as diverse as astronomy and French. I had looked forward to having another library to explore. Instead I would be hiding my own meagre collection of books from Uncle Ebeneezer, lest he decide to throw them on his bonfire as well.

'I suppose,' I said, clutching at straws, 'that there are plenty of pretty walks hereabouts?'

'Papa does not allow me to go beyond the gardens,' Ellen said. 'He says that the hills are dangerous.'

'I imagine that they must be so,' I said, 'if there are whisky smugglers roaming freely. You said that there was a still at the tea house? Where is that?'

Ellen pointed towards a gully thick with pine trees that cut deep into the hillside. 'The path is that way. The tea house is a hut up in the hills. We call it that because it provides refreshment to the drovers driving their cattle over the mountains to Kinlochewe.'

'Refreshment of an alcoholic nature,' I said, understanding. 'I see.'

Ellen nodded. 'You will not tell anyone, will you, Catriona?'

'It seems to me,' I said dryly, 'that everyone hereabouts already knows.'

'Oh, hereabouts that it true,' she said. 'But should the excise officers come—' She broke off, colouring.

'If the excise officers come,' I said, even more dryly, 'it will be because of you, Ellen, and nothing to do with the whisky.'

She blushed even more. 'I'll agree that Lieutenant Graham was a handsome gentleman,' she agreed.

'And quite incapable of hunting smugglers,' I said.

'Since it would without doubt require more effort on his part than he is prepared to give.'

She giggled. 'He *is* very indolent.'

'He is bone idle,' I said. 'Your father is fortunate in that at least.'

'Oh, Papa is not the ringleader,' Ellen said. 'That is—'

'Do not tell me!' I said hastily, trying not to wonder if it was Neil Sinclair. 'The less I know of it the better.'

She nodded. We talked a little more about Glen Clair, and her intermittent schooling at the hands of a series of governesses who had been able to stand the isolation and Uncle Ebeneezer's drunken violence for periods varying from one day to six months.

'Miss Sterling stayed for two years, from when I was ten to when I was twelve,' Ellen said wistfully. 'I liked Miss Sterling, but in the end she ran off with Lord Strathconan and there was a terrible scandal.'

'Lord Strathconan would be Mr Sinclair's uncle, would it?' I asked, unable to avoid mentioning him any longer. 'They did not have children?'

Ellen shook her head. 'Miss Sterling was past child-bearing years when she eloped with the Laird. I think that was why there was so big a scandal. Had she been young and comely no one would have been surprised, but everyone wondered why he had thrown himself away on a middle-aged woman.'

It seemed to me that Ellen, for all her sweetness and her intermittent schooling, could be as shrewd as her mother in her observations. It would not do to underestimate my cousin.

'Perhaps he loved her,' I said.

'I think he must have done,' Ellen agreed. She smiled faintly. 'She was very lovable. She smiled a great deal, and was warm and motherly even though she had no children of her own. And she was well read, and could hold a very educated conversation. I'm told the Laird likes a woman of decided opinions, which is another thing that many hereabouts could not understand.'

Lord Strathconan was beginning to sound like the sort of man I admired, if he gave credit to a woman for being more than a henwit. It did not seem much of a mystery to me as to why he had snapped up the attractive Miss

Sterling and carried her off. Women of distinction were probably as rare as hen's teeth in these parts.

My heart ached for Ellen, though, losing such an affectionate companion and being left with no one but a sickly, complaining mother and a brute of a father.

'So Mr Sinclair is nephew and heir to the Earl of Strathconan?' I said. 'That would account for the high opinion in which the Miss Bennies held him when he came to Applecross.'

'That and his looks,' Ellen said. She looked at me sideways from under the brim of her bonnet. 'Did you not think him handsome, Catriona?'

'No,' I said untruthfully. 'He is not a good-looking man in the sense that Lieutenant Graham is.'

'No,' Ellen agreed, 'but he has something more than mere good looks.'

Something of wickedness and striking attraction. I viciously pulled the heads off a couple of innocent daisies and shredded them between my fingers.

'Does he come to Glen Clair often?' I asked. 'I understood him to be a cousin of your mother's?'

Ellen smiled. 'My grandmother on my mother's side

was a Strathconan, and it is true that Mama delights in the connection. But Neil Sinclair seldom calls here, and Lord Strathconan never. Not after the scandal Mama talked about Miss Sterling.'

'Oh, dear,' I said, seeing how it had been.

'It was very short-sighted of her,' Ellen said with a sigh. 'She should have realised that His Lordship would not wish his bride to be slighted, even if she had once worked for Mama. I am sorry for it, for I should have liked to see Miss Sterling—Lady Strathconan—again.'

'Yes, of course.' I digested this information in silence. So Lord Strathconan had cut himself off from his cousin over a family scandal, and thereby denied poor Ellen the pleasure of ever enjoying her former governess's company again. And Neil Sinclair, for all that he thought Ellen delightful, was not drawn to Glen Clair to see her. I wished that I did not feel so pleased to realise it.

'I like Neil,' Ellen said suddenly. She looked up. 'I do not mean that I like him in the sense that your Miss Bennies would, Catriona, but I enjoy his company. He is an interesting man. Did you not find him pleasant?'

Pleasant was hardly the word I would have used to

describe my emotions towards Neil Sinclair. I cleared
my throat. 'I spent little time with him.'

'Several days!'

I shrugged. 'I do not think it long enough to form a
fair opinion of a man.'

Ellen's blue eyes were very perceptive. 'So you do
not like him?' she said.

I frowned. It came hard to me to prevaricate. Usually
I am open to the point of folly. 'It is not that,' I said.
'He…I…we did not agree on certain matters.'

She looked fascinated. 'Indeed? Well, you will not be
troubled much by him here. As I said, he seldom calls.'

I ripped the top off another wild flower. 'I imagine
that his uncle wishes him to make a grand match?'

Ellen looked amused. 'Aye—which is rich, is it not,
since Lord Strathconan ran off with a penniless governess? But Neil seldom does what any man wishes other
than himself, or so I have observed.'

'Very true.'

She laughed. 'So you have observed it too, in the
short space of your acquaintance? It seems you know
him better than you pretend, cousin.'

'I have certainly observed that he dislikes opposition to his plans,' I said coolly.

Ellen raised her brows. 'Then clearly you know him very well indeed, if he has proposed a plan and you opposed it. What did he do? Try to elope with you?'

'Like uncle, like nephew,' I said lightly. 'Only Mr Sinclair was not proposing marriage at the end of it.'

She gave a squeak and clapped her hand to her mouth. 'No! He is no gentleman, then!'

I laughed at that. 'So I told him.'

Ellen's eyes were as round as saucers. 'Did he kiss you?'

I blushed. I could hardly tell her the truth of that, not without revealing that I had met Neil the previous night. Ellen did not, however, need words.

'I have sometimes wondered,' she said slowly, 'what it would be like to be kissed by a gentleman.'

'Then do not look to Mr Sinclair for the answer,' I said. 'For he may be a nobleman but he does not deserve the title of gentleman.'

Her eyes were bright with amusement and curiosity. 'You are very harsh, cousin,' she said. 'Was it then so bad?'

'No,' I said. 'It was nice. I imagine he has had plenty of practice.'

'Nice!' she said. 'You have a fine line in understatement, Catriona Balfour.'

I laughed, and she opened her mouth to ask another question, but Mrs Grant was running towards us across the lawn, her apron flapping. She was a round body of a woman, and hurrying had made her out of breath. Her face was flushed and her expression agitated.

'Mistress Ellen! Soldiers at the door!'

She made it sound as though the Army was besieging the house—though I assumed that she meant that Lieutenant Graham and Lieutenant Langley had called, as they had promised they would. We stood up, and Ellen slipped her hand through my arm.

'Speaking of gentlemen,' she murmured, 'are either of these two worthy of the title, do you think?'

'Who can tell?' I said. 'In this instance my acquaintance with them is very short indeed, and I am happy to report that I have no insights at all. I leave that to you, cousin.'

And we went in together to meet the gentlemen.

Mrs Grant had shown our visitors in to the oak drawing room—which, as its name suggested, was a long, dark room adorned with carved panelling. She had also provided tea, cooling rapidly in a battered silver pot. There was a much cosier parlour across the stone flags of the hall, but clearly this would not do for visitors. Aunt Madeline had her standards, even though she was not there in person.

Lieutenants Graham and Langley were standing by the window, talking in low voices. It was clear that both had taken an inordinate amount of trouble with their appearance. Lieutenant Graham was a symphony in dress uniform and silver lace, whilst his colleague had at least brushed his hair and pressed his jacket. All this for Ellen! I wondered idly what it must be like to have so much power. Not that Ellen was the type of woman to manipulate a man. She was far too gentle and honest.

As we went in I saw both men focus on her as though they had never seen anything quite so pretty. Indeed they might not have done, for this morning she was dressed in sprigged yellow muslin—not in the first

stare of fashion, perhaps, but fresh and bright—and
with her blonde hair curling in ringlets about her face.
As for me, I was in an old dress of hyacinth blue and
merited not a first glance, never mind a second.

Lieutenant Graham came forward eagerly. 'Ladies.'
He was still looking at Ellen. 'We called to see if you
had recovered from your ordeal last night.' He took
Ellen's hand, bowing over it. 'Indeed, you look radiant,
if I may say so, Miss Balfour. It is good to see that your
nerves have not been overset by your experience.'

Since Ellen had not suffered any ordeal the previous
night, other than the worry that her father might be ap-
prehended as a whisky smuggler, I thought this a bit
much. However, I was not one to resent her the attention. Not much, anyway.

Ellen thanked Lieutenant Graham very prettily, I
thought, and brought Langley, who had been brooding
in the background, into the conversation. Neither gentleman thought to ask after my health, so I went and sat
on the window seat and watched Ellen pour tea whilst
she dealt with them. She had far more social graces
than I had. Miss Sterling had evidently schooled her

well in matters of etiquette whilst I was running wild at Applecross.

'Are you stationed at Kinlochewe for long, Captain Langley?' Ellen was asking.

Langley shook his head. 'Just passing through on our way back to Ruthven Barracks, ma'am,' he said.

'But staying long enough to call on you again, if we may, ma'am,' Graham added, winning a glare from his colleague.

'I am surprised that the Army can spare you both from your duties for so long,' Ellen said, with a warm smile.

'Oh, we are here to hunt smugglers,' Graham said, stretching his long legs and leaning back with his hands behind his head, in the kind of nonchalant gesture that I thought would probably break Aunt Madeline's spindly chair. 'So we have leave to come and go as we wish, ma'am.'

'And have you had any success, sir?' I asked politely.

Graham smiled at me as he passed me a teacup. I could tell what he was thinking—keep the plain companion happy, and then she will speak kindly of me to her beautiful cousin.

'Alas, no, madam,' he said. 'For they are cunning and wily, and they have the connivance of the local populace.'

'Shocking,' I said.

'Indeed, madam,' Lieutenant Graham said. 'I beg you not to distress yourself.'

'I am sure,' I said, with a glance at Ellen, 'that if either my cousin or I knew any information likely to help you in your search we would disclose it at once.'

'Of course,' Ellen said, smiling with limpid innocence.

Both men looked suitably dazzled.

The door opened, and Mrs Grant appeared once more in the aperture. She had a smudge of flour on her cheek and a flustered expression on her face. I could tell she was unused to such frequent interruptions to her daily routine.

'Oh madam,' she said unhappily to Ellen, 'there is another gentleman here now. It is Mr Sinclair! I don't know what your papa will say to see so many visitors.'

Chapter Seven

In which I give Mr Sinclair a piece of my mind.

I was so startled to see Neil Sinclair that I almost overset my teacup. He strolled into the room with an assurance that immediately made both the lieutenants seem at a disadvantage. Lieutenant Graham looked like an overdressed popinjay next to Neil's dark elegance, and Lieutenant Langley simply seemed gauche.

I know it is customary on these occasions for a young lady to be immediately assailed by the memory of her embrace with a gentleman, and to be so overcome by her emotions that she can scarcely look at him and certainly not speak to him. And it is true that I had spent a fair proportion of the time before I had fallen asleep the previous night thinking about Mr Sinclair and the way he had kissed me. I will not deny it. But now I was in no danger of swooning at his feet. On the contrary, I was ready to tell him exactly what I thought of him.

Neil bowed to the room in general. 'Ladies…gentlemen…' A nod to the redcoats before he turned back to Ellen. 'I heard you had visitors, Ellen, and apologise for intruding, but as I was passing and can claim a cousin's privilege—'

'It is lovely to see you, Neil,' Ellen said, tilting her head so that he could kiss her cheek. She looked at me thoughtfully.

'You know my cousin Catriona, of course, and these gentlemen are Lieutenants Graham and Langley, from Ruthven. Gentlemen—my cousin Mr Neil Sinclair.'

Mr Sinclair smiled at me. 'You are well, Miss Catriona?'

For a moment I thought he was going to have the audacity to claim a cousin's privilege with *me,* and come across to kiss me. Something of this must have showed in my face, for I saw his smile deepen. He remained where he was.

'I am very well, thank you, Mr Sinclair,' I said starchily.

I knew that his claim to have been passing was all a pretence. I did not flatter myself that he had called to see me, either. No, I was sure that he had known the excise men were calling, and had deliberately walked in to discover how much they knew about the smuggling incident the night before. His eyes met mine with a dark gleam. He was daring me to say something, to give him away.

You go too far...

I saw the fleeting smile on his lips as he read my thoughts.

An interesting by-play now arose between Mr Sinclair and the two lieutenants. I sensed that both of them had taken Neil Sinclair in immediate dislike, and the reason for it was sitting only a few feet away. Where Ellen was concerned Graham and Langley were already possessive, and barely prepared to tolerate each other let alone an interloper. But Graham was also a strategist. Neil Sinclair, as a lieutenant commander in the Navy, was the senior officer. And even more important to Graham was the fact that Neil Sinclair was heir to Lord Strathconan, and therefore doubly influential. Such a man could not be ignored.

So when Langley burst out, 'And who the devil might you be, sir?' Graham kicked him sharply on the ankle.

'Sir.' He gave Neil a respectful bow, and Neil inclined his head in acknowledgement, a cold smile on his lips. I could tell that they disliked each other.

Ellen passed Neil a cup of tea. 'Lieutenant Langley and Lieutenant Graham are here to catch the whisky smugglers, cousin,' she said. 'You may not have heard, but poor Catriona had her coach stopped last night, after you had parted with her at Sheildaig.'

Mr Sinclair had taken his tea and strolled over to the window, so that he was now standing beside me. His leg brushed my skirt and I moved ostentatiously away, along the seat. He looked down at me.

'How vastly disturbing that must have been for you, Miss Catriona.'

'Vastly,' I said. 'But I have no doubt that I shall survive.'

He smiled. 'Perhaps you should have permitted me to escort you on to Glen Clair instead of rejecting my company?'

I narrowed my eyes. 'You are all concern, sir,' I said, 'but that would have been most improper without Mrs Campbell's chaperonage.'

'Of course,' he murmured. His gaze moved over my face and seemed to linger on my mouth for a moment. I knew that he was thinking about the kisses we had shared there in the wood, with the shadows falling and the scent of the pine needles as they were crushed beneath our bodies. 'You are the soul of propriety,' he added.

I shifted. 'Besides,' I said sweetly, 'I did not expect the Navy to be able to spare you for yet another day. How comes it, Mr Sinclair, that you are here today, once more so far from the sea?'

In truth I had remembered that Mr Sinclair had said he had been granted leave but I was happy to pretend that I had forgotten.

There was a smile in his eyes as he took my purposes and realised that I was going to make this very, very difficult for him.

'I am running an errand for my admiral,' he said easily. 'He had despatches for my uncle, Lord Strathconan, so I offered to carry them.'

'Carrying messages!' I said. 'Do they not have a servant for that?'

'You are on your way to Glen Conan now, sir?' This was Lieutenant Graham, interposing with respectful enquiry.

Neil turned courteously towards him. 'I am. And yourself? How does your work progress, Lieutenant? Catching smugglers in these mountains is a devilish tricky business.'

'We almost had them last night,' Langley said eagerly. 'We pursued them—'

'But lost them in the high passes,' Graham finished, smoothing his lace cuffs. 'And, alas, we found no trace of the still.'

Probably because you were not looking, I thought.

Neil was all sympathy. 'Very likely they signalled ahead to warn of your coming,' he said comfortingly. 'And it is hard to find the stills at the best of times, amongst all the nooks and crannies of these hills.'

'You seem disturbingly well-informed on the ways of smugglers, sir,' I said. 'Do you know any of these desperate scoundrels in person?'

Neil laughed. 'Who knows? They say that the parsons hereabouts hide the whisky in their pulpits, so widespread is the defiance of the law.'

'You do not surprise me,' I said. 'I thought as much last night.'

He looked at me with the same challenge in his eyes that I had seen before.

Denounce me if you dare...

I was about to take it further, but then I caught sight of Ellen, looking piteously white and worried by now, and I did not have the heart to make her suffer further. I turned the subject to how beautiful the glen was looking in the summer sunshine.

'I was thinking on much the same lines, Miss Catriona,' Neil said, smooth as silk. 'Perhaps you would take a stroll with me in the rose garden on such a beautiful morning? I think we have matters of business still to discuss.'

'There is no point in asking me to show you the rose garden, Mr Sinclair,' I said, barely civil, 'when I have been here a mere day and do not even know where it is. You must allow me to be excused and apply yourself to my cousin, I think.'

Both Graham and Langley were positively bristling at the thought of Ellen showing Neil the rose garden, whilst Neil himself merely looked amused and slightly bored by their posturing.

'It would be delightful if we were all to stroll down to the loch, would it not?' Ellen said quickly, rising to her feet. Lieutenant Langley leapt forward to offer her his arm, but only succeeded in knocking over the little tea table. Graham took advantage of his confusion and *sotto voce* swearing to step forward and guide Ellen towards the door. When they had gone out, trailing a dejected Langley in their wake, Neil turned to me and offered his arm.

'Shall we?'

'Must we?' I said. I sighed. 'I suppose we must.'

'Unless you would prefer to stay and talk with me here?'

'I do not want to talk to you *anywhere*, Mr Sinclair,' I snapped. 'I would have thought that was obvious.'

'I do not think,' Neil murmured, 'that a lady has ever been so reluctant to have my company the morning after I have held her in my arms. You are a salutary lesson, Miss Catriona.'

I glared at him and, ignoring the proffered arm, swept past him and out into the hall. The others were already outside. I could hear their steps crunching on the gravel, and Langley's eager conversation and Graham's more languid tones.

'I hope,' Neil said, 'that those two will not come to blows over our cousin.'

'Can you be surprised at their admiration?' I asked. 'Ellen is vastly pretty, and most agreeable, too.'

'I suppose so,' Neil said. 'Though there are some men who prefer substance over style.'

'Your uncle Lord Strathconan for one, so I hear,' I said, ignoring the little voice inside me that whispered he was talking about *me*. I was not going to allow Mr Sinclair's flattery to turn my head. 'I hear that your aunt by marriage is an admirable woman.'

'Did Ellen tell you that?' Neil asked. His lips twisted

in a sardonic smile. 'Either she is all generosity, or she is a poor judge of character.'

'Maybe she is both,' I said. I was curious about Lady Strathconan now, but not quite ill bred enough to ask a direct question. Had Ellen been wrong in thinking the Earl had made a love match? Had she misjudged the admirable Miss Sterling? I glanced at Neil, but he looked abstracted, locked deep in thought.

We were following the others down an overgrown path towards the loch. I heard Neil sigh and glanced at him curiously.

'It pains me that Glen Clair is so neglected,' he said in answer to my unspoken question. 'I love this place, and have done since I came here first as a boy. Your uncle has let it go to rack and ruin—' He broke off.

'Uncle Ebeneezer seems to drink away any profit he makes,' I said. 'A pity, for it could be a beautiful house if only it were cared for again. I would like—' I, too, stopped. For what was the point in telling Neil that I already loved Glen Clair and wished I could fill its corridors with warmth and happiness and laughter? That was never going to happen whilst Uncle Ebeneezer ruled here.

We watched Ellen and her admirers as they reached the water's edge, and then Neil drew me aside through a little rickety wooden gate into the orchard. It was cool beneath the trees.

'The roses are in the walled garden to the west of the house,' he said. 'Should you ever require to know.'

'Thank you,' I said. 'Should a gentleman ask me to show the roses to him in future, I will be sure to remember.'

Neil smiled. He rested a hand against the trunk of the nearest apple tree. 'You seem out of charity with me today, Miss Catriona,' he observed.

'You are perceptive, sir.' Through the lattice of the branches I could see Lieutenant Graham take out his handkerchief and solemnly dust the log on which Ellen and I had sat earlier before he permitted her to sit down. Neither he nor Langley seemed to have remembered that there had originally been two other people in the party. Neil and I might well have been on the moon for all they cared—though I saw Ellen cast a quick glance over her shoulder towards us, and gave her a little re-assuring wave.

'I suppose,' Neil said, 'that you are angry with me for kissing you last night.'

I looked at him. He did not look regretful. He was smiling slightly. In fact he looked as though he would do exactly the same thing again, given the slightest opportunity. It was time to depress his pretensions.

'How like a man to think that,' I said scathingly. 'How like *you!*' I swished away from him through the ankle-high grass beneath the trees. 'I don't care about the kiss,' I said, not entirely truthfully. 'At least no more than I would if any insolent fellow thought to steal a kiss from me.' I turned to face him. 'What I *do* care about is these games you play, Mr Sinclair—turning out as a whisky smuggler one night and then arriving in your guise as Naval officer the very next day.'

As soon as I started to speak my anger with him flared into so tight a ball in my chest that I was afraid I would not be able keep my voice down. I did not understand why I was so upset, but it was something to do with the fact that, despite what had happened between us, I liked him. I liked him very much, and I could not seem to help myself. And so in some complicated way I wanted him to be a better man, a man of integrity. Now, with the proof of his dishonour clear, I felt cheated—and far, far more disappointed in him than I should, than I had a right to be. What was it to me, after all, if Neil Sinclair chose to while away his time breaking the law? I had not trusted him from the start.

'I do not understand you,' I said. 'Is it so tedious serving in the Navy that you must seek out other excitements—illegal ones, irresponsible ones? Do you *want* to be caught? What sort of a man are you, heir to the Laird of Strathconan, to take the King's commission and flout his laws?'

After my first few words Neil stiffened and listened to me in silence, his eyes dark, narrowed and intent, never leaving my face. When I stopped, short of breath and mortified, he did not speak for a moment.

'You do not understand,' was all he said.

I stared at him, baffled. I had expected some kind of excuse at the least. Not even to bother to offer one seemed lazy in the extreme. It suggested that not only did he see nothing wrong in breaking the law, but also that he did not care what I thought either. That hurt me.

'How do I not understand?' I burst out. 'Because I do not connive at your deceit like everyone else does?'

'You drink the whisky,' he said. 'I wager you eat it in your marmalade. You know a dozen people and a dozen more who benefit by the smuggling trade. Of course you connive, in your own way, and it is hypocritical of you to deny it.'

That silenced me for a moment, because it was true. I thought of Uncle Ebeneezer, and of Ellen's desperate desire to protect him, unworthy as he was of her loyalty. We were all of us culpable in one way or another. I shrugged, wrapping my arms about me for comfort.

'That is so,' I said. 'I concede it. But that does not make what you do right.' There were other words in my head, words that were more impassioned, words that were more of a betrayal of my feelings for him.

I wanted you to be better than the rest. I wanted you to be an honourable man...

'You will not give me away.' It was a statement, not a question, and his arrogance angered me.

'What? To that man milliner down by the lake?' I jerked my head in the direction of Lieutenant Graham.

'Even if I did tell him about you he would not be able to catch you.'

Neil smiled. 'That's true.'

'So you have nothing to fear,' I said. 'Do you?'

He was still watching me, his face intent and serious. 'I do not know,' he said slowly. 'With you, I really do not know.'

A little ripple of victory went through me that he was not sure of me.

'Give me your word,' he persisted.

I raised my brows. 'No. You do not deserve it. You deserve nothing from me.'

A shadow of a smile touched his mouth. 'But you like me, Catriona Balfour. You know you do. You would not wish to see me hang.'

I thought of bodies strung up in their cages, rotting as they swung in the wind at a crossroads. No, I would not wish to see Neil Sinclair hang, scoundrel though he undoubtedly was.

'Besides,' he added, 'you would be bringing danger on yourself and to others were you to speak out.' He took a step forward, caught my hand. 'Promise me…'

He was very close to me now, and I looked up into his face and saw a conflict there, a mixture of concern and calculation. There was something else in his expression as well. Perhaps it was a shadow of regret. Perhaps he was sorry that he did not have my good opinion. Or perhaps I deluded myself that it mattered to him.

'Very well,' I said after a moment. I freed myself from his clasp and moved away towards the wicket gate. 'I give you my word I won't betray you. But it is for Ellen's sake, not for yours. She has already been so kind to me, and I know…'

I stopped.

'You know of the whisky still on Sgurr Dhu, and of her father's involvement in the trade,' Neil finished. 'The two of you have indeed exchanged many confidences in so short a time.'

'I like Ellen,' I said. 'And exchanging confidences is what young ladies do.'

'Did you talk about me?'

'Only about how conceited you are,' I said coolly. 'I said so, and she agreed with me.'

I put my hand on the latch of the gate but Neil moved quickly to put a hand over mine and stop me.

'One other matter…'

I turned. Now he was even closer to me—so close that I could see the golden flecks in his dark eyes and feel the hard press of his lower body against mine, trapping me against the wooden panels of the gate. If the group down at the water's edge had turned around my reputation would have been in tatters to be seen in such intimate proximity with a man.

Neil cast them one glance and then ignored them. He bent closer to me still. His breath raised goose pimples against the sensitive skin of my neck. His lips brushed my ear, stirring the tendrils of hair that had escaped from my rather carelessly tied ribbon.

'About ill-mannered fellows who steal meaningless kisses…' he murmured.

'Yes?' I said. My voice sounded slightly husky to my own ears.

'That was not the way of it at all.'

I held his dark gaze for what seemed like for ever. 'Truly?' I said, marvelling at the lightness of my own tone. 'When you are heir to Strathconan and destined for a grand marriage? What else could your kisses be but meaningless?'

'I told you just now,' he said, and his mouth curved into that wicked smile. 'You are different, Catriona. You are an enigma, a challenge. I cannot be sure of you, and that…intrigues me.'

The air beneath the trees was warm and thick, heavy with the scents of high summer. It matched the heavy beat of my blood. Slowly, very slowly, he traced the line of my jaw with the tips of his fingers. I jerked my head away in a vain attempt to escape the hot, tempting pleasure of his touch.

'And yet you have all those beautiful women begging for your notice,' I said sarcastically. 'You are spoiled, Mr Sinclair. You want only what you cannot have.'

His lips brushed my neck in the lightest of caresses, dipping down to linger in the hollow above my collarbone. I trembled. I could not help myself. He was very good at this, whereas I was unpractised in fending off a rogue's seduction. His voice was so quiet I could barely hear him.

'You know that I wanted you from the moment I first saw you,' he said.

'Which changes nothing,' I said. 'It makes you a scoundrel who wants more than mere kisses.'

'Much more.'

'Well, you cannot have what you want, Mr Sinclair,' I said. I slipped the latch and stepped back through the gate. 'This goes no further. But you do. You go straight down that path to the lake and make your farewell to my cousin, and then you leave Glen Clair. And pray do not return whilst I am here—not if you do not wish to be denounced to the excise men. Goodbye.'

He looked at me for a long moment. The sun was on his glossy black hair and in his dark eyes, and I could not read his expression, but I had the strangest feeling that he wanted to say something else. Then he bowed and walked away, and I was left with nothing but a lump in my throat and the light off the loch dazzling my eyes—for I swear that was what it was, and I certainly was not crying. But I will not deny that I felt bereft. I had sent Neil Sinclair away, and I felt very alone.

Chapter Eight

In which I should have been more suspicious and more careful than I was.

Aunt Madeline was very sorry to have been abed on the morning that the gentlemen came, and declared that when they next visited she would rise from her couch like a phoenix and make a grand entrance. Alas for her, Lieutenants Graham and Langley were ordered back to Ruthven Barracks the very next day and she never had the chance to meet them. Lieutenant Graham sent Ellen an elegant note thanking her for her hospitality and wishing her well. Lieutenant Langley sent nothing. Ellen seemed sad, and I hoped it was not because she had conceived a *tendre* for Lieutenant Graham. When I asked her she laughed, so then I worried that she might have conceived a *tendre* for Mr Sinclair instead. And then I felt annoyed that I cared one way or the other.

After that day, our time at Glen Clair fell into something of a routine, and I realised what Ellen had meant when she told me that one day was very much like another. No one called and we never went anywhere. I wrote to Mr and Mrs Campbell—long letters filled with descriptions of Glen Clair and of my friendship with Ellen. I hoped it would reassure then that I was happy in my new home, for I did not wish them to worry about me. I would also read to Aunt Madeline sometimes, for she said that she liked my voice, which was so much clearer than Ellen's gentle tones. I helped Mrs Grant in the kitchen because the poor woman was cruelly overworked. Ellen exclaimed over the blisters on my hands, but I told her that I would rather keep busy than fidget away in idleness.

I kept out of Uncle Ebeneezer's sight. I am not sure what he did all day, for he seldom seemed to work on the estate, which was in a shocking condition of disrepair. He would disappear off to the stables or into his gunroom for hours at a time, and I knew better than to disturb him there. When I felt like a walk to escape the oppressive atmosphere of the house I would venture into the hills, amidst the bracken and the heather, but I made sure that my path took me far away from the whisky still on Sgurr Dhu.

July slipped into August, and the red of the bracken started to pale and the sun was a little cooler. Soon I had been at Glen Clair for more than a month, and it was starting to feel a little like home. I still missed my mama and papa with a fierce ache that could strike painfully at any time, and I longed for Applecross and the wild tumble of the sea, but with Ellen's friendship and hard work to keep me busy I managed to get by. I also tried not to think of Neil Sinclair, but in a strange way I missed him, too, and the spark of excitement and challenge that he had brought into my life. I thought it unlikely that I would ever see him again, and imagined that one day in the far future word would come to Glen Clair that he had married some irreproachable aristocrat approved by his uncle to be the next Countess of Strathconan.

One night at supper Ellen whispered to me that the whisky smugglers were coming again, and that she and I had to be abed with the covers up over our ears, or Uncle Ebeneezer would have our hides. Naturally I did not want to fall in with Uncle Ebeneezer's wishes, but I could see the sense in what Ellen was saying, so I stayed in my room with the candle blown out. I thought I heard Neil's voice amongst the others, and my blood prickled with the same mixture of anger and frustration that I had felt that day I confronted him in the orchard. By a great effort of will I stayed in my bed, and did not slip across to the window to watch for him when the smugglers left. But I lay awake for a long time after the horses' hooves had echoed away down the road.

But I digress. I was intending to write of the fateful day that was to lead me into such deep trouble with my Uncle Ebeneezer.

It was on account of Mrs Grant's lumbago that I was

cleaning the library one morning, for the poor woman was so bent with pain that she could barely lift a dish-cloth. I was taking the cobwebs down from the high rafters with a bunch of feathers tied to a stick, the poor fowl that had provided them having graced our dinner table the previous Sunday. The room was called the library, but of course Uncle Ebeneezer had burned all the books, so it was in fact nothing more than a cold, bleak space with empty shelves. I hated being in there and was hurrying in order to get back to the relative warmth of the kitchen. And then I saw the family bible. It was not hidden away, but was sitting in plain view on the shelf. Its once black leather cover was grey with clinging dust, and the gilt letters that spelled out the words 'Holy Bible' were worn almost away. I only opened it on a whim.

Actually that is not true. I opened it because I remem-bered Neil's words about his being third cousin twice removed to Aunt Madeline, and I wanted to read the details of his ancestry. Even when he was not there, Neil's presence seemed to stick in my mind like a burr.

Inside the cover on the very first page of foolscap was

a family ancestry, written in a thin scrawl in faded black ink. It seemed that the Balfours were as ancient a family as my papa had always boasted, for despite their poor estate, the list of their antecedents went back to 1353 and a relative of King David II. Tracing my finger down the line of names I saw that the firstborn son had always been called David until the generation before my own. But when I reached the line where my father's name and that of Uncle Ebeneezer should have been, the names were crossed through heavily and the thin parchment was yellowed and torn. I could just decipher my father's name and his date of birth—1754. Uncle Ebeneezer's name was listed afterwards but his birth date was unreadable.

I suppose that I should have been suspicious then, but it never occurred to me that my father had been the elder son and that Uncle Ebeneezer might have swindled me out of my inheritance. Even had I known my uncle was the younger son, I would probably have assumed that my father, learned and bookish, had given the estate of Glen Clair to his brother outright, so that he could be free of the responsibility and could pursue his scholarly interests in peace. I suppose that I might have asked some difficult questions, for I am fatally inquisitive, but at that moment, looking down at the family bible and feeling the history of the Balfours stretching back over the centuries, I felt no more than awe that I belonged to that long procession of names.

There was a movement behind me, and I spun around to see that Uncle Ebeneezer himself was standing in the open doorway of the library, watching me with cunning in his bloodshot eyes. Although he did not appear to be drunk this morning he had not washed, still less shaved, and his shirt and breeches reeked of stale whisky and smoke. I repressed the urge to open a window there and then, to let in the fresh air and sunshine, for somehow my uncle always brought with him a shadow of darkness and misery, as well as the more tangible smell of the still and the stable.

I dropped him a small but respectful curtsey, making sure at the same time that I kept out of his reach. Uncle Ebeneezer was free with his fists, though I had never seen him strike a member of the family, only the servants. I had no illusions that he had any affection for me, though, just because we shared a name. Sometimes he looked at me as though he would like to hit me across the room. This was one of those moments. There was violence in those blue eyes alongside the calculation.

'Davie's child,' he said now, head on one side. 'Reading the bible, are ye now?'

I was tempted to reply that we needed all the spiritual succour we could get in that house, but I knew that would only provoke him.

'I was looking at the family history, sir,' I said.

His eyes narrowed on me. 'Were you indeed?' he said. 'The great line of the Balfours, and nothing but two miserable girls to bring it to an end.'

I bit my lip to prevent myself from telling him what I thought of him for that.

'One girl was bad enough.' His tone was musing. 'Sometimes I wonder why I felt the need to take you in as well, Davie's child.'

I had often wondered that too, given that he so clearly disliked me and hardly had the money spare to feed another dependent.

'It's the blood,' he said. He sounded bitter. 'Ye canna escape the demands of the blood.' He looked directly at me. 'Glen Clair should have been yours, Davie's child,' he said. 'But you are only a girl. 'Tis better I keep it myself.'

I had no idea what he was talking about, although I could have argued with the fact that he was in any way better for Glen Clair. He had come close to me now, and all I wanted to do was escape the malevolence that seemed to envelop me whenever Uncle Ebeneezer was near. I tried to slip by him, but he caught my arm in a grip so tight I dropped the feather duster with a clatter on the stone floor. I could feel anger in him, and violence and something strange that felt like conflict.

'You'd be better off dead, Davie's child,' he said, 'than reliant on me.'

'I've no complaints, sir,' I said. My heart was thudding now. 'I'm only grateful to have a roof over my head.' They were craven words, but he was a deal bigger and stronger than I was, and I had to escape his hold before I could do anything else. For a moment I stood there, locked in his grip, and then his clasp on my arm loosened. He let me go, and I was so relieved that I almost fell, for my legs were shaking so much. I did not need to check my arm to know that there would be bruises.

'You've an easy tongue in your head. I'll say that for you, girl,' he said. 'But I've seen the insolence in your eyes. You're not like Ellen—she has no fight.' He scowled at me. 'I'll break you, too, in the end, though. You'll see.'

Poor Ellen. She had never had a chance of developing any spirit in the first place. She had grown up in that house, accepting Uncle Ebeneezer's curtailment of her freedom from the earliest age. In fact it was a surprise to me that she was still sane. Aunt Madeline was no longer sane, with her pretty toy dolls and her bedroom that was a museum to her lost beauty.

'You've had a long time to mould Ellen to your ways,' I said, unable to hold my tongue now I was free and with a clear run to the door. 'But I have only been here a month, and I do not bend easily.'

He made a grab for me, his face contorted with sudden hatred, but I ducked beneath his arm and ran away down the corridor, hearing his roar of fury behind me. I made for the kitchen, on the principle that if the worst came to the worst there would always be a rusty old knife I could grab from a drawer. I slammed the door behind me and stood with my back to the dresser, panting and shaking.

Mrs Grant looked up from peeling the potatoes and turnips, and shook her head at me.

''Tis madness to defy him,' was all she said before she went back to her peeling, head lowered, eyes averted from trouble.

But Uncle Ebeneezer did not follow me, and after a few moments I began to breathe a little easier. I heard the back door slam, and out of the kitchen window I saw him making his stumbling way down the path towards the stables—no doubt to vent his anger on the poor wretch of a groom. I set the kettle on the hob to make a cup of tea to revive myself, and vowed that the next time I cleaned the library I would keep the iron poker within reach. I even slept with a knife under my pillow that night, but I did not think any more of the family history or the ancient line of the Balfours. My encounter with Uncle Ebeneezer had put it from my mind. I should have been suspicious. I should have been careful. But I was not.

* * *

Ellen woke me the next morning by sitting on the edge of my bed and shaking me until I came to. I was so startled to be roused thus that I almost stabbed her by accident.

'What on earth is that for?' she asked me, looking at the dirty kitchen knife I had concealed beneath the covers.

'Mice,' I said.

She looked surprised, then apprehensive. It always made me laugh that a girl who had grown up in the middle of the Highlands should be afraid of small mammals and insects, but that was what Ellen had been taught was acceptable behaviour for a lady.

'Don't worry,' I said, hiding the knife away. 'What was it that you wanted to tell me?'

'Oh, yes!' Her face lit with a smile so bright it felt as though the sun had come out. 'The most exciting news! We are to go to Gairloch for the day! Papa has matters to attend to there—he says he is to meet the Captain of a trading ship with whom he does some business.' She frowned momentarily. 'Which is odd, now I come to think of it, for this is the first I have heard of him having commercial interests. At any rate, he has said that you and I may travel with him and visit the shops, and perhaps even buy some new gloves or a shawl or some lace…'

She was so animated that she could not still the flow of words, and chattered all the while I dressed.

'This is the first time I have left Glen Clair in three years,' she kept saying, as though she could not quite believe it.

She was too excited to eat breakfast, and sat at the table staring at her plate as though entranced. In the end I ate her bowl of porridge and mine as well, and followed it up with some honey and oatcakes. As I have said before, very little affects my appetite— neither good news nor bad—and despite the promise of Uncle Ebeneezer's generosity I could not imagine being treated to dinner, let alone a new pair of gloves.

I had almost finished eating when Uncle Ebeneezer himself came striding into the kitchen. He grabbed the last of the oatcakes from the plate and stuffed them rudely into his mouth, talking through the crumbs.

'Come along, girl! I've been waiting this half hour past!'

Ellen jumped up so abruptly she almost overset the table. Uncle Ebeneezer did not even glance my way, which made me wonder if Ellen had mistaken the invitation and it was for her alone. But when she dragged me out into the stable yard—I was still chewing the last of my breakfast at the time, and shrugging myself into my coat—the gig was drawn up with cushions for two, so from that I gathered that I was to travel with them. I was glad, for I had been away from the sea for over a month and was happy to be bound for it again.

Uncle Ebeneezer drove. He did it as he did most things: carelessly, dangerously and with absolutely no consideration for Ellen and me. We hung on to the sides for dear life as the gig rattled over the bridge and swung onto the road to Gairloch, which was scarcely less rough and rutted than the track to Glen Clair.

The autumn wind tugged at our bonnets, and I was extremely grateful for the thick tweed rug about our knees, for the breeze off Loch Maree was stiff and cold. All the same this counted as a fine day in the Highlands, because it was not raining. There was blue sky and high white clouds and, praise be, very few midges.

As the road climbed towards the Kerrysdale Pass, Uncle Ebeneezer pulled out to overtake a peddler riding a pony, and almost collided with the Ullapool mail coach in the process. There was much swearing and trading of insults, but Ellen did not appear to notice the commotion because she was busy exclaiming over the beauty of the scenery. To our right rose the sandstone bastion of the mountain Slioch, vast and red against the sky. In the valley the waters of Loch Maree sparkled and danced. Ellen was of a mind to be enchanted by everything, and perhaps if I had not left Glen Clair for three years I would have been too, but although I thought the mountains looked vastly pretty in the sunshine, I was still cold and travel-sick with Uncle Ebeneezer's driving.

By the time we rolled into the little seaside town of Gairloch the poor horse was exhausted, and my fingers were stiff from gripping the side of the gig to avoid being thrown on the floor. Uncle Ebeneezer drove into the yard of the Five Bells, muttered something about seeing a man about some business, jumped down and disappeared into the inn.

'Perhaps we could take some refreshment here

before we walk around the town?' I said to Ellen, for the journey had taken a good couple of hours, despite our speed, and I was already sharp set again. The scent of broth was wafting from the inn and it smelled good. My stomach rumbled in an unladylike manner.

Ellen's face fell. 'I do not think we should,' she said. 'This inn is accounted very rough, and Papa's business is private and anyway, I wished to visit the gown shop on the Parade.' She glanced over her shoulder in the direction that Uncle Ebeneezer had disappeared. 'Papa was supposed to have given me some shillings to spend,' she said sadly, 'but I think he has forgotten.'

This did not surprise me. I suspected that Uncle Ebeneezer had forgotten on purpose, never having intended to waste his meagre fortune on ribbons and bows. Ellen probably thought this too, but being a far sweeter natured person than I, was refusing to acknowledge it.

'I could go in and ask him for the money—' I began, but she turned pale and her eyes looked stricken.

She grabbed my arm. 'No!' she said, casting another

fearful glance towards the inn door, as though something dark and dangerous dwelt inside. 'No, don't
disturb him. We shall window-shop instead.'

It seemed to me that pressing our noses against the
glass of a dress shop like the penniless urchins we were
would be poor entertainment, when we could buy a
paper twist of clams for a few pennies and eat them
down by the harbour. The sight of the ships bobbing at
anchor in the bay lifted my heart, reminding me of
home. Nevertheless I allowed Ellen to pull me along the
narrow pavement and through the jostling crowds, past
sedate villas and fishy alleyways, until we reached
Madame Aimée's gown shop.

Gairloch was crowded: fine ladies drew back their
skirts to avoid the uncouth sailors from the merchant
ships. The air was full of the scent of the sea, the cry
of the gulls as they hung on the wind, and the shouts
of street sellers in the market on the quay.

Ellen wrinkled up her nose. 'The smell of fish is
quite dreadfully strong,' she said, stepping delicately
over a couple of severed heads that a fishmonger had
thrown from his basket to a lurking stray cat. I forbore

to point out that this was probably because Gairloch was a port built on the fishing trade.

The gown shop was a pretty little building on the promenade, an avenue that was set back from the quayside and bordered most attractively by gardens. It had bow windows, with an artful show of gowns and shawls, gloves, scarves and reticules to tempt even the most parsimonious of purchasers. Everything was pale pink and green and blue and spring yellow. As soon as Ellen saw the display a faraway look came into her eyes.

'Oh, Catriona, are these not fine? Oh, if only Mama could see the pale pink silk and lace gown! It would suit her so well.'

She looked at her reflection in the windows and her smile slipped a little. I knew that she was thinking that even her best spencer was five years old, probably more, and that in this company she looked shockingly dowdy. As though to underline the fact, a lady paused beside us on her way up the steps into the shop, and looked us up and down as though we were exhibits in a freak show. Her hair was auburn, like mine—though not in the least like mine, in fact, for it had seen the ministrations of a comb more recently, and was piled up beneath a striped green and gold bonnet, whilst my curls had escaped their ribbon and were blowing in the breeze. Her eyes were green and her nose especially designed to look down. She wore a matching gown and spencer in emerald-green and gold, and little green slippers peeped from beneath her hem.

A haughty smile curved her lips. She inclined her head to us with just the right degree of condescension, and I saw myself through her eyes as a tumbled waif in a faded gown, a pauper without a feather to fly. I could almost smell the scent of money on her. Even Ellen's glowing prettiness faded into shadow beside her.

'Oh, how fine!' Ellen said reverentially, when the beauty had passed by.

'How gaudy,' I said. 'How brash.' Envy beat in my blood.

On a wild impulse I ran up the steps and pushed open the door of the gown shop. 'Come along!' I called to Ellen over my shoulder. I think she was almost too scared to come, but in the end, unable to resist, she followed me inside.

The shop smelled divinely of fresh flowers and perfume. There was a low hush of voices as ladies discussed their purchases with the smiling shop assistants. The patronising beauty was over at the counter, sorting through a pile of embroidered silk stockings that cost seven shillings a pair. She had already put at least half a dozen on one side to buy. Madame Aimée swam towards us, her expression of warm welcome cooling slightly as her needle-sharp gaze took in the shabbiness of our clothes, and in particular my darned pelisse.

'How may I help you, ladies?'

Ellen shot me an agonised glance.

'We would like a pair of the pale blue silk embroidered gloves, if you please,' I said recklessly.

'Catriona!' Ellen said, looking as though she would like to sink through the floor.

'They will suit you,' I said. 'They match your spencer.'

In fact they far outshone poor Ellen's outmoded spencer, but I was determined to have them. Something in Madame Aimée's gaze, contempt barely masked by courtesy, brought out the very worst in me.

'They are seventeen shillings a pair,' she said.

'Splendid!' I proclaimed. 'And I will have matching ribbons and bows, to make it up to a round guinea.'

Those of you with a good memory will recall that not only was I in possession of Mr Campbell's pound from the collection plate, but that I had also left Applecross with no less than an additional five pounds from the school trustees and five from my father's colleagues. It was certain that they did not intend me to spend this money on anything as frivolous as feminine fripperies. Nevertheless, as I gazed on a pale bronze evening gown with matching slippers, shawl and reticule, I was sorely tempted to squander the entire amount. I knew that the colour would suit me, and I could see myself wafting up an imaginary staircase in an equally imaginary mansion on the arm of some devastatingly handsome gentleman whose face was disturbingly familiar…I even stretched out my hand to touch the material…

'Catriona,' Ellen said again, and this time there was warning and dread in her tone.

The shop door opened, the bell gave a 'ping'—and I was facing the image of my dreams.

'Neil!' Ellen cried, beaming. 'How delightful to see you here!' Her relief that my purchasing madness had been stopped in its tracks by Mr Sinclair's arrival made her far more fulsome than she would normally have been.

'Neil!' cried the lady in the green and gold stripes, only a second after Ellen. She stopped, glared at Ellen with something close to hatred, and looked at us as though we belonged in the gutter with the fish heads.

'Do you know these…ladies?' she asked Neil, with arctic chill.

Now, although I am not always the most observant of people, being in far too much of a hurry to take action before I have thought matters through, it did appear to me that Mr Sinclair disliked the lady's proprietorial attitude towards him. A hard expression came into his eyes, and his firm mouth set in a slightly disdainful curl. The other ladies in the shop had all stopped talking now, in order to listen. Or perhaps they were just struck dumb by the sight of Mr Sinclair, for he did look far too dark and dangerous and virile for such delicate and refined surroundings.

'These are my cousins, Celeste,' he said, his tone bored.

'Miss Ellen Balfour and Miss Catriona Balfour.' He bowed to us. 'Ladies, may I introduce Miss McIntosh?'

That placated the lady nicely. She even smiled at us.

'Cousins!' she cooed, as though we were still in the schoolroom. 'How charming!' Once again her gaze appraised us. 'Distant ones, I assume? I had heard that none of the Balfours has a penny to rub together.'

'I will take both the gloves and the ribbons, if you please,' I said, producing a guinea in the manner of a magician with a rabbit in his hat.

Celeste McIntosh smirked and turned back to her stockings. 'Come and give me your opinion of the quality of these, Neil,' she said, smiling at him over her shoulder. 'After all, you *are* paying for them.'

Well, *that* was fairly self-explanatory. I felt a strange stab in my stomach akin to indigestion. So this gilded creature was Neil Sinclair's mistress. Truly I did not care except to deplore his bad manners in introducing her to us, his relatives, as though she were a *lady*. I stole a glance at her from under my lashes. This was how elegant and burnished and bright *I* would look if I had accepted Neil's utterly indecent proposal and used his money to turn me from an ugly duckling into a pampered swan. But I had not, and he had moved on to Miss McIntosh quickly enough. Or perhaps he had already had her in keeping when he made his offer to me… Yes, very probably. Neil Sinclair was just that sort of unscrupulous, arrogant man.

Neil leaned forward close to my ear. 'I would take the bronze gown as well,' he murmured. 'It will become you vastly.'

'Don't let me keep you, Mr Sinclair,' I said coldly. 'Miss McIntosh is waiting to discuss stockings with you and your wallet.'

His smile was mocking. 'I do believe you are jealous,' he whispered.

I felt the same squirm of excitement inside that he had always been able to arouse in me. 'I do believe you are conceited,' I said. 'Good day.'

Madame Aimée had already passed my purchases to an underling to wrap, and had hurried away to tend to Miss McIntosh's every need. It seemed to matter nothing to her that Miss McIntosh was a *demi-rep*. In fact I imagined that tending to the fashionable needs of mistresses was far more profitable for her. Husbands were probably less inclined to spend generously on their wives than they were on their lovers.

Neil strolled over to join Miss McIntosh at the counter, and Ellen and I went out onto the street, the precious parcel tucked under her arm.

'You should not have done it, Catriona,' Ellen said. 'That money was meant for your dowry.'

'Dowry?' I laughed. 'When am I going to have the chance to wed? Far better to use the money to bring you some happiness, dearest Ellen, when you have made me so welcome in my new home.'

Ellen turned pink and looked very gratified. 'You are very kind, cousin,' she said. She caught my arm. 'Miss McIntosh,' she whispered. 'Do you think that she is… intimate…with Mr Sinclair?'

'I am sure of it,' I said tartly. 'Unless he is so generous a gentleman that he buys stockings for all the ladies of his acquaintance.'

Ellen looked disapproving. 'I know that gentlemen are permitted to indulge their desires in such a way—'

'So society decrees,' I snapped.

'But even so I would like him better were he not to be so…'

'Licentious?' I said crossly.

'I suppose so,' Ellen said sadly. 'Only think, though, Catriona. That could have been you!'

I paused. Indeed, it could have been. I thought about being Neil's mistress and felt a mixture of virtuous pride at refusing him balanced by an equal amount of unmaidenly curiosity in what the role might entail. Actually, the curiosity was rather stronger than the virtuous pride. I admit that now. Although I would never have admitted it to Ellen then. But I had always had an inquisitive nature.

'That gold and green gown would have suited me well,' I said solemnly. 'I suppose it is not too late to change my mind…'

For a moment I think Ellen actually thought I was about to run back to the gown shop, push Miss McIntosh out of the way and throw myself at Mr Sinclair's feet. Then she saw my face and burst out laughing.

'For a moment I believed you,' she said.

It was in a state of high good humour that we arrived

back at the Five Bells. The church clock was striking the hour of two, and this time I was absolutely determined to eat before Uncle Ebeneezer dragged us back to seclusion at Glen Clair. This might be the last time Ellen and I saw the outside world for another three years. But as soon as we walked through the door of the inn parlour Uncle Ebeneezer grabbed the parcel from Ellen and tossed it onto the table.

'What's this?' he said contemptuously.

Ellen shot me a terrified look. 'Gloves and ribbons, Papa. Catriona bought them.'

Uncle Ebeneezer picked the parcel up and threw it casually into the fire. Ellen gave a little horrified scream. I ran forward as the paper curled in the heat and started to blacken and char. I could see the ribbon starting to burn, orange flames leaping and dancing in the grate. But it was the smell of the gloves burning that made me dart forward and plunge my hand into the flames in a hopeless, desperate attempt to save them. I knew it was stupid and pointless. The silk was so delicate, and it was already flaking away into ash, but I was damned if I would allow Uncle Ebeneezer's careless cruelty to beat me.

Ellen screamed properly when she saw what I was about, but it was Uncle Ebeneezer who moved, grabbing my arm and dragging me back so brutally that my shoulder wrenched.

'Papa, no!'

'Too much spirit,' Uncle Ebeneezer said. His face was a mottled grey colour. I could smell the sourness of wine on his breath. 'I said I'd break you, girl. And so I shall, before you take back all that should have been mine.'

He spun me around to face him and I saw his upraised hand too late. I did not have time to think, or even to feel fear. He hit me hard, and I went out like a blown candle.

Chapter Nine

In which I am kidnapped.

'Catriona!'

Someone was calling my name in a tone edged with urgency. Through the terrible ache in my head I wondered if it was my papa. He felt close.

'Catriona! Wake up!'

Papa's voice again. I wanted very much to please him and obey, but his very insistence drew me back to places and thoughts I would rather escape.

I opened my eyes reluctantly.

It was dark. I tried to move and realised that I was bound hand and foot, trussed up like a chicken for the plucking. My head ached fiercely. I gave a small, heartfelt groan and wished myself unconscious again. Unfortunately my wishes were not answered.

The noise was deafening, and now that I was awake I could not blot it out. The sound of water roared in my ears, along with the thrashing of waves, the crack of sails, the shouts of men and the scrabbling of what sounded to be rats' claws on wood. The whole world rocked and tumbled around me, first up in a giddying heave and then down in a rush that made my stomach somersault.

We were out at sea. The knowledge slid into my mind as my stomach gave another sickening lurch. Furthermore, I knew enough about ships and had sailed enough in my childhood to realise that I was lying somewhere in the depths of the hold, and that we were already out of the shelter of the harbour with the wind blowing a gale. The ship groaned and juddered about me, and I rolled with each blow of the waves against the side.

Someone moved beside me—moved and spoke.

'Catriona,' he said for a third time. 'Thank God. I was afraid he had hit you so hard you would never recover your wits.'

I recognised Neil Sinclair's voice, though I could see nothing of him in the darkness. He shifted a little, and I realised dimly that he was tied up next to me. This seemed odd, but even as I tried to grasp the thought it slipped from my mind like water. Strange, disconnected memories drifted through my mind. I thought that I had seen Neil recently, but could not recall the circum-stances. I remembered going to a gown shop with Ellen and buying the beautiful gloves. I remembered a little stray cat in an alleyway and the sights and smells of Gairloch, ships bobbing at anchor in the harbour. I saw all of this as a series of images flashing across the surface of my mind in quicksilver colours, but I did not seem able to thread the whole together and recall what had happened to me.

My thoughts dipped and swooped with the move-ment of the boat. My head ached horribly and my face felt stiff. My arms were bound behind me in a most un-natural and uncomfortable posture, and my ankles were tied so tight the ropes bit into my skin. In short, it was not pleasant, and the easiest thing to do was ignore it and slip away back into unconsciousness.

'I don't want to talk,' I said, and even those words felt like an inordinate effort. 'I'm tired. I don't like it here and I want to sleep.' I think I sounded cross and childish. At any rate, Neil laughed.

'I daresay you do,' he said. 'But if you go to sleep now they may come for you and you may never waken again.' His tone hardened. There was something in it that I had never heard before. I had thought him a scoundrel, a man of straw, but now he sounded tough and uncompromising.

'Your uncle hit you, Catriona,' he said. 'He knocked you unconscious and then he paid for you to be kidnapped and put aboard this ship. He planned it all along. It was the only reason he brought you and Ellen to Gairloch today. He wanted to be rid of you. Now, are you simply going to go to sleep and let him get away with that?'

His words were like a dousing of cold seawater. Suddenly I remembered everything. Fury washed through me so hot and fierce that it is a wonder I did not combust spontaneously there and then and burn the ship down. You may already have noticed that I have a fine temper, and this time I was enraged. So this was my uncle's doing. Cunning, deceitful Uncle Ebeneezer, plotting to be rid of his brother's child! He had tricked me and injured me and paid to be rid of me, and I was *damned* if I was going to roll over and simply let it happen.

'You are right, Mr Sinclair,' I said, sounding a deal calmer than I felt inside. 'I suspected that he did not like me, but this is going too far.'

Neil laughed again, and this time there was relief in it. 'I knew that would get through to you,' he said. 'I knew all I had to do was make you angry.'

'You have quite a talent for it,' I said, and despite everything I smiled, too. The fury had cleared my head quickly, burning away all confusion. I held on to it because it was the only thing that warded off my despair. My uncle had deliberately, callously brought me to this. I was cold, I was damp, I was in pain, and I was desperately hungry, and I doubted that any of those factors would change in the near future. In fact it seemed to me that the prospects of a decent supper were fairly bleak.

'So,' I said, 'what ship is this? Where are we going? And what is your connection to all this, Mr Sinclair?'

'How like a woman to start at the wrong end,' Neil Sinclair said. 'I will ask the questions, if you please. Why did your uncle see fit to get rid of you like this?'

I did not know the answer to this for sure, of course, but I remembered the bible, with its family tree defaced and torn to erase the record of my father's generation, and the expression in Uncle Ebeneezer's eyes when he saw me standing there looking at it. Suddenly a great many things made sense. Uncle Ebeneezer had not liked me, nor wanted me at Glen Clair, but it was unlikely that that alone would have been sufficient to make him take such pains to get rid of me. No, there had to be a greater reason for his hostility. I remembered his words then, too late.

'Glen Clair should have been yours, Davie's child... but you are only a girl. 'Tis better I keep it myself.'

And then again, that very day, before he had struck me down. *'I said I'd break you, girl. And so I shall, before you take back all that should have been mine.'*

'I am not perfectly certain,' I said slowly, 'but I think it is because I must be the rightful owner of Glen Clair. I think my father was the elder son, and that I should inherit the property after him. Uncle Ebeneezer told me as much, in a roundabout way.'

Neil gave a low whistle. 'Men have died for less.'

'And women too,' I said tartly. 'Even for a small, neglected parcel of land in the middle of nowhere.'

'Glen Clair could turn a tidy profit if it was properly run,' Neil said. He shifted again, and I had the fleeting impression that he was in some pain. 'It is no mean inheritance, and I do not suppose your uncle wished to give it up. Did you challenge him about your suspicions?'

'No,' I said, 'for I had not realised that he might have swindled me.' My head ached all the more as I thought about it. 'I cannot be sure of it, and I do not understand how it might have happened, but I imagine that Mr Campbell must know the truth. He is my godfather and my father's oldest friend. Oh, if only he had told me!'

'Mr Campbell is a good man,' Neil said, 'but he is

also unworldly and thinks the best of everyone. Perhaps he thought that it was your uncle's place to tell you of your inheritance, or perhaps your papa requested him to keep silent. We shall not know unless you get the chance to ask him—'

'Which is looking increasingly unlikely at the moment,' I finished.

It was very odd, talking to Neil like this. I could not see him except as a darker shadow against the blackness that pressed all around us. He was not touching me, and I was not even sure how near to me he lay, though from the sound of his voice it was a matter of no more than a few feet. I could see nothing, yet I could feel his presence. It felt strong and comforting. It was warm and reassuring to have him there. He made me feel safe and protected, there in the intimate dark.

This was strange, for I also knew without asking that Neil was probably in as great a state of discomfort as I was, if not worse, for although he had made no mention of it there was an underlying strain in his voice that constantly suggested pain. It is difficult to explain, but it felt as though he was obliged to think past some barrier in order to concentrate on talking to me. It felt as though he was only conquering his pain through sheer force of will. I wondered if he, too, had been knocked unconscious and brutally manhandled into this prison. I wondered if he would tell me.

'What about you?' I said, trying to keep my tone light. 'I think it only fair that you should tell me what happened to you now that I have told you why I am here.'

He sighed. 'I got into a fight,' he said, 'and I was on the losing side.'

'I hope it was not over Miss McIntosh,' I said, 'for I suspect she would not be worth it.'

He gave a snort of laughter. 'Unlike you, Catriona,' he said softly. 'You are well worth fighting for.'

That stole my breath for a moment—until I told myself that I was sitting bound and helpless, a prisoner in the hold of a ship, and there were far more pressing matters to concern myself with than a flirtation with Neil Sinclair. Even so, there was some sweetness in pretending otherwise.

'I do not believe I gave you permission to address me by my first name, sir,' I said.

'Well, you'll just have to let it go on this occasion,' Neil said, 'as there are more important matters to discuss.'

'Yes,' I said. 'So you were in a fight. Were you hurt?'

He was silent for a long time. 'No,' he said, at last. 'Not much.'

'Liar,' I said. 'If I could see you…'

He laughed. 'Ah, well, if you could see me you would realise that I am not perhaps looking my immaculate best. But the damage is only superficial.'

'I don't believe you,' I said baldly. 'But I know you won't tell me the truth. Tell me instead who the fight was with.'

The smile was still in his voice. 'Your uncle.'

'He's a busy man,' I said.

'Plus three or four others.'

'You are only saying that so that I do not think you too easily overpowered,' I said.

'Perhaps I am. Yes, there were ten of them…'

'And the reason? It was not because of me, was it? Did you see what Uncle Ebeneezer had done to me—?'

'And you think that *I* am conceited!' He sounded amused. 'Do you think I would trouble to disturb the set of my coat over you, Miss Balfour?'

'You have just told me that I am worth fighting for,' I said. 'Now you are changing your tune.'

'Well, in principle you are correct,' Neil said. His voice changed, became brisk. 'You *are* worth fighting for. But on this occasion I was attacked by your uncle and his cronies because I had upset them in a business arrangement.' He stopped.

'Why don't you tell me the whole tale?' I said crossly. 'Instead of me having to wheedle it out of you with endless questions. It is not as though we lack the time.'

'True,' Neil said. He sounded rueful. 'The only reason I hesitated was because…' He stopped again.

'Because you do not trust me,' I said. 'Or perhaps—' I was hit by sudden inspiration '—it reflects badly on you and you fear my poor opinion?'

'You have always had a poor opinion of me,' Neil said, still sounding rueful.

'Well, first you propositioned me to be your mistress,' I pointed out helpfully, 'and then I discovered you to be a whisky smuggler. I only base my opinion on experience.'

'Quite,' Neil said. He sighed. 'Well, it may do my cause some good with you if I tell you that your uncle and his henchmen beat me up because they discovered that I was no true smuggler. They found out that I was working for the excise.'

'You were an excise man pretending to be a smuggler?' I said. 'No wonder they were angry!'

'They always had their suspicions of me,' Neil said. 'After all, I was an officer in the Navy. But corrupt officers are nothing new, and I was also a Sinclair and a Highlander, so…' I sensed a shrug in his words.

'So they trusted you and then found you to be false,' I said. 'I can imagine how that would be. How did they find out?'

'I am not sure,' Neil said, 'though I think it was that tailor's dummy Arlo Graham. I suspect that he genuinely *was* in the pay of the smugglers, and laid information with them that I was secretly working for the excise.'

'He was certainly very slow in pursuing you the night

I first arrived at Glen Clair,' I said, remembering. 'I thought it was because he was downright lazy and did not want to spoil the line of his uniform with physical exercise, but perhaps he had been paid to be blind, deaf and idle as well.'

'Perhaps,' Neil said. 'And perhaps he was also the man giving your uncle secret intelligence to pass along to the French—under cover of smuggling the whisky.'

That took the breath from me. I had wondered why a man like Neil Sinclair had been deputed to work secretly for the excise, but now I saw that it was a great deal more serious than that. He had been working against those who spied for the French.

'Uncle Ebeneezer is a French spy?' I said. I think there was a fair degree of unflattering surprise in my voice. 'I can scarce credit it.'

'Hence his success,' Neil said dryly. 'It is a certainty that he was passing information along with each consignment of whisky. He had a well-established route by which the whisky was smuggled out. Messages were passed along it too, from the barracks at Ruthven to the coast.'

'But I thought we were at peace with the French now,' I objected.

'The Treaty of Amiens will not hold,' Neil said. 'There was never a chance of it. We will be back at war within the year.'

I would have shaken my head at the shock of it all if I had been able to move.

'So you were betrayed, and they set a trap for you,' I said.

'Yes,' Neil said. He sounded bitter. 'Fool that I was for not seeing it. I had been smuggling alongside the gang for six months and thought your uncle trusted me.' He sighed. 'He bade me meet with him at the Five Bells in Gairloch. I left Miss McIntosh at the tea shop, with the promise of returning to her shortly, and followed you and your cousin along the promenade.'

'Poor Miss McIntosh,' I said. 'I wonder if she is still there? Perhaps she will be if she believes that you are worth waiting for?'

'I doubt it,' Neil said. 'Miss McIntosh has never lacked for masculine admiration and she has a short attention span.'

'Dear me,' I said blandly. 'I think I may have made a mistake when I turned you down, Mr Sinclair. You could have been a mere stepping stone to so many others.'

I felt him looking at me through the darkness. Strange—when I could not see him—that I knew that his look was intense and hot enough to send sparks through my blood even in the dark. Especially in the dark. I shivered, and this time it was from neither the rats nor the cold.

'Pray continue your tale,' I said hastily.

'I walked into the inn parlour a bare few minutes after you,' Neil said. 'The first thing I saw was you, insensible on the couch, and Ellen in hysterics. Before I could even open my mouth to ask what was going on your uncle turned on me and denounced me for a traitor. Someone hit me, and we had a fight that ended up with me here, with no escape and nothing but a slip of a girl as an ally.'

'Well,' I said tartly, 'since I *am* the only ally you have, you might be a bit more grateful.' I sighed. 'I might have known that Ellen would have the vapours,' I added. 'Was there ever such a helpless girl?'

'I'm not sure that she could have done anything more practical,' Neil said. 'There were four or five burly men there, and she is at the mercy of her father.'

I was not particularly impressed, either by Ellen's behaviour or by Neil's defence of her, but I let it pass since there were more pressing matters in my mind. But you may be sure that had I been in Ellen's place I would have found some way of saving the day—or so I like to think.

'What manner of ship is this, Mr Sinclair?' I asked. 'Is it a slaver? Am I bound to be raped or sold into servitude or worse? Are we to be thrown overboard? You had best tell me the truth. I need to prepare myself.'

Neil was silent, which did nothing to reassure me. Despite my attempts to remain calm my imagination was by now running riot. The crew, I was sure, must be rough, uncouth men, to take such a commission from my uncle, and as such they would clearly be criminals engaged in smuggling, slaving and worse. Besides, a rat had just scurried over my skirts in the dark, its feet pattering away on the bare boards of the ship. There is nothing like being down among the rats in the darkness to encourage the mind to run wild.

'I fear I cannot offer much comfort,' Neil said. 'I know the Captain of this ship. Whilst he may sail on the wrong side of the law, he has never dealt in slaves before, but…' He let the sentence trail away.

'He may not deal in slaves, but he deals in bribes,' I said. 'And he has agreed to rid my uncle of the two of us. What does he mean to do—murder us?'

'He may,' Neil said. 'Though I suspect he would not care to sully his hands with such work unless your uncle has paid him a vast sum of money. The Navy have had their eye on him for a while. We suspected he was a French sympathiser.'

'Then it is a pity you did not do something about it sooner,' I said, testing the ropes at my wrists and ankles and feeling them burn me. 'I have a bad feeling about this whole business. Since you recognise him, Mr Sinclair, he cannot run the risk of you returning to tell your Navy colleagues what he has done. Nor can I be allowed to return with some wild tale of kidnap. He might as well kill us and have done with it.'

'You may find out soon enough,' Neil said, 'for I hear someone coming.' There was the beat of footsteps above our heads. Neil shifted beside me and his voice became urgent. 'Catriona. Be careful what you say. You are right in that we do not know what fate is intended for us.'

'I know you think me foolishly outspoken—' I started to say, but he interrupted me.

'No,' he said. 'No, I do not. You are courageous to a fault. That is why you have to be careful.'

There was no time for any more, because with a creak of protest a trap door opened above and a lantern glimmered in the gap. I saw first of all the strong dark beams of the ship, like a cage about us, and a wooden ladder descending from a small square gap in the roof. A man came down, lantern in hand. He was small and young, younger than I, and he had a thatch of unkempt hair, darting eyes, and a merry smile that seemed singularly inappropriate given the circumstances.

But as soon as the light fell around me I forgot everything else because then I could see Neil, and I will never forget what he looked like. His uniform was filthy beyond recognition, his dark hair matted and dull with dust. There was an evil looking cut to his forehead that was still crusted with blood, and a bruise on one cheek-bone that looked angry and raw. But it was the way that they had tied him up that caused me to catch my breath on a gasp. I had thought that they had been cruel to me, with the rope tied so tight that I had lost the sensation in my limbs, but Neil had been tied like a bow, his wrists bound to his ankles so that he was bent into the most painful and unnatural shape imaginable.

The man with the lantern heard me gasp. He looked across at Neil with dislike. 'Don't waste your sympathy on him, lassie. No one likes him very much.'

He threw down a hunk of bread and a pannikin of water in Neil's general direction, although it must have been obvious to him that Neil could reach neither, and then he knelt by my feet and cut through the ropes that bound my ankles.

'Captain wants to see you, lassie,' he said, with another inappropriately merry smile. 'Follow me.'

I hesitated, looking at Neil, wanting to help in some way, but he looked straight back at me, his dark gaze forbidding me to interfere. I bit my lip hard, to prevent the furious words from spilling out. The lantern bobbed ahead of me as my guide shinned up the ladder and through the hatch, plunging the hold back into darkness. I followed much more slowly, because I was cold and stiff and my legs were shaking and reluctant to work.

'Remember,' Neil whispered, 'be careful, Catriona.'

And then the trap door closed, condemning him to the darkness, and I was standing on the deck, blinking in the pale evening light, shivering and shivering, and wondering if I would ever see him alive again.

Chapter Ten

In which I meet Captain Hoseason and hatch a plan for escape.

It was cold on the deck, and there was a fresh breeze rattling the rigging, although the gale that had battered us earlier had blown itself out. As far as I could see, our ship was alone on the ocean. It was my bad luck that the recently signed peace treaty had lifted the requirement for merchant ships to sail in convoy, protected by a naval vessel.

Night was falling and the moon was full, illuminating the islands to the west. The brig was rounding the north-west point of the Isle of Skye. I could see the outline of the wickedly sharp Coullin Mountains against the deep blue of the twilight. Applecross lay beyond, across the Inner Sound, and I felt such a sudden and sharp bite of homesickness that for a moment tears closed my throat. But my escort had no patience and had a hand on my arm, beckoning me to follow him.

The Captain's cabin was warm and lit by a couple of lamps that swung from an overhead beam. After the dark horrors of the hold it looked calm and welcoming, but I knew that I was not among friends here. This was the man who had taken my uncle's commission to get rid of me. He was seated at a desk, writing, and did not look up when I entered, which was no doubt intended to make me feel insignificant, but only succeeded in making me feel annoyed.

Whilst he was rude enough to ignore me, I studied him; he was tall, dark and sober-looking, studious and self-possessed, far from the image of a pirate brigand involved in kidnap and deceit. Eventually he looked up and his eyes, dark and deep-set, rested on me for a moment. I looked back at him directly. Although I remembered Neil telling me to be careful, I was damned if I would be servile.

'Thank you, Ransome,' the Captain said. 'Pray fetch Mr Riach.' Then, as the cabin lad scampered off to do his will, he turned to me. 'Mr Riach is my second officer,' he explained. 'Mr Struan, the First Officer, is navigator, and needed on deck at present whilst we sail these treacherous waters.' He sketched a slight bow. 'I am Captain Hoseason, Miss Balfour.'

It seemed remarkable to me that he was treating this as though it were some sort of social occasion and he expected me to curtsey in return. I gave him a cool look instead.

'Treacherous waters, indeed,' I said coldly. I held out my bound wrists. 'I'll thank you to remove these ropes.'

He hesitated a moment, before taking a dirk from his belt and cutting through the ties. The rush of feeling as the blood returned was sharp enough to drag a gasp from me, and he poured a measure from the brandy bottle on his desk, holding the glass out to me. I took it reluctantly. I have never liked brandy, and

I did not want to take anything from him, but I did need it now.

'Thank you,' I said.

'Take a seat, Miss Balfour,' Captain Hoseason said, waving me towards a battered leather armchair that was lashed to the floor. 'In a moment Mr Riach will escort you to his cabin, which is yours for the duration of your voyage. Ransome will bring you hot water to wash…' His gaze lingered on me—and no doubt I was rather dirty and smelly by now. 'And hot food as well.'

'That all sounds delightful, Captain,' I said, 'and I thank you for it. But…my voyage to where, precisely?' By now I was fuming at the Captain's suggestion that I was an honoured guest on this journey rather than a prisoner who had spent the last several hours trussed up in the hold. I imagined he had locked me up to try and break my spirit, so that I would accept whatever fate was intended for me. The thought made me angry.

Captain Hoseason smiled, though his eyes were cold. I understood then that he was a ruthless man, a man who would take an unsavoury commission simply for the money and that no appeals to his sentiment would work because he *had* no sentiment. I straightened instinctively, recognising him as an adversary. I did not sit, for that would have placed me a great deal lower than he was, and I had no desire to look up at him like an adoring puppy gazing on its master.

'We are headed for Hispaniola,' he said. 'It is my intention to put you ashore there, Miss Balfour.'

I did not like the sound of that. Being abandoned, alone, unprotected and with no money in a foreign land was a terrifying prospect when I was eighteen years old and had travelled no further than Edinburgh in my life. By the exercise of the greatest self-control I kept absolutely quiet. I think Captain Hoseason had expected me to protest, to beg him to spare me, but I did not, and after a moment he resumed.

'Your uncle wished your fate to be rather more conclusive, Miss Balfour, but I am a generous man and would not wish to have such a matter on my conscience...' He shrugged. 'I decided you might fare better in the colonies. There is a gentleman there I know who is looking for a young wife.' His gaze lingered on me in a way that made my skin crawl. 'He is willing to pay well, so it will benefit both of us for you to arrive unharmed, in good health and strength… All will be well with you, and your uncle need never know.'

The nausea rose in my throat. So I was a slave, then, in all but name. I was to be sold off like a virginal sacrifice to some rich colonial to warm his bed and meet his every whim. It was vile.

'I see,' I said. I did see too; I saw that he had taken my uncle's money to kill me and then cheated him. I saw that there was no point in begging for clemency when there was none to be had.

'And Mr Sinclair?' I asked. 'Where does his journey take him?'

Somehow I did not think they would be taking Neil all the way to the Caribbean.

'He goes straight to the bottom of the sea,' Captain Hoseason said, and I could not suppress a wince.

'You have a fondness for the gentleman?' the Captain asked.

'He is my cousin,' I said.

The Captain raised his brows. 'Is he so? I never heard that the Balfours and the Sinclairs were related.'

'My aunt is his mother's cousin thrice removed,' I said.

'That may be the case,' Captain Hoseason said, 'but his journey still takes him directly to the bottom of the sea. We wait only to be well clear of land.' His tone hardened. 'I want to run no risk of Mr Sinclair being picked up by another ship or managing to reach the shore.'

It was as I had feared. The smugglers had paid well for Neil to be murdered, and this time Captain Hoseason had no scruples because his own survival depended on it.

'You know, of course,' I said, 'that Mr Sinclair's uncle is a rich man, who will pay well for his heir to be restored to him—twice, maybe four times the money you were given to kill him?'

The Captain looked pained at my bluntness. 'I had thought of it,' he admitted after a moment—of course he had, for he was motivated by nothing if not money. 'But sadly it would not serve. I could not trust Mr Sinclair to hold his tongue. He is a Navy man, and they would hunt me down to avenge one of their own. There are too many reasons why he has to go, and soon.'

There was a knock at the door and Mr Riach, the

second officer, appeared. He was tall and he had start-
lingly bright green eyes, a tangle of fair hair and a long,
thin, melancholy face. I put his age at about thirty years.
He looked like a gentleman but I doubted he could be,
being one of Captain Hoseason's crew. As he stood
swaying in the doorway I also realised that he was
drunk. The smell of rum hung about him like a cloak.

The Captain did not look pleased. 'Been at the stores
again, Mr Riach?' he said.

Mr Riach bowed rather insolently, I thought. 'There
are precious few privileges aboard this old tub, Captain,
and even fewer when you take payment for murder and
the rest of us do not have a share.'

I sighed. For a moment there I had hoped the second
officer was a man of principle, but it seemed that he did
not object to murder as such, only that he had been
cheated of a share in the spoils.

'It adds insult to injury,' Mr Riach continued, 'that
I have to give up my cabin for the duration of the
voyage as well.'

'For which I thank you,' Captain Hoseason said
quickly, 'as I am sure Miss Balfour does, too. And let

us have no talk of murder, Mr Riach. You will show Miss Balfour to her cabin, if you please. Miss Balfour—' he turned to me '—you may have the run of the ship, for there is nowhere for you to go and no way to escape.'

'The men don't like it,' Mr Riach said, shooting me a dark look from those melancholy eyes. 'They say having a woman aboard brings bad luck. They say it is worse than having a P-I-G—' he spelled it out '—on the ship.'

The Captain snapped his fingers. 'Superstitious fools, the lot of them. Nevertheless, Miss Balfour—' once again he turned to me with exemplary courtesy '—it might be worth staying out of the way of my sailors. I could not guarantee your safety if they decided to toss you over the side.'

'Thank you for the warning, Captain,' I said, nose in the air. 'If there are books to read, and if I may walk on the deck when it is quiet, then I shall be very content.'

He looked at me as though he could not quite understand my attitude. 'You seem mighty calm, Miss Balfour, for one who has been kidnapped aboard ship and is being taken from all that is familiar. Why is that?'

'You have met my uncle, Captain,' I said. 'Do you think that life at Glen Clair was preferable to forging a future in a new land? In all likelihood the man has done me a favour.'

I did not believe it, of course, and I am not sure the Captain believed *me,* but Mr Riach gave a snort of sardonic laughter.

'Miss Balfour has a point, Captain,' he said. 'That old miser must be hell to live with.'

The captain looked sour. Matters were not working out quite as he wanted, I suppose. He had a drunken second officer who was pressing for a share in his profits, he had a restless crew who did not want a woman aboard and he had a prisoner who was not behaving in the manner he felt a prisoner ought. He was probably thinking that he had not been paid enough for this. I hoped he was not thinking it best to despatch me to the bottom with Neil and have done with it, for I had every intention of using my time and my liberty to plan an escape.

The Captain shrugged. 'You will wish to inspect your new quarters, Miss Balfour. Mr Riach will escort you. Riach, send Ransome for hot water and food to be served to Miss Balfour in her cabin.'

'I know what befits a lady better than you, Captain,' Mr Riach said huffily, standing aside to permit me to precede him from the cabin.

On the way to my new quarters I asked Mr Riach some artless questions about the ship. I learned that she was nineteen years old, was seventy-seven foot long with a beam of twenty-four foot and a depth of twelve, and that she was not a bad piece of work. Mr Riach had sailed with the Captain on three previous voyages, and on this trip they were carrying all manner of mixed goods. The crew numbered fifteen men. It was this last piece of information that interested me the most, and I filed it away in my mind for future reference. Fifteen men was a great many to overpower if Neil and I were to be free, but I was optimistic that I would think of a way of managing it.

You will have seen the flaw in my reasoning, I expect: the flaw that I am sorry to say did not leap out and strike me when it should have. If by some miracle I could overpower sufficient of the crew to set Neil free, and if he were to despatch the rest, there would be no possible way that he and I could sail the ship between us. Yes, I admit it—it never even occurred to me.

Anyway, by the time that we reached Mr Riach's cabin, which I could see had been hastily tidied against my arrival, Mr Riach and I were on fair terms.

'There is nothing but sea blankets for the bunk, Miss Balfour,' he said apologetically. 'I am afraid you will find them rather rough.'

'I am extremely grateful, Mr Riach,' I said truthfully, 'and make no complaint. I am sorry to evict you from your own quarters.'

He shrugged and looked a little uncomfortable. 'The Captain does as he wishes,' he said, 'and the berths in the roundhouse are not so bad.'

The cabin boy, Ransome, brought my food then, and water to wash in, so Mr Riach excused himself and I sat down at the tiny table to eat. The thick chicken broth was better than anything I had eaten at Glen Clair, but I could not be comfortable thinking of Neil down in the hold beneath me, shackled so cruelly to the bulkhead.

When Ransome came back to collect my dishes I

asked him how long it would be until we were in open water. He looked doubtful—I think the Captain had told him not to answer any of my questions—then muttered something about two days at the most, depending on the weather, and scuttled off.

So there it was. There were no more than two days until we were free of the coast and the Captain was free to send Neil to a watery grave.

I did not sleep well that night.

The following day there was a strong westerly blowing, penning us close to land and setting Captain Hoseason in a very bad mood indeed. A Navy cutter had been sighted to the north, and he was like a cat on hot coals at the thought of it pursuing us. I confess I could understand his difficulty. If the *Cormorant* was boarded I could not see how he might easily explain away an unwilling female passenger and a Navy captain tied up in the hold. But as matters turned out the cutter disappeared, the crew breathed a little more easily and Neil took a step closer to his doom.

After my breakfast of porridge and a hard ship's roll,

I took a turn about the decks. I had washed and pressed my clothes and made myself look as respectable as possible, even going to the extent of borrowing a thick coat from Mr Riach's tiny wardrobe to muffle myself against the wind and make me appear as shapeless and unfeminine as I could.

I had already observed that the crew were orderly and polite, if not particularly well drilled in seamanship, and despite what Mr Riach had said they did not seem disposed to dislike me. They touched their forelocks most respectfully when I passed, some even lending a hand to steady me when the swell of the waves had me clinging to a rope or handrail to avoid falling. Although I had been seasick on ships in the past I now found that I was not the least affected by the motion of the swell, and I think that that too commanded the respect of the crew, who must have expected me to cower in my cabin or behave like a helpless female. Perhaps I had too much to think about to have time to spare for sickness. At any rate, my mind was fully occupied, running backwards and forwards over the opportunities to free Neil and to escape.

These were, admittedly, very limited. In fact they were practically non-existent, but I did not want to be defeatist. There were fifteen men crewing the ship and I had no weapon to use against them. In my wanderings I had discovered that all the firearms and cutlasses, along with the best part of the food, were stored in the round-house, a cabin occupied for the most part by at least two sailors, one of whom was always an officer. There was not the slightest chance of my slipping in there unnoticed and lifting a dirk from one of the lockers. And even if I did I still had to overpower the man who guarded the trap door down to the hold. It was a problem.

I ate my lunch alone in my cabin, staring through the tiny porthole at the land slipping along rapidly to the east. The wind had turned to the north and the brig was cutting along at a rare pace now. I could feel the seconds of Neil's life ticking down inexorably and the panic tightened inside me. Once we were beyond the Outer Hebrides I knew we would turn westward into the Atlantic Ocean, and then there would be nothing between us and America and nothing between Neil and death.

I felt so helpless and so angry, and so many other

emotions that I did not want to explore. If I was going to lose Neil I could not bear to open up all those feelings and acknowledge how I really felt about him. So I told myself that I barely knew him. I told myself that he was a handsome rogue—arrogant, devil-may-care, charming and dangerous—and that dangerous scoundrels had a habit of coming to a bad end. But I knew now in my heart of hearts that he also had honour and principle and courage, and I could not simply dismiss him nor my feelings for him.

I loved him.

I loved him for all those qualities that I had told myself I deplored. I loved his honour and his bravery but I also loved his arrogance and his charm. I also knew that this was not the time to sit around idly reflecting on my feelings for Neil Sinclair.

I am the only ally you have…

I felt hopeless, frustrated, impotent as though I had already failed him. I paced the little cabin, trying to think of a way to help Neil and trying to find something—anything—that I could use as a weapon. There was not even a mirror that I could break to use a shard of glass as a knife. But that was probably a good thing, for not only was I superstitious enough to wish to avoid the seven years of bad luck, I also had no real wish to see how bedraggled I was looking. It was probably vain of me even to be thinking of such a thing at a time like that, but, well, if that was vanity then I stand condemned.

By the time the sun was setting I reckoned we were west of the Isle of Barra and heading out into the open sea. Mr Struan, the first officer and navigator, was a man of few words and did not answer me when I slipped into the roundhouse after dinner and asked our location. The Captain was there as well, but he spared me barely a glance. The two of them were whispering together and seemed anxious about something, and I quickly heard from the other sailors—who had forgotten that they were not supposed to talk to me—that the wind was dropping and there was the chance of fog. Sure enough, by the time darkness came down the wind had fallen to no more than a whisper, and gradually, like little white wraiths, the threads of mist rose from the sea and wrapped themselves around us until the stars vanished and there was neither sight nor sound but a thick white blanket and the muffled slap of the waves on the hull.

The Captain's expression grew longer and gloomier, and Mr Riach looked ever more mournful and started talking about the vicious reefs of the Western Isles and how we might drift to our doom. Mr Struan still said nothing, but looked annoyed at this slight on his navigation skills.

The fog had not lifted the next morning, and the only indication that it was day lay in the fact that the air was a lighter grey. It pressed close, as though to suffocate the ship, and even I started to feel the creeping gloom that possessed the sailors. They had taken refuge in rum, and first they were cheerful. Then they were gloomier than ever, the drink having that effect on them, and finally they were insensible. It astounded me that the Captain made no more than a half-hearted attempt to stop them, but he too seemed infected by the general despondency, and I swiftly realised how shallow was his grip on the crew and how fragile his authority. When he forbade them more rum they simply defied him, taking the keys to the locker from Mr

Riach, who was himself so cast away that he seemed not to notice.

It had not occurred to me at first that I might turn this to my advantage, but as the sailors grew more inebriated and the Captain shut himself in his cabin, and Mr Struan pored over his maps and Mr Riach started quoting the psalms, I had an idea. I liberated a bottle of rum from the hand of a sailor who had slumped on the deck, snoring, and wandered innocently away down the corridor towards where Neil's guard stood.

The man was in a foul humour. I saw it as I approached, for his face in the lamplight was scowling and hard. I quickly realised the cause. Whilst his comrades were all sitting around in various states of drunken stupor, he had kept to his post here, and they had forgotten to share the rum rations with him. When he saw me, the suspicious expression on his face started to change to one of faint hope. I smiled winsomely and held out the bottle to him. He snatched it from my hand and gulped down the spirit, the excess running off his chin and dripping onto the floor.

It was my bad luck that he had the hardest head of all

the fellows on the ship. Twice I checked back to see if he had drunk himself into unconsciousness and there he was, still standing at his post above that damned trap door. It seemed the drink had left him completely unaffected.

Matters were now getting desperate. I made one final sortie along to see how Neil's guard progressed, and bless me if the man was not still fully upright, dirk in hand, as though he were expecting an attack. Then I noticed his eyes. They were glazed and unfocussed and he was swaying a little. I walked right up to him. He did not raise the dirk. He did not even seem to know I was there. He was, to all intents and purposes, asleep with his eyes open. I placed one hand on his chest and pushed very gently. He crumpled up without a sound. I took the dirk from his hand, opened the trap door—with much puffing and blowing for breath, for the catch was stiff and the door heavy—and pushed his body swiftly and silently through the space into the hold below.

Once the sound of his fall had died away there was an absolute silence from below. Fear gripped me that within the space of two days Neil had died—from starvation, from wounds that I had not realised he had suffered, from fever, from any number of dire causes. Then I realised that there was no point in my standing there wondering. I had to go and find out. I set my foot on the first rung of the ladder, grasped the lantern in one hand and started to descend into the dark.

I had taken no more than two steps down the ladder into the hold when someone grabbed me about the waist and pulled me down into the darkness. I felt the prick of a dagger at my throat.

Chapter Eleven

In which we are shipwrecked.

'No!'

The lantern had gone out and it was pitch-black. I
was a second away from death. I knew it was Neil who
held me. Some deep instinct within me recognised his
touch, but I recognised also, and with terror, that he was
utterly ruthless and determined to survive. There was
no mercy in the hands that held me.

I felt the shock go through him at the sound of my

voice, and then he had loosed me and I sensed him pull back.

'Catriona?' He sounded angry and incredulous. 'What the hell—?'

'I thought that you needed rescuing,' I said crossly, teeth chattering with a mixture of reaction and fear. 'I did not realise you could do it all on your own, or I would have left you to your own devices.'

There was a hairsbreadth of silence and then he laughed.

'You came to rescue me,' he said, and there was a tone in his voice I could not place. 'You really are the most extraordinary girl.'

My spirits soared, but I did not tell him that he was worth fighting for. I had my pride.

'Someone fell,' he said. 'Before you came down the steps.'

'The guard,' I said. 'I made him drunk and then I…I pushed him. I had his knife, but I dropped it when you grabbed me.'

'Damnation.' Neil sighed sharply. 'We need all the weapons we can get.'

'But where did you get the dirk?' I asked. 'I thought that they disarmed you before they threw you in here.'

I felt his self-satisfaction and knew he was smiling.

'You had not hidden it in your stocking?' I questioned. 'For pity's sake, that is a trick they teach us in childhood!'

'Not if you are not a Highlander,' Neil said, 'and Hoseason's crew are a ragbag mix who do not know such ruses. They took my sword but did not even think to look for a dirk. It took me a long time to work myself free of those bonds you saw, but when Ransome came down with his pitiful tin of water this last time he was drunk and easy to overpower, even though he had a pistol.'

'Oh dear,' I said. I had quite liked Ransome. 'Is he dead?'

'No,' Neil said. 'Not yet. So that is two of them out of the way, and a dirk and a pistol between us.'

'And thirteen crew left,' I said. 'All as drunk as lords at present. The Captain's discipline fell apart when the fog came down.'

'Fog,' Neil repeated. He shifted a little. 'I thought so when we stopped moving. The weather in these parts in early autumn can be very treacherous. Where are we?'

'Just west of the Isle of Barra,' I said. 'Or at least that was our location when we were becalmed.'

He sucked in his breath. 'A bad place to be. Even with no wind the swell will take us eastward and there are some nasty reefs. I don't like this.'

'Neither does the Captain,' I said. 'Neither does Mr Struan, the navigator. And now that the crew are blind drunk there is no one on watch either.'

'We had better get out of here,' Neil said.

I looked up at the small patch of light above our heads. We had been talking urgently, in fragments, to exchange all the most important information that we needed as quickly as possible. We could not have been there longer than a few minutes, but suddenly it seemed imperative to get out of this trap and for Neil to hide before his absence was discovered. I shuddered with a mixture of fear and panic as the wooden walls of the ship pressed in on me, and Neil put out a hand and clasped mine. His was warm and rough and reassuring and his grip tightened on mine, more eloquent than any words.

He pulled me to my feet.

'I'll go first,' he said. 'In case there is anyone in the passageway.'

There was no one. Neil leaned down to give me his hand and pull me up through the hatch, and we stood in the passage, looking at one another. He looked terrible, filthy and battered. The bruising to his face was livid, and the gash on his forehead stood out angry and red. There was three days of stubble on his chin.

I bit my lip to smother an unexpected smile. 'Oh, dear. Not so handsome now, Mr Sinclair.'

'Well,' he said, 'if it comes to that, your coat smells of seaweed, Miss Balfour, the rats have made nests in your hair and you have cobwebs on your cheek. But—' The expression in his eyes changed and suddenly he grabbed me, seaweed-smelling coat and all. His mouth crushed mine, hard, fierce and utterly demanding.

'With thanks for your aid,' he said, as he let me go.

'There's no time for that,' I said, pushing him away to cover my confusion and the dizzying emotions that threatened to swamp me.

He grinned at me with all the blazing charm I remembered. He was alive and in control now, and I sensed the hard, masculine force that was driving him. He looked dangerous. I felt my love for him race through my body in an irresistible tide.

'If not now, later,' he said, and smoothed the tumbled hair back from my face in a gesture so tender I felt my heart turn over.

'I hope you do not thank all your colleagues that way,' I said, and he laughed.

'Only the pretty ones, so you need have no concerns.'

The *Cormorant* had become like a ghost ship. Even when we dropped the trap door back into place, and the thud seemed to echo through the whole ship, no one stirred. It was as though the fog had brought a sickness with it that had infected all the men. We straightened up, and Neil took my hand and drew me softly, carefully, along the side of the corridor. When we reached the doorway through to the deck I caught a flash of movement away to my right and cried out. Neil turned and hit the man who was coming through before the poor fellow even knew what had happened. It was Mr Riach, drunk and unsteady on his feet even before Neil's ministrations. We dragged him to the nearest storeroom and locked him in.

'Twelve men left,' Neil said.

'Poor Mr Riach,' I said. 'He was kind to me. He gave me his cabin—' I patted my jacket '—and his smelly coat.'

Neil looked at me, and there was a possessive glint in his eyes that suggested that if he had the chance he would hit Mr Riach all over again. I trembled to see it.

The deck was even more of a shambles than it had been the last time I passed that way. There were men slumped insensible against the mast, and some even prone on the deck. Neil stirred one of them with his foot, but the man just groaned and rolled over. There were ropes uncoiled untidily, waiting to trip the unwary or the drunk. There were empty bottles rolling in the slight swell. I saw Neil look around and his expression set with disgust. I could not imagine the Navy running such a ramshackle ship as this.

There was no one on watch.

The wind was starting to rise again, stirring the mist so that it eddied and whirled about the mast. A gust caught the topsail, so that it filled for a moment before hanging limp again. I was no trained sailor but I knew what that meant. Soon the fog would clear and we would see just how far the *Cormorant* had drifted towards the treacherous reefs of the Western Isles.

'The Captain is in the roundhouse with Mr Struan,' I whispered in Neil's ear. I had seen the two of them moving about in there, still studying the charts, it seemed, impotent in the face of their crew's drunkenness. 'What are you going to do?'

Neil took the pistol from his belt and smiled. 'I'm going to talk to them,' he said. 'Watch my back, Catriona. If anyone approaches—'

'I'll push them over,' I said.

'It is a pity we do not have another pistol,' Neil said.

'Not really,' I said. 'I am a schoolmaster's daughter. I did not learn to shoot. And my papa disapproved of violence.'

'I hope you were thinking of him when you pushed that fellow down into the hold,' Neil said dryly.

Neither the Captain nor the first officer saw us coming. The Captain had his back to the door, and Mr Struan was poring over the maps on the table as though they held the answer to the secrets of the universe. Neil walked in through the open door of the roundhouse.

'Good afternoon, gentlemen,' he said, cool as you please.

The Captain swung around so quickly he almost tripped himself up. 'Sinclair!' he said. 'How the devil—?' His gaze fell on me. 'I should have guessed,' he said. 'I knew you had a fondness for him.'

I felt Neil look at me quickly, but it was hardly the moment for protestations of undying affection.

'I told you he was my cousin four times removed,' I said. 'Blood counts for something in the Highlands, Captain Hoseason.'

Neil went over to the rack of cutlasses on the wall and tossed one to me. 'I remember your aversion to violence,' he said, 'but take this just in case, and cover the door.'

I grasped it in my hand. It would, I supposed, deter a drunken sailor from launching an ill-advised attack, but I prayed I did not need to use it. I stood with my back to the roundhouse, my gaze searching the decks. There was still no movement other than from the wind, which was strengthening now. The fog was slipping away across the water.

'Now, Captain,' I heard Neil say, 'I want you to set a southerly course and put in at Oban, where Miss Balfour and I will go ashore.'

'I'll put you ashore wherever you wish, sir,' the Captain said with weary courtesy, 'as long as it is deep enough for the ship's draught. But for the present I have no notion of our whereabouts and no hands to sail, so we are all in the same predicament.'

'You run a disorderly ship, Captain,' Neil said coldly, 'and have no one but yourself to blame for that.'

It was at this moment that Mr Struan, who had remained silent and motionless, crouched over his maps and charts, decided to try to disarm Neil. Perhaps Neil's description of the ramshackle crew had offended him, even though it was no more than the truth. At any rate, he lunged forward with a sudden roar, reaching for Neil's throat. Neil shot him in the shoulder—a flesh wound that barely grazed him and was meant more as a warning than anything else. There was the smell of singed cloth and Struan went down with a bellow of fear and surprise, fainting dead away. The Captain took advantage of the mêlée to reach for a cutlass from the rack, and I cried out a warning to Neil and tossed my sword to him. He caught it one-handed and spun around to face the Captain's attack.

The roundhouse was too small for a proper fight, for there was not enough space to use a sword to full effect, and soon both men had tumbled out through the door and were fighting on the deck, the clash of steel on steel sharp and vicious. The Captain was desperate and determined, but his anger made him careless, and Neil was by far the better swordsman. I stood watching in a frenzy of anxiety, my nails digging into my palms, but I knew better than to try to interfere in a sword fight. Suddenly there was a movement beside me, and I saw Mr Struan struggling to his feet.

'Can I help you, sir?' I said, which, I suppose, shows that I had no real stomach for fighting. 'If you will let me wash and bind your shoulder wound—'

His only reply was a grunted obscenity as he stumbled towards the rack of pistols. I doubted they were loaded, but I did not really have the time to check, so with an inner sigh at succumbing to the lure of violence once again, I grabbed one of the enormous books on navigation that were on the table, raised it in both hands and brought it down on the back of Mr Struan's head. He crumpled up again.

'Nice work,' Neil said from beside me, and I saw that he had disarmed Captain Hoseason, who was sitting on the deck, head bent, chest heaving so hard that I was afraid he would expire before our very eyes. His face was a greyish colour and he looked ill. He had had neither youth nor fitness on his side. Neil leaned on his sword. He was barely out of breath. 'Come, Captain,' he said. 'This is downright madness. We may carry on like this until you have no crew left, but that is a foolish way to conduct business.'

Captain Hoseason had no breath to reply, but he did not look as though he was going to argue. He sat on his deck, with his snoring crew all about, and he looked old and broken. And all the while the mist was lifting like a curtain, and now I saw the sun setting away to the west in a pool of pink and gold, and the wind filled the sails, snapping and cracking like a live thing.

'Neil, look!'

I ran across to the rail. As the mist vanished land came in sight on the larboard bow, so close it made my heart jump to see it. Before the fog had come down we had been many miles west of the Outer Hebrides, heading for the open Atlantic. It seemed impossible that we had drifted so far east on a calm sea. And yet there was no doubt, for a mountain rose high above us from a barren and rocky shore, with a wisp of mist still upon its peak.

Neil had joined me at the rail and now he swore. 'That's Ben Tangoval, to the south west of the Isle of Barra,' he said.

'But how can we be so close?' I questioned. 'When the fog came down we were twenty miles to the west!'

'Treacherous weather, treacherous currents,' Neil said. He looked away to the west, where the sky was clear and the moon was rising. 'There's a gale brewing,' he said. 'Captain!' He turned abruptly. 'Wake your men. The brig is in danger.'

If there were any words that could rouse Captain Hoseason from his torpor these were the ones, for he was on his feet within seconds, shaking the men, overturning buckets of seawater over their heads, so that they emerged rubbing the water from their eyes and blinking in the fading daylight. Suddenly the deck was bustling with activity.

Neil despatched a man to free Mr Riach and his colleagues from the hold, then strode to the roundhouse to check the navigation charts. The Captain took the wheel and sent a man up to the foretop to keep watch for reefs. I hoped he was sober enough to climb the rigging. The wind was strengthening even as I watched, and now the *Cormorant* was suddenly tearing through the seas, pitching and straining, rising on the swell and thundering down. Away on the lee bow I saw what looked like a fountain rise up from the sea, and I called out at the same time as the man in the topmast shouted.

'Rocks!'

Almost immediately another plume of water spouted to the south, accompanied by a roar.

'Reefs,' Captain Hoseason said bitterly. 'If only the fog had not come down, and the men had not got so drunk and Mr Struan were not still pretending to be injured because he is too damned afraid.'

'I can navigate,' Neil said, 'but you do not need a navigator to tell you that the brig is in trouble, Captain. These reefs stretch for near ten miles to the south and west. The only way through is to stay close to the land.'

'The wind is blowing us in to land anyway,' Hoseason said. 'We'll all be fortunate to come out of this in one piece, Mr Sinclair.'

As we got closer to the southern tip of the land the reefs began to appear more frequently, sometimes directly in our path. The man on watch would shout to direct us to change course, and sometimes we were so close to the breaking water that it would spray across the deck. I was cold and wet by now, but something kept me up on the deck, for I could not bear to go below, where the ship's wooden walls would close about me like a coffin. I knew we were in deep trouble indeed, for the mist and the crew between them had done for us, and unless we could pick our way between these rocks we would all end our days here and now in the sea.

The steersman had sobered up by now, and both he and the Captain stood by the wheel. Captain Hoseason's face was grave but steady as steel, and I could not but admire him for his courage when facing death and ruin. For myself, I was terrified, but did not want to show it. For Neil was as cool and composed as I would have expected him to be in such a situation, and I was not going to show my fear by running screaming for my cabin.

We passed the little island of Vatersay. The light was fading now, but the rising moon illuminated everything as clear as day. The tide around the islands was strong, and tossed the brig about like a cork. The captain put his hands to the wheel alongside the steersman as we sheered to one side and then the other to avoid the rocks. Even Neil set his weight with theirs against the tiller as it struggled like a living thing, and the wind and waters drove us inexorably towards the rocks. My fingers were white and tight on the ship's rail.

'Reef to windward!' the man in the rigging called out, and at the same moment the tide caught the brig and turned her about. She spun into the wind like a top. The sails filled and she hit the rocks with such a blow that it threw me flat on the deck.

Neil grabbed my arm and dragged me to my feet. 'To

the longboat!' he shouted, above the sound of the hissing spray.

The brig shifted on the rocks with a terrible groan of timbers, and Neil half dragged, half carried me across to where Mr Riach and a couple of men were busy throwing various bits of equipment out of the longboat and attempting to pull it across the side ready to launch. This was no easy task, because the waves were breaking over the brig now, and every few moments we were forced to stop and hold on for dear life as water raced across the deck. I worked with the others, and beside me Neil worked too, his expression dark and set, his hands touching mine, desperation in both our hearts.

'Hold on!'

The shout came from the man on watch and we braced ourselves, but then a wave so huge lifted the brig clean off the rocks and smashed it down again on its side. Whether my hands were too numb to grip by now, or whether I reacted a second too late I am not sure, but the water caught me and swept my wet skirts about my knees, knocking me down. The sea carried me away as though I weighed nothing, and I was cast over the side into a choking, whirling pit.

I went under, blinded, terrified, my lungs bursting, and gulped a mouthful of salty water. I came up and heard a shout, saw for a moment Neil's face and his outstretched hand so close to me, but even as I reached for him I sank again, and the water closed over my head. After that I was so battered and beaten by the movement of the sea that I was only half-conscious. I had learned to swim as a child, but it was no use to me now in that pounding maelstrom, and after a few half-hearted splashes I gave up and went with the tide. I knew I was going to die, but somehow the thought no longer troubled me.

Eventually I started to dream. I dreamed that someone was holding me and guiding me into calmer waters. When I struggled a little he murmured soothing words in my ear and I felt peaceful even though I was so cold and so tired and could not stay awake. I let my mind float free of the storm and thought of my childhood at Applecross, with the sun sparkling on the sea and the warmth of it beating down on my head, my father calling me in from the garden and my mother wrapping me in her scented embrace…They were here now, lifting me, holding me, and I felt so safe and knew I need worry no more.

And then someone slapped me hard on the back, and all the water left my body in a choking rush. I was lying on a sandy beach, staring at the stars, and little waves were still breaking over me. I had no strength and felt sick, and wanted to lie there and die. But Neil was not going to let me. He grabbed me and dragged me upright, shaking me so hard I thought my neck would break. His eyes were burning with a fierce dark light and he looked angrier than I had ever seen him; angrier than I had even imagined he could look.

'You are *not* going to leave me now, Catriona!'

I wanted to respond but my eyes were closing. It was too much effort.

'Open your eyes!' He jerked my chin up, his fingers hard against my cheek.

My eyes snapped open. 'How dare you—?' My words came out in an infuriated croak.

'That's better.' He looked grimly amused. 'Don't you *dare* go to sleep now or you will die. Do you hear me?'

He picked me up as though I weighed less than a feather and strode up the beach. I bit my lip to prevent myself from groaning. I did not want to show any further weakness, and given the way that Neil had treated me up until now I suspected that he would have very little sympathy for me anyway. My sore cheek chafed against the soaking collar of his coat. All of my body ached with a pain that was deep, deep in my bones. Every inch of my skin felt bruised and torn. I felt cold and racked with shivers, but hot and feverish at the same time, as though I wanted to rip off my soaking clothes because they were too warm for me.

I lay still. I remembered now the moment that someone had caught me and held me, pulling me away from the murderous reef and into the calmer waters of this little bay. Neil must have jumped into the water to rescue me. He had put his own life in danger to save mine. My mind struggled with the enormity of it. The love I had had for him before was as nothing to what I felt now—now that he had risked everything to save me.

'Thank you,' I whispered. My lips felt cracked and

salty, and my throat was so sore, but I knew I had to make him understand that I realised what he had done.

He paused in his step for a moment and looked down at me. 'I'd like to say it was a pleasure,' he said, and I could hear the wry humour in his voice, 'but that hardly covers the situation.'

I turned my head slightly to see if the *Cormorant* was still visible. I could just see her in the distance, black and white in the moonlight, lying low on the rocks now. There was a wide tract of calm water between our cove and the reef, but nothing moved on it. I wondered if they had managed to launch the longboat.

My head bumped against Neil's shoulder as he strode up the shingle. I could see heather and machair and white sand. Little white stars of mica sparkled in the rocks. It looked extremely pretty—except that it all seemed to be fading from before my eyes.

I had begun to shiver in spasm after spasm that I could not control. My head felt so heavy I could not hold it up. My eyelids were weighted with lead.

'Hold on, Catriona,' I heard Neil say. 'We are almost at shelter.'

He did not sound angry with me any more, but he did sound worried. I tried so hard to hold on. I wanted to please him, and to banish that anxiety from his voice, but I could not stay awake. My strength was exhausted. I gave in to the darkness and it rushed in to claim me. I felt nothing but the most enormous relief.

Chapter Twelve

In which my heart is broken.

The first sensation that I recognised was warmth. I was warm and I was dry and it felt wonderful. I lay for several seconds simply savouring the feeling. Then I opened my eyes and tried to move. This was a mistake. Immediately every last inch of my body screamed with pain. My skin felt scoured by rock and sand, and my bones ached and groaned like those of an old woman. I gave a gasp.

Someone moved beside my bed. It was Neil. He had been sitting close by and now he turned towards me.

The firelight was behind him, and there seemed no other light in the room, so I could not see him properly other than to realise with a tremendous shock that he looked as tired and worn and old as I felt. His eyes were sunk deep and his face was lined and grey. In that moment I realised he must have been sitting beside me from the time he had first brought me here, and I had no notion of how long that was.

'How are you feeling?' His voice was brisk, but for a moment I thought I had seen the shadow of quite a different emotion in his eyes.

'Beastly,' I said, and he smiled at me, and the tiredness lifted from his face for a second.

'But I am glad to be alive,' I added, 'and I think I have you to thank for that.'

'You have already thanked me.' He had turned away. His voice was gruff. 'Would you like some water?'

'Please.' My throat was parched and sore from gulping down so much salt water. I moved a little, recognising now that my body hurt from being pummelled and battered on the rocks, and thrown around in the current like a rag doll. I imagined I must be covered in bruises. Soon, I thought, when I felt strong enough to face the shock, I would look.

I moved slightly as Neil brought some water over to me in a dented tin beaker. The covers fell back—actually they looked like grain sacks, and felt as rough—and as the cold stung my bare arms I realised that I was naked. I made a grab for the nearest sack and saw Neil grin.

'I'm sorry,' he said. He sounded both amused and rueful. 'I had to do it. It was the only way to tell whether or not you were badly injured—and most of your clothes were ripped to shreds anyway.'

It said something about my feelings for Neil that even when I was in such extremes of discomfort the thought of him stripping me naked and examining my body made me feel hot all over, made my skin prickle with something very different from pain. It was fortunate that the room was so dark he could not see my blushes, or I would have been obliged to plead a fever to hide my reaction.

I took the cup gingerly, preserving my modesty with a carefully placed sack, and gulped down the water within. I could tell it was spring water, and it tasted delicious.

'So I have no clothes?' I asked, looking at him over the rim of the beaker. 'What am I to do?'

Neil laughed. 'Some of them are still wearable, and they will have dried out by now. And I am sure we can fashion you a skirt from one of these sacks.'

I rolled over in order to get a better look at our shelter. If there was sacking for blankets and sacking for clothes as well, I had guessed that this was not a very luxurious lodging. There was no light other than what the one window could provide, and at present it was closed and barred with a wooden shutter, so I assumed it was night. Neil had coaxed a fire in the grate, and by its light I could see we were in a rough, one-roomed croft that was presumably used as a fisherman's shelter. The narrow cot I was lying on had heather for a mattress, which poked and prodded at me in a way my bruises disliked intensely. But beggars could not be choosers. At least we had a roof over our heads and one, moreover, that did not appear to leak.

'How long have I been asleep?' I asked.

'Two days and two nights,' Neil said. He had sat down again on the stool that was beside my cot. 'I was afraid you had taken a fever the first night, but you shook it off. You must come from strong stock, Catriona Balfour.' Our eyes met and held, and his were dark with emotion. 'You were very brave,' he added, 'both in the shipwreck and before. I will never forget…'

His voice faded away, and for a long moment we looked at one another. The feelings seemed to tighten like a coil within me and tug at my heart until I felt breathless. Neither of us could break the moment.

The fire hissed as the dampness in the peat fought the flame, and Neil wrenched his gaze away from mine. I felt shaken, both by the force of my feelings and the expression I had seen in Neil's eyes.

'You do not look as though you have slept in all the time we have been here,' I said, a little at random.

Neil shrugged, ill at ease. 'I confess I did not fancy sleeping on this floor,' he said. 'I have been out once or twice to fetch water and take a look around.'

He did not say that he had not dared to leave me for fear I would relapse into the fever and never awaken, but I knew that was in his mind.

'The brig!' I said, suddenly remembering. 'Is there any sign—?' But I stopped as Neil shook his head.

'I don't know if they were able to lower the boat and paddle to safety,' he said. 'The ship has gone, and although there are plenty of goods washed up on the shore I have seen no one.'

I knew he meant that he had neither seen men alive nor dead bodies, and I did not know whether to be sad or thankful.

'If they were able to escape to safety,' I said slowly, 'do you think that they would send anyone back to look for us?'

'No,' Neil said. 'I do not.' He looked at me, his face stern in the firelight. 'Hoseason would face arrest and trial if the truth of his kidnapping attempt became known,' he said. 'He will not risk that to see if we are safe.'

I was silent. I knew he was probably right. Even if the crew had survived they would not wish to face difficult questions by admitting that we had been on board the brig. We were abandoned.

We sat quietly together for a while, on my part because I was exhausted simply from drinking a little water and asking questions, and on Neil's because he was probably thinking over all the difficult things I had not yet had chance to consider, such as the fact that we were alone on the isle and had no food and nothing but spring water to drink, and that there was only a rough croft to shelter us and no means of escape.

Presently I told Neil I needed to get up and go outside, which was accomplished by my wrapping several sacks around myself and him tying them together with twine, since my fingers were too sore to do it. I did not much care what I looked like, and to Neil's credit he managed not to laugh at the sight. He insisted on coming with me in case I fell down in a faint, and as I staggered back inside, clutching his arm for support, I reflected ruefully that I had no secrets from him now—and no doubt very little allure left either.

The little croft was cosy, though, for all its simplicity. Neil helped me back into the cot and banked the peat fire down, but when he made to take his seat on the stool again I put out a hand to stop him.

'This is folly,' I said. 'There is plenty of space in this cot for two, if we lie like spoons, and if you do not rest soon I will be the one tending to *you,* for you look fit to fall down.' I was nervous, and so my words got faster and faster as I spoke. I had never invited a man to my bed before.

He was silent for so long that I was sure he was about to refuse, but then he heaved a huge sigh.

'I suppose…'

'Good,' I said, covering my embarrassment with briskness. 'If I wear these sacks and you keep all your clothes on then we will be most respectable. Besides, I am too ill for this to be anything other than a practical arrangement.'

Neil glared at me. 'Very well,' he said fiercely. 'But it is only until I can retrieve some of the driftwood from the beach tomorrow and make another bed.'

'Of course,' I said.

A part of me was shocked by his vehemence, and yet another part was not. Something had changed between us from the moment that I had helped him escape.

Yet, despite our best intentions, it felt scandalously *unrespectable* when Neil slid into the bed behind me and lay against my back. Though he tried to hold himself apart from me, and I held myself stiffly away from him too, I was shockingly aware of his proximity, and of the unfamiliar hard lines of a man's body so close to my own. I could feel the movement of his chest as it brushed my back. His breath stirred my hair, raising goose pimples on my neck. I felt hot and disturbed. Evidently I was not as ill as I might have imagined.

After we had lain tensely that way for quite a long time, Neil gave a sigh and said, 'Neither of us will get a wink of sleep like this.'

I wriggled a little with discomfort. 'What do you suggest?'

He did not reply, but slid an arm about my waist and drew me very gently back into the curl of his body, so that my back was against his chest and his legs curved close against my buttocks and thighs. It felt warm, delightful—and utterly improper. For a moment I allowed myself to imagine what it might be like if there were not three sacks and Neil's clothes separating our bodies—if we were both naked and were lying together this way—and I felt light-headed at the thought. Clearly I was no lady to be thinking such wanton thoughts, particularly when I was so sick.

'I am afraid,' Neil said in my ear, 'that you are going

to learn some things about men that will probably shock you, Catriona. But I should reassure you that although my body might…um…desire you, I would never abuse your trust. I swear it.'

I was already shocked, but I was intrigued too. Lying there with the fire dying down and the sound of the sea on the distant shore, and Neil's arm about my waist and his body against mine, I could imagine how easy, how utterly pleasurable and how completely natural it would feel to give myself to him. Then I thought of my aching, bruised and lacerated body, and of the impossibility that it could give either of us pleasure at this moment, and was almost tempted to laugh.

'Thank you,' I said meekly. 'I knew you could not be as much of a rake as you claimed.'

Neil sighed sharply. 'I am every bit as much of a rake as I claimed, Catriona, which is why you are in the gravest danger, with only my honour standing between you and ruin.'

'Well,' I said, 'if your honour lets you down pray have some concern for my poor, bruised body. I cannot believe that even the greatest rake in Scotland could find so pitifully injured a woman to be attractive.'

Neil laughed, and I felt him relax a little. 'You have a point. I am not so depraved.'

I yawned. My body warmed and softened against his and I relaxed, too. I felt his lips brush my hair, but in a gesture of sweet affection rather than seduction. Then I fell asleep.

When I woke in the morning the croft was full of daylight and Neil had gone. I missed the warmth of his body next to mine. I had a vague memory of half waking in the night to find his arms about me, and one of his legs entangled with mine. I remembered that it had hurt to feel the weight of him on my aching bones and the friction of his skin on the soreness of mine, but in truth I had not minded very much. In fact I had wanted to be closer still. Neil could have seduced me without a word of protest from me.

The exhaustion had left me and I was ravenously hungry. I lay for a little while, looking around the interior of our shelter. It was little more than a hut, really, with one room inside, where the fire was now burned out in the grate. My bed and the rickety stool took up most of the space, although there was a small table over beneath the window.

I got out of bed slowly, because I was still very stiff and sore, and dragged myself across the room to wash in a tin basin that the fisherman had evidently left behind. There was fresh water in the tin mug, which Neil must have supplied before he disappeared. And there was a tin plate, which I held up and used as a mirror—then wished I had not. Even though it was dull and speckled it showed enough of my face to make me realise that I looked a dreadful fright. I had a cut on my cheek and another at my temple, a series of bruises along one cheekbone that were turning a most unattractive purple colour, and my hair defied description. I suspected that I was going to have to ask Neil to cut it off if we could find a knife, because it was knotted beyond salvation. The rest of my body was not much better, covered in multi-coloured bruises, cut, scratched and scored by rocks and sand.

I found my clothes hanging on a makeshift line across

one corner of the room. They were bone-dry and crumpled, but at least my bodice was wearable, even if my skirts were tattered and in shreds. I set my teeth as I re-tied the sacking around my waist, for the twine was rough on my hands, but I managed it through sheer will power. Once that was done I felt able at last to go out to investigate my surroundings.

The sun was shining on our croft, which was small and primitive, whitewashed, with a thick turf roof. It might once have been a nice little dwelling, for it was set back from the cove on a low plateau of machair, where the grass grew through the sandy dunes and the last of the summer wildflowers bent in the soft breeze. It was protected from the westerly gales by an outcrop of rock that was almost big enough to be called a hill. Behind the house I could hear the splashing of the spring from which Neil must have fetched the drinking water. I walked barefoot and wincing around the outside, found the water, which poured into a crystal-clear pool, and saw that beyond it the land rose to another high point to the south, a bare quarter mile away. It was immediately apparent that there were no other buildings on the island, and that it was in fact so small it barely deserved the name of island and was more of an islet.

My shoes had been lost long since in the shipwreck, so I walked carefully in my bare feet to the top of the rising land. From here it was possible to see the whole of our isle laid out about me. It was rocky and heather clad above, where the low cliffs met the blue sky and the seabirds wheeled on the edge of the breeze. To the east there was clear water for what I reckoned to be almost fifty miles across to the mainland at Ardnamurchan. This was the Sea of the Hebrides and, recalling the maps on my father's schoolroom wall, I knew that north of here lay the islands of Barra, the Uists, Benbecula, Harris and Lewis, whilst to the east lay Skye and Mull with their scattering of smaller islets.

My mind was already running on the idea of escape, for although our temporary home seemed a very earthly paradise on this calm and sunny day, it lacked food and just about everything in the way of supplies. And although I am not the sort of woman who requires hours before the dressing table with her pots and potions, I do need good food and a proper skirt to wear rather than a sack. It might be possible, I thought, to attract the attention of some passing ship if we lit a beacon on this small hill. Certainly a crofter on the island of Barra might see our smoke and come to investigate. Of course there was the small problem of a lack of firewood, for there were no trees that I could see, and I remembered that Neil had built up the fire with peat the previous night. Frowning over this latest setback, I made my way gently down to the white sand beach, where I had glimpsed Neil, scavenging amongst the rocks.

The beautiful curving beach was littered with debris from the ship. More of it bobbed in the lagoon behind the huge reef, where the *Cormorant* had been wrecked. Little lazy waves were washing things up on the shore—spars of broken wood that I immediately realised we could dry out and use for the fire, rope and rigging, and a couple of barrels.

'Look at this, Catriona!' Neil shouted as I drew closer. He was brandishing what looked like a long bale of tartan cloth in one hand and a bottle in the other. 'We have rum and salted pork, and beef in the crates!'

My stomach gave a long, loud rumble at the thought of this delicious feast. I caught Neil's excitement and darted about on the sand, finding all sorts of treasures: a bone comb here, a spoon there, ship's biscuits, bread and oatmeal. Finally, when we had gathered together a magpie's hoard of goods, we collapsed on the sand to prise open the crate of beef and eat our fill, washing it down with the rum. Then we dozed in the sunshine.

'I am so relieved,' I said, 'that we will not have to live on seabirds. I hear they taste both salty and fishy.'

'I'd like to see you try to catch one,' Neil said lazily.

'I could catch a fish if I had a line,' I said, stung.

'We must make one for you, then,' Neil said. 'For a diet of salt meat will not be good for us.'

'There are berries amongst the heather,' I said, 'and there is oatmeal for porridge, and bread.'

'The bread is ruined by sea water, I am afraid,' Neil said.

'Well, there are biscuits,' I argued, 'and shellfish in these pools.'

'Poisonous,' Neil said. 'I almost died from eating raw shellfish when I was a child.'

'You are such a Jonah,' I said. 'It is no wonder that the ship sank.' I started to try to pull the comb through my hair, wincing as it caught on the tangles and knots. As fast as I managed to unravel one, another caught on the teeth, making me flinch again. I could not even reach around to the back of my head, for my shoulders were too stiff to raise.

Having watched my struggles for several minutes, Neil shifted closer to me.

'Here,' he said, 'give that to me.'

I handed the comb over reluctantly, I confess. There is nothing worse than a ham-fisted person pulling on one's hair. But Neil was extraordinarily gentle as he plied the comb, patiently teasing out each curl and tendril, loosening the knots. The sun was hot on my back and the rum was warm in my blood, and I felt soft and melting and breathless beneath his ministrations.

'You have done this before,' I accused, glancing at him over my shoulder as he worked, the intent, concentrated look on his face making me smile. 'You are a most accomplished lady's maid.'

He looked up, his fingers still in my hair, and his dark gaze trapped and held mine. Slowly, very slowly, he drew me closer to him, until my lips were touching his. The kiss was different this time, gentle and sweet, because he was being very tender and careful of my injuries. But it was different in another way too; it felt deeper, more profound, and it hit me with all the emotional power of a storm wave. This was not the calculated seduction of a rake. Nor was it the triumphant possession of the victor saluting his comrade-in-arms. It was hot and sweet and terrifying, and yet the summit of my most tender and secret desires.

I pressed even closer to Neil, seeking urgency beneath the sweetness until we both tumbled backwards into the bed of a sand dune and he kissed me harder, his tongue tangling with mine in an intimate dance. His hand was inside my bodice, the palm warm against my breast. I felt so soft and sensuous, and so desperately in need of something I barely understood and yet ached for with the very essence of my being.

Then Neil wrenched himself away.

'Catriona,' he said, and his voice was very rough. 'There is no power on earth that is going to keep you a maid if we do this.'

He got to his feet, tension in every line of his body, and turned his back on me. After a few moments he strode away along the beach without another word.

I struggled into a sitting position and watched him walk away. Now that the beat of excitement was fading from my blood I felt bruised and cold and confused. I understood well enough what Neil had meant, and I also knew I had my share of the responsibility in helping him. If Neil was trying to do the honourable thing and keep away from me to avoid seducing me, it ill became me to tempt him to do otherwise. It was hard; I was young, I was in love with him, and my body wanted him. But I had to remember that one day soon we would be going back to a life and a society that made rules that a young unmarried girl broke at her peril.

That was why I had turned Neil down when he had first asked me to be his mistress. I could not have had him and kept my honour, too. And though I might now be swept away in the heat of the moment, life had already taught me harsh lessons about how vulnerable was a woman on her own, with no money and no connections and nothing standing between her and ruin. I might be impulsive, but I also have a strong streak of practicality in me. I loved Neil, and I wanted to make love with him, but I was already thinking about what would happen when he tired of me—as surely he would. Neil had a short attention span when it came to women. I knew that. So when his gaze wandered from me what would I do? I did not want to be a professional mistress, moving from lover to lover. He was the only man I wanted, but if I could not have him for ever then better not at all.

I wandered slowly back towards the croft, carrying the bolt of tartan and another bolt of muslin. All afternoon, until my feet were too sore to carry me, I carried bits and pieces of stores back from the beach, and fetched fresh heather for the bed. I left Neil be. He had collected a pile of timber from the beach, but I knew it was not for a beacon. I could see that he was making himself a cot, so that he would not be obliged to share a bed with me or take the cold stone floor.

In order to help I fetched a piece of rigging that had snarled itself on the rocks and fastened it across a corner of the croft, so that it partitioned off the space that had my bed in it. Then I draped the bolt of muslin over the rigging like a sheet. Well pleased with myself, I lit the fire and heated some water in a battered pan I had found on the beach.

When Neil came back he was carrying a very neatly made wooden bunk. He looked from my makeshift bedroom to the tiny space left for him beside the window and his lips curved into a rueful smile.

'I have the better billet,' I said. 'I am afraid you are in the draught.'

He laughed, and some of the tightness went from his face.

'I am glad to see,' I continued, nodding at the bed, 'that you are not an inadequate aristocrat who cannot fend for himself.'

'That is Navy training for you,' Neil said dryly. He looked about the croft. 'You have scarcely been idle yourself.'

'There is porridge for supper,' I said, 'and hot water

to wash.' Then, feeling I was sounding a little too wifely, I said quickly, 'Neil, I *do* understand—'

'Do you?' he said swiftly. 'I am not sure that I even understand myself.'

I waited. He put the bed down slowly and stood there, looking at me. There was confusion in his eyes, and anger, and desire. My heart did a slow somersault to see it.

'When I first knew you and asked you to be my mistress,' Neil said, 'I was trying my luck. I used to do that with women.' He sounded disgusted with himself. 'Sometimes it worked and sometimes it did not. It was a game to me and I seldom cared. I thought it was what young men did.'

'I understand,' I said again. 'I met Miss McIntosh.'

Neil laughed harshly. 'Yes. I tried my luck with her. She agreed. You did not. You and Celeste McIntosh...' He shook his head. 'So different. *What* was I thinking?'

'It doesn't matter,' I said, not really sure what he was trying to say, but moved by the violence of his tone. I thought about Celeste McIntosh, with her sleek auburn hair and her slender, rounded body. 'Actually,'

I added, incurably truthful, 'I can quite imagine what you were thinking.'

'Yes,' Neil said, 'because I am a man and I desired her and I did not really care that she was avaricious and spoilt and calculating. In fact I never really cared for her at all.' He looked at me. 'You were different from the start,' he said. 'I told you that at Glen Clair, didn't I? I never knew where I stood with you. It fascinated me.'

His gaze was dark and intense on me and I could scarcely breathe.

'If you had agreed to my proposition…' he said.

'I would not have been the woman I am,' I said, trying to be brisk. 'The porridge will be burning.'

Neil caught my hand as I would have moved past him to the fire. 'I like thick porridge,' he murmured. He cupped my chin, and his eyes searched my face as though looking for the answer to some question. 'I did not really know you then,' he said. 'Now I do, and I admire you even more, Catriona.' His face darkened. 'I admire you so much that I could never take you and discard you at whim, as I had once planned to do, paying you off like a cheap whore. The idea is abhorrent to me.' Once again his gaze scoured my face. 'I care for you so much, Catriona, and you know that I desire you, but…'

It was that 'but' that prevented me from pouring out my love for him there and then. I can be appallingly frank with my feelings at times, but I do have my pride, and in that one small word lay all the difference between us.

I care for you so much, Catriona, but I do not love you.

That was what Neil had been trying to find the words to say. And I sensed in his wariness and hesitation that there was more. Neil did not *want* to love me, and he did not want my love in return. If it had not seemed so absurd I would have said that love frightened him in some way. I looked at him and saw the conflict in him, and I felt so old and wise, for all that he was eight years my senior.

'I cannot offer you what you deserve,' Neil said. His hand dropped from my cheek. He sounded tortured. 'You deserve someone who will love you utterly for the woman you are, and I can never love like that. I do not even wish to. So I will not spoil matters for you, Catriona, by taking what I want selfishly and in the process ruining your life.'

'Neil!' His name burst from me in shock and instinctive denial, but already he was withdrawing from me, turning away, his whole figure stiff with the force of his own denial.

I went back to the fire and stirred the porridge pot vigorously. My throat ached with unshed tears because he did not love me, but I knew I could not let him see how much it hurt me. Somehow I had to protect myself and build a different relationship with Neil—at least whilst we were trapped here together.

I had no thought to try and change his mind. I knew that I would be able to seduce him easily enough if I tried, but that would be unfair when he had done the first unselfish thing ever in his relationship with a woman by repudiating me now, before it was too late. Besides, I knew that though we might know physical passion together I would always want more, always want his love as well, and so in the end I would feel unfulfilled. There would always be something missing. There was nothing so sad or so unequal as unrequited love.

Love. All the poetry and prose I had read had warned me it could be painful. Now I knew it was true.

Chapter Thirteen

In which I attempt to fall out of love and fail miserably.

After that I think that both Neil and I held back from each other a little. It felt awkward at first, particularly when we were obliged to share so small a living space, and I missed the intimacy that had been building between us. Neil was better at withholding himself than I was, for I am so spontaneous and open a person that I could no more be cold and distant with him than I could fly off that island. Neil, in contrast, seemed adept at keeping some part of himself locked away. I suspected that he had always been able to do this, especially with women, and it frustrated and hurt me. A part of me wanted to force him back to the intimacy we had once shared, to demand that he be himself again. At times I was almost bursting with the things that I wanted to say to him. Yet I knew that the only way we could survive this exile together was with a workable truce, so I held my tongue. I suppose you could say that I grew up.

During the day we both went our separate ways, insofar as that was possible on such a small island. I would sweep the croft and fetch fresh heather for our bedding, air the covers—our sacking blankets had been replaced by a motley collection of materials salvaged from the wreck—and forage for shellfish in the pools and berries on the hillside. I had persuaded Neil to eat the shellfish, and so far we had both survived.

Neil collected wood and built the beacon. This was more complicated than it might sound, since every time we had dried the wood out in the wind and the sun a rainstorm would come along and threaten to soak it all again, or the wind would blow up a gale from the west and scatter the timber like firewood. Sometimes we did get it to light, and the fire puffed and hissed fitfully, but if anyone saw our smoke they never came. Occasionally we would see sails far out on the horizon, and the smoke from homesteads to the north on Barra, so we knew that we were not alone in the wide world, but still no one came.

On the days when the wind blew the storms in, Neil would disappear off to some makeshift shelter he had built, where he worked the driftwood into fantastical shapes, or constructed bits of furniture to make our croft more cosy—a shutter for the window that fitted properly and kept out the draught; a chair with a back and arms to replace the rickety stool. I decorated the little house with shells from the beach and the wood Neil had carved, and even with bits of coloured net washed up on the rocks, until he complained that there was scarcely room to move in there with all the ornaments.

At night I retired modestly to my bed behind the muslin wall and Neil waited politely until I had disappeared before undressing and taking the cot beside the window. I would lie listening to the sound of his breathing as he fell asleep, feeling so close to him, wanting to reach beyond the barrier that was between us. Neil was scrupulously careful to avoid touching me except in the most impersonal way when he passed me a plate at supper, for example, or helped me over the rocks on the rare occasions that we might take a walk together.

There was no repeat of that sunny day lying together in the dunes, and the rum remained largely untouched, as though it represented a temptation that might lead us into indiscretion. I will confess, though, that on one occasion I was walking back to the croft when I caught a glimpse of Neil washing in the pool by the spring and chose not to walk on or to avert my eyes. We both washed in the freshwater pool occasionally, because although sea bathing was delightful it was also salty and sandy, so that by the time you had walked back up the beach you needed another wash.

On this occasion I had been collecting loganberries from the far side of the island and came upon the pool from the windward side, which was probably why Neil did not know that I was there. He was standing with his back to me, naked to the waist, sluicing the clear water over his head and shoulders. The lines of his body were hard and clear cut against the pale blue of the twilight sky. As I watched he raised his hands and smoothed his black hair down, so it was as sleek and wet as an otter's pelt. The low sun glistened on the droplets of water running down his shoulders and back. I stared, my mouth as dry as though it were full of sand, my heart thumping.

I must have made some sound, for he turned and for a long moment his eyes met mine. My legs trembled so much I thought I was going to tumble over in the marram grass. Still holding my gaze, he strode out of the pool and reached very deliberately for his shirt. He shrugged it on and the material clung to his damp torso. Then he walked away without a word.

We did not speak at all that evening, and the air between us was so thick with tension that you could have cut it with a knife.

It was the following day, in an effort to break the strain between us, that I asked Neil to make a wooden chessboard. Now that September was well advanced the evenings were drawing in, and I was reluctant to sit with Neil night after night in silent unease. I collected shells from the beach to use as the pieces—scallop shells for the pawns, limpets for the knights, cockle-shells for the rooks and beautiful fan shells for the kings and queens.

'You do play, don't you?' I asked, after we had eaten salt pork stew for our supper and cleared a space on the floor for the board.

'Of course,' Neil said. 'I've played chess since I was a child. I'll wager I could beat you easily.'

This, naturally enough, raised my competitive spirit. My papa had taught me chess, and I had been accounted quite good, but of course I brought to my chess-playing the same recklessness that categorised other aspects of my behaviour. I was so desperate to win that I was careless, and I soon discovered that Neil was a strate-gist when he had me and my queen in check.

'Let's play the best of three,' I said quickly, setting the pieces back to their original places. I could see that Neil was laughing at me, and thought he would have another easy win, so I tried really hard and concentrated hard as well the second time. I almost beat him.

'Did you learn woodwork as a child as well?' I asked,

when I had at last conceded and was running my fingers idly over the smooth surface of the board he had made. 'It does not seem the type of occupation I would expect in the grandson of an earl.'

'I learned my woodworking from the gardener at Strathconan,' Neil said. His face was grave in the firelight. 'My father did not approve.'

'You never speak of your parents,' I said. I drew my tartan shawl more closely about my shoulders and huddled nearer the fire, for a storm was blowing up outside and the wind was chasing little piles of sand across the floor, setting them dancing in the draught.

'No,' Neil said. He shifted a little. 'I was a disappointment to them. They wanted me to be the sort of sprig of nobility who spends his time mindlessly oppressing tenants and shooting feathered creatures. My interests were all more practical than that, and they thought it beneath me.'

I picked up one of Neil's driftwood carvings. He had polished it smooth, so that it felt like silk beneath my fingers. In the dim light of the cottage the wood looked ghostly pale.

'I think your work is beautiful,' I said. 'And I thank God you *are* practical, for I do not know how we would have managed these weeks past had it not been for you making things to ease our life here.'

I stopped and looked up. Neil was smiling at me, and my heart gave a little flip before I blinked and looked away.

'I only have book learning,' I said, a little randomly, 'for that is what I was taught. But at least my papa was always proud of me.'

'My parents died years ago, when I was barely sixteen,' Neil said. 'And although it was a shock when it happened there was a part of me that was relieved to be free of the burden of their disapproval. But you—' He tilted his head to look at me. 'You must still miss your parents very much, I think. There are times when you look so sad.'

My grief felt painful in my chest. 'I do miss them,' I said gruffly. 'There have been times recently when I would have welcomed my father's wise counsel and my mother…' I paused. 'Well, she was simply the most beautiful, loving and generous person in the world, and it was so hard to lose her.'

Neil did not offer any platitudes or false comfort, but he took my hand and linked his fingers with mine. His touch was warm and strong and comforting, and it made me feel better even as it undid almost all of the flimsy defences I had placed in my heart against him.

I knew then. I knew I could not stop loving him just because I willed it. I knew it was going to be a long, hard journey for me.

'What about your uncle, the Earl?' I said. 'Does he approve of you?'

Neil laughed and let me go. 'He has little choice, since I am the only heir he has.'

'But you said that he is a good man,' I persisted.

'He is a good man in that he works with his tenants rather than throwing them off his land and enclosing their pastures,' Neil said. His voice was hard. 'I admire him for that, when all about us we see landowners grabbing whatever they can get.'

I thought of Squire Bennie, enclosing the common land at Applecross, and of some of the crofters moving away to find other work because there was no way they could provide for their families otherwise. If the Earl of Strathconan was more considerate of his tenants than the majority of his peers there would no doubt be those who thought him soft and foolish, but I admired him for it.

'And does he approve of you being a Navy man?' I asked.

'Not in wartime,' Neil said. 'When I was a troublesome sixteen-year-old and he did not know what to do with me he thought it a fine idea. But now he is afraid I will do something foolish and end up dead.' He threw a piece of driftwood on the fire, and in the spurt of flame that followed his expression was moody.

'It is natural that he should worry if he cares for you—' I began. But Neil shook his head and that silenced me.

'He cares that the Strathconan title should not die out,' he said abruptly. 'That is all he cares about.'

It seemed to me then that Neil had never had anyone who loved him for himself alone. His parents had wanted a pattern card son. His uncle wanted a dutiful heir. Miss McIntosh had wanted someone rich enough to buy her a dozen pairs of stockings on a whim. Love was unfamiliar to him, unknown and strange. It had had no place in his upbringing. Instead there had been pale imitations—approval when he pleased his family, respect for his money and status, physical desire and admiration from women—but no pure love given unconditionally. He was not loved and he did not know how to love in return. Whereas I had been materially the poorer, but had known every day of my life that my parents loved me unreservedly.

For a moment I was so close to throwing myself into his arms and demonstrating to him all the love that I had for him. I looked at him, at the pure, clean line of his jaw in the firelight, and the hard curve of his cheek, and the silky softness of his hair, and I was submerged in my feelings of love and lust. Then the wind rattled the shutter and I shivered and drew back. I could not weaken now, for both our sakes. If Neil did not want to love—if he was afraid of love—then I could not push him towards somewhere his heart did not lead.

The shutter banged again and the wind howled. Sometimes on stormy nights—and days—I would go out onto the strand and let the rain wash my face, the wind knit my hair into knots again. I would stand on the hill and feel the raw power of nature, and think of the *Cormorant* in her watery grave on the seabed below. But tonight I wanted to sit tight beside the fire and feel safe, until the storm had swept by and the sun rose on our island and the raindrops twinkled in the machair and the breeze was calm again.

'I wonder what is happening in the world,' I said suddenly. 'I wonder if we are at war again. And, if we are, will we win?'

'Of course we will,' Neil said. 'I was with Nelson at Copenhagen last year. There is a man to inspire his fleet! Such daring and courage and skill! He makes his men believe he can conjure victory from nothing, and when we believe anything is possible.'

We talked long into the night, until the wind died down and the island was calm again. That was the start of it, and after that Neil and I would spend the autumn evenings in talk or playing chess. Sometimes I even won a game, and I do not think he let me win on purpose. We talked of his childhood and mine, and the places we loved and the things that we believed in. We spoke of everything and anything other than how we felt about one another and what would happen after we left the island. I kept my feelings for him locked away as though they were in a padlocked box, and yet every conversation we had only helped me to fall more deeply in love with him, just as I had known I would. Love was not always a matter of passion and desire, but sometimes an outcome of shared adversity and day-to-day intimacy. I had not realised that before, but I understood it now.

As the October days slid towards November, and we had been on the island for over a month, I think that both of us started to assume that we might be there for the winter. We had enough food salvaged from the wreck to see us through, although it was becoming rather monotonous to eat salt beef or salt pork or biscuits or porridge. I had had to throw the cheese away when I had found things living in it. We supplemented our diet as best we could with berries, and some potatoes I had found growing in a neglected vegetable plot behind the cottage, and even with seaweed on occasion.

Sea fogs were becoming more common at night now, their grey shroud pressing around the cliffs and

outcrops, smothering all sound. The fine days were few
and far between, and when it was not foggy it seemed
to rain with either a soft drizzle that was penetratingly
wet or with great sheets of water flung in on the wind.
Even the sunny days had a cold, cutting edge.

It was on one of the rare sunny days that I was
watching the beacon whilst Neil was fishing from the
rocks. The wood was damp, as it always was now, and
had been slow to burn and was now hissing spitefully
and sending out great belches of smoke. It was probably
this that saved us, for the smoke was caught on a brisk
breeze that carried it northwesterly. I was not really
paying much attention to the sea, for I was watching a
lizard that was sunning itself on a sparkling mica rock,
when suddenly a sea eagle cast its huge long shadow
over us and I looked up. The bird was already soaring
away, but beyond it, nearer than the horizon, I caught a
flash of colour from the sails of a ship.

Panic and excitement gripped me and at the same
time a fear that I would see the ship turn and slip away
and once again our hopes would be lost. I fed the fire
feverishly, desperately trying to fan the meagre smoul-

dering to a blaze, throwing as much wood as I could find onto the pyre with no thought for what we might do if the ship vanished and the beacon had to be built up again. But the ship did not disappear. It came closer and closer, until I could see the sails and the flag of St George. It was a small Navy cutter, a reconnaissance ship. I remembered Neil saying when we were on the *Cormorant* that the Irish Squadron were patrolling these seas against Napoleon's fleet.

I shouted for Neil then, even though I knew he was away to the east and could not hear me, and I ran across the heather in my bare feet to find him, tripping and stumbling, all the time throwing backward glances at the treacherous beacon in case it went out and the ship turned and left. Neil came running up from the rocky outcrop when he heard me, a couple of salmon dangling from one hand and the line in the other, and I fell into his outstretched arms.

'A ship!' I gasped. I had one hand pressed to my side, where I had such a stitch I could barely breathe.

Neil turned and ran up to the beacon, and when I finally managed to lumber back up the hill to his side the cutter had dropped anchor a respectful way out from the reef and they were lowering a boat over the side.

Neil gripped my hand so tightly that I thought the bones might crack. Neither of us spoke. I think we were both terribly torn then, knowing that the rescue we had hoped and prayed for was here, and yet realising that this meant the end of our island life. Everything was going to change.

When the longboat reached the lagoon we went down onto the beach to meet the sailors. There was a lieutenant who looked pin neat and elegant in his uniform compared to our raggedness. I was acutely aware of the stares of the boatmen as they took in my rather unorthodox tartan-wrapped gown, but the Lieutenant did not betray by even the slightest twitch of an eyebrow that he thought there was anything amiss. He saluted Neil.

'Lieutenant George Rose of His Majesty's ship *Agamemnon,* sir!' he said smartly. 'Captain's greetings, and would you care to come aboard, sir?' Then his demeanour relaxed into a grin. 'The Captain is damned—sorry— dashed relieved to have found you, Mr Sinclair. Your uncle has been turning the Admiralty upside down this month past.' He bowed to me. 'How do you do, madam?'

Neil took my hand and drew me forward. 'This is my fiancée, Miss Catriona Balfour,' he said.

And that was how Neil Sinclair proposed marriage to me.

Chapter Fourteen

In which my stubbornness and pride prompts me to make a bad decision.

It was a shock. I admit it. And I am not sure exactly what expression showed on my face. Yet after two seconds thought I understood why Neil had done it. We had been living alone together for over a month. I had not a shred of reputation left. Truth to tell, my good name had been lost from the moment I had been carried aboard the *Cormorant*. Now we were back in the real world, and it was marriage or ruin.

Everyone was looking at me—Neil included. There was tension in his eyes, and I knew he was afraid I would refuse him point blank there on the beach, with half of His Majesty's ship *Agamemnon* in attendance. I knew he was only doing this out of honour, to save me, and for a moment my pride almost prompted me to tell him not to be foolish, that I cared not a rush for my reputation and would go and live in a bothy at Glen Clair and keep sheep and the world and its opinions could go hang.

But I did not. I did not contradict him. Instead I smiled graciously and accepted the sincere and slightly relieved congratulations of Lieutenant Rose. After that it was official, and there was no going back—at least not for now. I had every intention, however, of waiting until all the fuss had died down and the scandal was forgotten, and *then* breaking the engagement and going off to live in a bothy at Glen Clair and keep sheep.

You may be wondering why I intended to turn Neil down, given that I was hopelessly in love with him. It is true that I loved Neil so much that it was like a physical ache inside me. I loved him for his courage and his gallantry on board the *Cormorant,* I loved him for saving me in the shipwreck, and I loved him for having the principles that I had originally thought he lacked. But none of that changed the fact that he could not love me in return, and I was not going to sell myself short and settle for second best.

There was, however, no chance to talk to Neil about it now. Lieutenant Rose was anxious to get us aboard the *Agamemnon* before the tide turned. I insisted on dashing back to the cottage to collect my meagre belongings, such as they were. This amused the sailors mightily, but they provided a small oilskin bag for the purpose and in it I stowed some shells, the smallest of Neil's carvings, and a few other bits and pieces of sentimental value. And as I was standing there, looking around the little room that Neil and I had shared, a sudden pang of loss and sorrow hit me as I realised matters would never, ever be the same again.

I went out of the door one last time, then down the sandy path through the machair to the beach and to the future.

* * *

The *Agamemnon* was a neat little ship, and it was immediately clear how different it was from the *Cormorant* both in terms of tidiness and the discipline of the crew. As we went aboard Neil's face broke into a grin as we reached the deck and found the captain waiting to greet us.

'Johnny Methven! They have given you your own ship at last! Whatever possessed them?'

Captain Methven was only a few years older than Neil himself, with blue eyes bright in a tanned face and fair hair bleached pale in the sun. He shook Neil's hand, laughing.

'Thank God we found you, Sinclair. I'd never have been able to look Lord Strathconan in the eye again, had we failed.' His gaze swept over me thoughtfully. 'Trust you to be the one to be shipwrecked with a mermaid!'

Neil's smile faded abruptly. 'This is my fiancée, Miss Balfour, Methven. Catriona, this is my cousin, Lord Methven.'

'Your fiancée. Of course,' Captain Methven said, straightening. His tone changed to one of the utmost respect and he bowed to me. 'A pleasure, madam.'

But I had seen the surprise and speculation in his eyes, and I knew that as Neil's cousin and friend he would be aware of Celeste McIntosh, and all the other women, and would know, too, that Neil's marriage should be a very different business from this scrambled affair or should be a match with an heiress of good family, who had been approved by Lord Strathconan himself.

I raised my chin. It was at that precise moment, I fear, that I changed my mind about marrying Neil and I did it for all the wrong reasons. I decided that none of Neil's aristocratic connections had the right to look down their nose at me. I would marry Neil and be damned to the Earl of Strathconan and indeed to everyone else.

You see how it was with me—I had so much youth and determination, and so much pride. Enough to block out every difficult issue that I did not wish to confront, from Lord Strathconan's inevitable disapproval to the fact that Neil was not in love with me. My decisions are often swiftly made and, though I blush to admit it, are sometimes still based on as little sense as that one was even to this day. But at the time I had good excuse, for I was burning with indignation. In my opinion a Balfour was a good enough match for a Sinclair. In fact I thought that Neil was fortunate to be marrying me, not the other way around.

Everyone was most frightfully respectful to me after that. Captain Methven said that I should have his own cabin, and called a man to show me the way at once so that I might refresh myself. Although there were no ladies aboard he said that he was almost sure he could put his hand on a few items of clothing and toiletries for me which would, he hoped, make my journey more tolerable until we could put in to port.

The whole business gave Neil only a moment to grab my hand and say in a hasty whisper, 'Catriona? Is that all right?'

I whispered, 'Yes!' in reply.

If no proposal of marriage had ever been offered in so cavalier a manner, I suppose that no acceptance had ever been so rapidly and injudiciously given.

Neil and I did not meet again until dinner. I was in my borrowed plumes of a rather frivolous blue silk gown adorned with yards of lace. To this day I do not know where Johnny Methven obtained it from, but I can guess. The shoes they had found for me were too big, but that was a good thing, for my feet had been much abused, running around the island barefoot. Even the soft silk stockings that went with the dress seem to rub them rough and raw. My flat chest barely filled out the front of the gown, so I wrapped my tartan about me like a shawl, which created a rather comical but entirely respectable effect. Neil was also in borrowed clothes, a Navy uniform that made him look at once much smarter than me and somehow very intimidating. At least one of us did not look as though they were participating in a theatrical performance.

As I came into the wardroom Lieutenant Rose offered me a sherry and engaged me in conversation, and although half my mind was distracted by his pleasantries, the other half was entirely focussed on Neil. Captain Methven was talking to him most earnestly over in a corner.

'She seems a charming girl,' I overheard Methven saying, 'and I understand why you feel you must do this. But there is no getting away from the fact that she is unsuitable, Sinclair, and there is your uncle's opinion to consider—'

'Catriona is more than charming,' Neil interrupted. 'She has great courage and spirit. My uncle will grow to like her.'

'If you say so.' Methven still sounded unconvinced. 'I wouldn't have thought you the marrying type, though.'

'I know what I'm doing, Johnny,' Neil said shortly. 'And besides, in honour—' He looked up, caught sight of me, and bit off whatever he had been about to say.

He and Methven both came across then, and cut poor Lieutenant Rose out completely for my attentions. It was flattering, but I knew that since I was the only woman on the ship I did not exactly have a great deal of competition.

The cook had come up with a wonderful meal of lamb stew, for the ship had taken on fresh supplies on Barra, which was where the crew had also heard rumours of the wreck of the *Cormorant*. I tried to eat with some restraint, and not fall upon the meal like a castaway who had been eating nothing but porridge and salt meat for six weeks.

'It was all thanks to a relative of yours that we even knew where to look for you both, Miss Balfour,' Captain Methven said to me as we sat down to eat.

He was very gallant to me all of sudden, holding a chair for me and vying with Lieutenant Rose to fill my wine glass. Neil watched them falling over each other to be chivalrous to me, and there was sardonic amusement in his dark eyes.

'A relative of mine?' I said, thinking of Uncle Ebeneezer. 'I have barely any, and those that I do are mostly reprobates.'

Captain Methven laughed. 'I am speaking of a Miss Ellen Balfour of Glen Clair. I believe she is your cousin? She raised the alarm after you were kidnapped.'

I met Neil's eyes. I do not know which of us was the more startled. 'Ellen did?' I said. 'But how? What did she do—run away from Glen Clair?'

'So I believe,' Captain Methven said, nodding. 'As I heard it, she travelled to Kinlochewe in secret, went into hiding from her father there, and sent word to her fiancé, who is in the Army—'

'Her fiancé!' I burst out. I could not help myself. 'Surely she is not betrothed to Lieutenant Graham?'

Captain Methven looked puzzled for a moment. 'No, her fiancé is a Captain Langley. In point of fact I believe your cousin must be Mrs Langley by now, for I know the nuptials were close when we sailed three weeks ago.'

I was speechless—and that does not happen to me often. Neil's shoulders were shaking with laughter.

'I always thought that Langley was a dark horse,' he murmured. 'To steal the girl and the promotion from under his colleague's nose…'

'Never mind about Captain Langley for now,' I said. 'What about Ellen? She is the sweetest girl in the world, but I would never have guessed that she could be so intrepid as to run away!'

'Mrs Langley is much admired in Edinburgh,' Captain Methven agreed. 'As much for her sweet nature as her beauty.'

'I can see that you have met her,' I said, and he almost blushed.

'I have had that pleasure,' he murmured.

I could just imagine Ellen laying waste to the hearts

of His Majesty's Navy in the same way that she had cut a swathe through the Army, and I felt a most unpleasant stab of jealousy. Sitting there in my pantomime gown did little to restore my confidence. Then Neil smiled at me across the table. His eyes were still bright with suppressed amusement at the thought of Ellen's daring—Ellen who was scared of mice and thought the glen a terrifying place after dark.

'Actually, I think Ellen's behaviour is a tribute to you, Catriona,' he said. 'She is very fond of you, and perhaps she could not bear to sit by and do nothing when you were kidnapped.'

That made me ashamed of my jealousy. 'We are very fond of one another,' I said. 'I would have done the same for her.'

In point of fact I would have done more—hit Uncle Ebeneezer over the head with the poker and prevented her from being kidnapped in the first place—but one cannot have everything.

'Langley seems a sound fellow,' Methven said, picking up the tale. 'Apparently as soon as he heard that you had been taken as well, Sinclair, he sent word to the Admiralty and to Lord Strathconan. The soldiers marched on Glen Clair to arrest Mr Balfour.'

'Uncle Ebeneezer!' I said. I put down my knife and fork. 'Where is he now?'

'He is dead,' Methven said, not without satisfaction. 'He was killed resisting arrest.'

I looked at Neil. I was thinking of the charge of treason Uncle Ebeneezer would have faced for his spying, as well as the small matter of whisky-smuggling, and the kidnap of his niece and an officer of the crown.

'They would have hanged him, would they not?' I whispered, and though I had never had an ounce of affection for the man I still felt the chill and the horror of it. 'Perhaps it is better this way.'

Neil did not deny it.

'Poor Ellen,' I said. 'Poor Aunt Madeline.'

'As to that,' Lieutenant Methven said, 'I hear that your aunt is now very comfortably ensconced in a house in Inverness, and once she is out of mourning she may indeed find a new lease of life.' He frowned. 'The only thing that puzzles me, Miss Balfour, is why your uncle saw fit to have you kidnapped in the first place.'

'I believe it was because I am heir to the Glen Clair estate, Captain, and my uncle did not wish to give it up. I must set lawyers on the case as soon as I return to dry land.'

It was at that point that Lieutenant Rose, who had been respectfully silent whilst his senior officers talked, straightened up and pressed me to another glass of wine. I could see him thinking that if matters did not turn out well between Neil and myself once we reached dry land—if Lord Strathconan cut up rough and wanted to parcel me off quietly to another man, for example— he might almost be prepared to overlook my sullied reputation for the sake of my inheritance.

Captain Methven now turned the conversation to the hunt for the *Cormorant,* and enquired how Neil and I had managed to escape the shipwreck. Neil gave full credit to me for rescuing him from the hold of the ship before it went down, but he told the tale of my adventures so charmingly that I sounded a heroine rather than a hoyden. Ellen's achievements were quite eclipsed, and soon the officers were toasting my bravery and I was quite in danger of having my head turned. I stood up.

'Gentlemen,' I said, refusing Lieutenant Rose's offer of a third glass of wine, 'you must excuse me. I will leave you to your port.'

This decision of mine proved even more popular— I could tell that only my presence had restrained them from broaching further supplies already—but they all stood up very courteously as I left. Lieutenant Rose eagerly offered to escort me back to my cabin, but Neil stopped him.

'You will have to concede to my superior claim both as a senior officer and the lady's betrothed, Rose,' he drawled, and Lieutenant Rose backed down with a hasty disclaimer.

There was no privacy on the ship, and since Neil seemed determined to continue to behave with absolute propriety he escorted me gravely to the cabin door but would not come in.

'We should put in to Gairloch in a couple of days, if the wind holds from the west,' he said. He hesitated. 'I thought perhaps to arrange for you to travel from there to Applecross. I will need to go to Lochinver and give an account of myself to my senior officers, and from there to Glen Conan to see my uncle.' He stopped and took hold of my hands. 'I thought you might wish Mr Campbell to marry us, as he is your godfather,' he said, 'but if you wish for the wedding to be sooner than three weeks we may wed immediately.'

'It will be perfect to be married at Applecross,' I said. I was deeply touched that he had realised how important it was for me to have Mr Campbell be the one to officiate at my wedding. 'And we do not need to rush. That will only increase the speculation and talk of scandal.'

'There will be plenty of that as it is,' Neil said ruefully. His hands tightened on mine. 'I am sorry, Catriona.'

'You have nothing to apologise for,' I said, astonished. 'You have been all that is honourable—'

Neil shook his head. It felt as though there was something he wanted to say to me, and yet he did not seem quite able to find the words.

'This is not how I wanted it to be for you,' he said at last, fiercely. 'With people gossiping and your reputation at the mercy of the scandalmongers. It is not good enough for you. You deserve better.'

He stopped.

'I have said that to you before, have I not?' he said bitterly after a moment. 'On the island, on Taransay, when I said that I could never love you the way that you deserve to be loved.' He gripped my hands even harder. His eyes were dark with passion. 'Well, be damned to it. I find I am not so scrupulous after all when it comes to letting you go. I saw the way all those men were looking at you tonight, Catriona. Do you think for one moment that I would permit another man to court you, to touch you, to make love to you?'

His words set my head spinning. The desire in his eyes threatened to steal all my common sense.

'Neil—' I started to protest, though I had no notion what I was intending to say. But then he kissed me anyway, and my words were lost beneath the demand of his mouth.

I could not resist him. I did not want to. I thought of marrying him, and of the desire that would flare between us in the marriage bed, and I felt weak with lust. The fact that he did not love me I pushed to the very back of my mind. Silly little fool that I was, perhaps I had even started to believe—to hope—that I could make him fall in love with me over time, and that we would live happily ever after at the Old House at Glen Clair.

'I am never letting you go, Catriona,' Neil said against my lips.

He sounded very fierce, and there was a possessive look in his eyes that held me silent. For all that I can be as stubborn as a mule, Neil has an obstinacy that matches mine sometimes, and I knew that now he had decided he wanted me he would go to the ends of the earth to keep me, love or not. He loosed me and pressed a kiss on my palm, then left me, walking quickly down the corridor away from me.

It was too late to turn back.

Chapter Fifteen

In which Neil and I are married, despite the opposition of his family.

A week later saw me back at Applecross, in the familiar surroundings of Mr Campbell's study, and in some ways it felt as though nothing had changed since the last time I was there. There was the same musty smell of old books and dust in the air. The badly stuffed sofa was as uncomfortable as ever. And Mr Campbell was still looking at me with concern in his eyes, as though he would never be free of worrying about me.

'I blame myself,' he said, and he sounded bitterly regretful. 'I knew the truth of your inheritance, but your papa swore me to secrecy. He was certain that Ebeneezer would do the right thing and pass Glen Clair over to you.' He shook his head. 'David—your papa—always believed the best of people.'

'What happened between them, sir?' I asked, leaning forward in my anxiety to hear the truth at last. 'Why were they estranged? Did they quarrel over Glen Clair?'

Mr Campbell got up and moved stiffly across to the window. His faded blue gaze was fixed on the far mountains, which were swept with a misty purple haze that late-autumn day.

'David had no interest in the estate and wished to pursue his academic career. He went to Edinburgh to study, met your mother, and settled here…' He sighed, shoulders slumping. 'He had asked Ebeneezer to run the estate at Glen Clair in his absence and your uncle was very willing. Unlike David, he loved the land and he loved Glen Clair.'

I frowned, trying to imagine a time when Uncle Ebeneezer had cared as passionately about Glen Clair as I did.

'He let it go to ruin,' I said. 'How did that happen? *Why* did that happen?'

'After a while Ebeneezer came to visit David here, and demanded that he make Glen Clair over to him,' Mr Campbell said. 'He argued that it was he who had worked all his life to keep the estate running well and it was only fair that he should have the ownership of Glen Clair for his pains. The estate was not entailed—your papa could have made it over to his brother had he so chosen.' Mr Campbell sighed. 'I had some sympathy with Ebeneezer Balfour's position,' he admitted. 'David cared for nothing but his books—and his family, of course.' He smiled at me, a tired smile. 'Ebeneezer had worked his fingers to the bone to keep Glen Clair profitable, and yet in the end he was to get nothing, for David refused to give up the estate and insisted that it would one day be your dowry.'

My heart gave a lurch of pain and pity and understanding. At last I could see what my papa had intended for me, and I understood the reason why Uncle Ebeneezer had been so bitter and had hated me. He had known that one day I would take away from him everything that he had worked for.

'There was a terrible argument,' Mr Campbell said. 'Ebeneezer swore that he would do no more for a man who sought to deprive him of his livelihood, and from that day he never spoke to your papa again—and he drove Glen Clair into the ground.' He turned and looked at me. 'In the end, in his bitter madness, he tried to kill you, too.'

There was silence in the study. I breathed in the comforting, fusty smell of old books and dusty cushions, and thought about Uncle Ebeneezer, with his love and his ambition trampled in the dust, and I confess that I felt a great deal of pity for him.

'If your papa and I had only been more honest with you none of this would have happened.' Mr Campbell turned back to his desk and tapped the letter that rested there. 'Your kidnap and shipwreck, Catriona…a shocking business, truly terrible…. And now you are obliged to marry Mr Sinclair.' He shook his head, and I thought for a moment that he was about to declare that a terrible fate as well.

'That is not so bad an outcome, sir,' I protested, trying to lighten his mood. I sensed his guilt and self-reproach was dreadfully strong.

'Hmm,' Mr Campbell said. 'When a gentleman has the reputation with women that Mr Sinclair does one has to question his reliability, Catriona. However—' he tapped the letter again '—Mr Sinclair does write very properly of his regret that he could not accompany you here to see me in person, and asks formally for my permission to marry you, which is all very appropriate.'

He stood up again and walked across to the study window. I had seldom seen Mr Campbell so restless, and his mood made me restive as well. The November sun was shining on the silver trunks of the old apple trees in the garden of the manse and glittering on the sea out in the Minch. I longed to be outside. Since returning from Taransay I had found it fearfully difficult to settle to being indoors in a normal house. I felt strangely penned in. And I missed Neil dreadfully.

We had parted in Gairloch, from where I had taken a carriage south to Applecross and Neil had travelled back to the naval station at Lochinver. I knew he had to go. It was his duty to give an account of all that had happened in his investigation into the spy ring, and everything that had subsequently followed with our abduction and shipwreck. And when that was settled there was Lord Strathconan to visit, in order to placate him about our marriage. Indeed, there were a hundred and one reasons why Neil could not be at my side during this time when I needed him the most.

I told myself that I did not resent his leaving me to travel on to Applecross without him but I knew it was not true. I fiercely begrudged losing him to the Navy and to his family. And a small part of me, a little voice that whispered unhelpfully in my ear whenever I felt tired or lonely, told me that he might not come back to me if Lord Strathconan persuaded him against our marriage. I hated that voice, and I tried to close my ears to it, but it never quite left me in peace.

Before Neil had left me he had promised to meet me at Applecross in three weeks' time for our wedding. He had sent word on ahead of us, and Mrs Campbell had travelled up to Gairloch to chaperon me home on the last part of the journey. This seemed a little superfluous to me after all I had been through, but I was not going to argue. I had already realised that when Neil was determined to observe propriety he could be stricter than a Scots Methodist minister.

I sighed as I remembered our parting. We had stood in the courtyard of the Eagle Inn at Gairloch to say our goodbyes. Unsurprisingly I had refused to take the carriage from the Five Bells. It was a grey day, with the rain falling in a pale curtain. We stood under the dripping eaves and Neil drew me close to him. The rain was running down his face and his coat smelled of wet wool. It was not romantic, and yet I wanted to stay there in his arms for ever.

'I don't want to leave you,' he said. He sounded strained. 'Catriona, my heart, little cat.'

He spoke softly, in the Gaelic, and my heart leapt to hear it, for it was not often that Neil's civilised reserve broke to show the passionate Highlander beneath. I raised a hand to his wet cheek, and then he was kissing me with all the release of his pent-up desire, and he tasted of rain and salt, and a huge wave of love and need knocked me flat with emotion. I am sure that he could have made love to me there and then in the courtyard, without the slightest protest from me, but my chaperon, seeing the way that matters were going, stepped forward with a great clearing of her throat and practically grabbed me from his arms. I suppose she must have told Mr Campbell what had happened, now I come to think of it, and it was probably that which had confirmed the poor man's opinion of Neil as a shameless ravisher of women.

Mr Campbell sighed now, recalling me to the present. 'If you are in agreement, Catriona, I will make the arrangements at once. Mr Sinclair suggests the twenty-fifth for the wedding.'

'I am in agreement, sir,' I said. I hesitated. 'Forgive me, but you do not seem very happy with the match.'

Mr Campbell sighed again. He turned back to look at me. His face was set in deep lines, and once again, as on the occasion when he had first sent me to Glen Clair, I was aware of the burden I was to him, and how determined he was for both my father's sake and my own to do the best that he could for me. Dear Mr Campbell! It had not turned out so well the first time, and perhaps he was fearful that this might be as bad.

'I realise that this marriage has to take place—' he said.

I blushed a fiery red. 'I beg your pardon, Mr

Campbell,' I said, 'but it *does not*. There is no *necessity* for me to marry, if that is what you mean.'

He looked at me, and I think his lips almost twitched into a smile when he saw the depth of my sincerity and my indignation. 'Then I beg *your* pardon, too, Catriona,' he said mildly. 'I did not intend to offend you. If you tell me there is no need…'

'Not in the intimate sense,' I said, almost ready to sink with mortification now, for nothing in my life had prepared me for talking about such personal matters with the minister who had baptised me and known me from childhood. 'No need at all. Mr Sinclair has been the perfect gentleman, and I—' I stopped, for in truth I could not claim a great deal of virtue for myself. There had been several occasions when only Neil's self-control had stood between me and my ruin, and in those moments I would have welcomed his lovemaking with open arms.

'Hmm,' Mr Campbell said. 'Not that that will stop anyone talking scandal.'

'Unfortunately not,' I agreed. 'And most people would never believe me anyway.'

I knew this was true, because I had already had a visit from Lady Bennie and the Misses Bennie. They had ostensibly called to show their sympathy for the terrible ordeal I had suffered, but they had also implied, with a slight withdrawing of skirts, that that although it was all very well for the scapegrace daughter of the late schoolmaster to behave as I had done—indeed, it was almost to be expected with my ramshackle up-bringing—it would certainly not have done for the daughters of the squire. One look at the faces of the Misses Bennie had told the truth, though. It was clear when the wedding was discussed that they both wished *they* had had the opportunity to be ruined by the wicked Mr Sinclair.

'Which is the material point, unfortunately,' Mr Campbell said, once again drawing me back to the present. 'Your reputation is ruined, whatever the truth behind the situation.' He shook his head distractedly. 'Oh, dear, for all that Mr Sinclair has offered you the protection of his name, like the gentleman he is, I cannot quite believe that he is good enough for you, Catriona. He may be a very worthy young man—' Mr Campbell did not sound entirely convinced of this '—but you are special, and I am not sure that he deserves you.'

I got up and went over to kiss his cheek. I so wanted to smooth the worried lines from Mr Campbell's face. 'Pray do not concern yourself, sir,' I said. 'Mr Sinclair *is* a very good man, and I am happy to be marrying him.'

I think that I convinced him. Certainly his anxious expression lifted a little, and though I heard him sigh for a third time it was in resigned acceptance. I think that I almost convinced myself as well. I had resolved to marry Neil Sinclair and I am not the sort of person to waver and bend with the wind. So each time a doubt nibbled at the corner of my mind I would dismiss it. I dismissed my fears that Lord Stathconan would refuse permission for the marriage to go ahead, I dismissed my anxiety over what shape my future life would take, and most of all I dismissed the knowledge that Neil did not love me.

It was perhaps fortunate—or unfortunate, depending on your point of view—that I was given very little time for thinking between choosing my trousseau from the travelling peddler, Mrs Campbell fussing over dress fittings, Mrs McLeod, the cook, wishing to talk about the wedding breakfast, and Lady Bennie and her daughters calling every other day to check as to whether I had had news of Mr Sinclair. I had not. The time slipped away and I managed most successfully to keep my thoughts at bay.

Two days before the wedding, Neil came back. Lord and Lady Strathconan were with him. A whole procession of carriages and coaches followed them down the narrow road into the village. People spilled out of them—friends, relatives, acquaintances—all of whom Lord Strathconan had decreed should be present to witness his heir's marriage.

And I think it was then that everything started to go wrong.

'I had no choice,' Neil said. He had caught my arm and drawn me aside for a brief moment, whilst Lord and Lady Strathconan descended their carriage. 'I could hardly deny my uncle and aunt the right to attend my wedding.'

'No,' I said. 'No, of course you could not. Of course they had to come.'

But I felt the cold touch of reality intrude, for here was the first tangible sign that my life was going to be very different in future, and that I might not always have the ordering of it. The Earl of Strathconan wanted to see his nephew and heir wed, and when Lord Strathconan asked, no one gainsaid.

I did understand. Even so, my heart ached for the quiet little wedding I had wanted in the chapel at Applecross. I had thought that there would be no one but Mr and Mrs Campbell to hear Neil and me take our vows. I had imagined the autumn sunshine making pools on the ancient stone flags of the floor and the dust motes dancing in the still air, and the tranquil atmosphere conjuring memories of my father and mother so that in the peace I could have time to think of them and believe them to be there in spirit, watching over me and blessing my future.

Now all that had changed. Lord and Lady Strathconan and all their entourage were staying with Sir Compton and Lady Bennie, there being nowhere in Applecross village remotely suitable to accommodate the exacting requirements of an Earl. That meant that the Bennies must be invited to attend the wedding, as well as all of Lord Strathconan's friends and relatives, who included Johnny Methven, standing as Neil's groomsman, and his mother, Lady Methven, who was apparently Lord Strathconan's sister. The wedding breakfast would now be held at the Manor, putting Mrs McLeod's days of preparation to waste and her nose firmly out of joint.

It soon became apparent that my modest trousseau was completely unacceptable to Lady Strathconan and Lady Methven. Lady Strathconan, who seemed as charming as Ellen had once told me, sifted through the little pile of gloves and scarves and ribbons I had bought from the peddler and shook her head slightly.

'My dear child,' she said, smiling gently at me, 'I am afraid these simply will not do.'

Lady Methven was not so charming. She picked over my undergarments like a crow picking over a cadaver. She looked like a crow as well, with her sharp chin and darting eyes. 'Dreadful cheap quality,' she cawed, and as her gaze slid over me I knew she was expressing her opinion of me as well as the clothes.

'It is fortunate,' Lady Strathconan continued, determinedly ignoring her sister-in-law and smiling through, 'that I brought you some items from my own dressmaker in Edinburgh, dearest Catriona. As a wedding gift, naturally…'

Put like that, of course, I could not be so ungracious as to refuse the gift, but I looked at my sad little pile of purchases and felt an angry resolve that I would not throw them away.

'Never mind the fripperies, Emily,' Lady Methven said sharply. 'We must do something about the gown.' She flicked dismissively at the lace and lawn that Mrs Campbell had sewn with such loving care. 'Indeed, the chit cannot wear this! She will look utterly unpresentable!'

'Yes,' Lady Strathconan said, 'the gown…' She sighed and her plump, pretty face drooped.

I could see that Emily Stirling must once have been an extremely attractive woman, pretty enough to tempt Lord Strathconan into the indiscretion of marrying beneath him. And it seemed to me that on her marriage she must have moved from placating difficult children for a living to placating snobbish aristocrats instead, for I imagined it had taken a great deal of work and many years before Lady Methven had welcomed this former governess into the family.

Such was not going to be my fate. In that moment I resolved that I was not going to spend *my* future begging for favour from Lady Methven and her ilk. I would rather pull out my own eyelashes than bend to her will.

'What is the matter with my wedding gown, ma'am?' I enquired, all innocence. 'Mrs Campbell has worked her fingers to the bone to have it ready in time.'

Lady Methven snorted with disgust. Lady Strathconan sighed. 'It is very pretty, Catriona,' she said, and Lady Methven snorted again, 'but I am afraid it is a little too simple for the occasion. I have brought a gown and a veil from my own dressmaker that will require very little alteration…'

Of course she had. Somehow I had known that already.

'That dress will never be ready in time,' Lady Methven opined. 'The chit is far too skinny—the bodice requires taking in by several inches.'

'Then I shall wear my own dress, my lady,' I said, 'for

it is already made and, as Lady Strathconan says, is very pretty.'

And though Lady Methven bullied me and Lady Strathconan cajoled me, I would not be swayed. Mrs Campbell had worked with love to produce that gown for my wedding, and so many of our plans and arrangements had been overset already. I was not going to go quietly.

They must have realised it, for several times over the next day I saw Lady Strathconan looking at me with speculation in her eyes, and Lady Methven with deep disapproval in hers. I think they were wondering how long it would be before they could break my recalcitrant spirit. It is true that they held all the cards. But if they were spoilt tyrants I was headstrong, and disinclined to meet them halfway, so it was inevitable that we would clash.

As for Lord Strathconan, beyond his first greeting he had not spoken to me at all. He was a short, rotund man, with a complexion that argued ill health and a choleric manner that suggested that he was in constant pain. Secretly I had hoped to find him far more congenial, and was gravely disappointed. When Neil introduced us the Earl had not minced his words to me.

He had looked me over, and the flinty expression in his grey eyes had not softened one iota.

'So,' he said, 'you are the gel my nephew is obliged to marry. He tells me that you are well bred and well educated and charming. I sincerely hope so. You are a Balfour of Glen Clair, so I understand?' His bushy eyebrows bunched together as he frowned. 'I'll not pretend that you are the bride I would have chosen for my heir.'

Well, if it came to that he was not the uncle I would have chosen for myself. I seemed to have poor luck when it came to uncles.

'I am sorry that you feel like that, my lord,' I said, very politely, and saw his brows snap down further as he realised I was apologising for nothing other than his own lack of courtesy to me. He had stumped off, and Lady Strathconan had made haste to follow him to smooth matters over.

You may be wondering where Neil was in all of this. I was wondering much the same myself. After our brief, snatched conversation on the day he had arrived, I had barely seen him. The ladies had informed me that it was bad luck for me to spend time with my groom until the day of the wedding itself, and had surrounded me like a witches' coven, never letting me out of their sight. I had never been so closely chaperoned in my life, and it drove me mad always to have someone at my elbow, and to have no privacy nor any time to myself. Lady Bennie had given me a bedchamber that could only be accessed through an outer room, and Lady Methven had stationed a servant there at all times as though she suspected I would be creeping out for an assignation with Neil—or he would be creeping in—if we were not close-guarded. It was ridiculous.

I wanted to find Neil and suggest that we elope some-where, taking Mr Campbell with us to perform the wedding ceremony, to get away from this circus of guests and gowns and wedding breakfasts. The Neil Sinclair I had known on Taransay would have run off with me in an instant. Of that I was certain. But this Neil Sinclair? The man who was heir to all this pomp and ceremony was a stranger to me.

That was when I started to have second thoughts. Suddenly I was crippled with shyness and doubt, wishing desperately that Neil and I could go back to how we had been in that little white hut by the sea, just the two of us alone in all existence. But that seemed impossible now. The kidnap, the shipwreck and our lives on Taransay seemed like a dream. It had been another world, and one that I had lost. All that excitement and adventure was gone now. We were back in a place with rules, regulations and reputations.

I almost ran away from the wedding. I was so miserable and afraid that I almost left Neil standing at the altar. I know his horrible relatives would have been glad to see me scampering away up the glen in my poor-quality wedding dress.

What was it that stopped me? It was my pride, naturally. I could not bear for all those stiff-necked aristocrats to believe I had run because I thought I was not good enough for them. For that was what they would have thought. That was the one thing that prevented me from backing out, and it was a poor enough reason to go through with the wedding, but that, alas, was typical of me with my Balfour pride.

And so I married Neil. And *then* I ran away.

Chapter Sixteen

In which I run away and Neil runs after me.

Actually it was not as melodramatic as it sounds. I ran away from the wedding breakfast, not from my marriage.

By the time that the dessert had been consumed and the guests were dissolving into alcoholic merriment I could stand it no longer. Neil had sat by my side throughout that interminable meal, but we had not had a single private conversation. He had helped me to the food, most attentively, had poured my wine himself and had complimented me on my appearance—in my second-rate gown—he had smiled at me frequently but we had not said one meaningful thing to one another. How could we, with Lord Strathconan on my other side and Lady Methven seated next to Neil and de-manding the best of his attention?

I began to see how it was possible for a married couple never to have a moment to themselves. And I also saw that no one thought this odd; indeed none of the married couples around the table appeared to *want* to speak to one another, for they were either busy getting drunk or flirting with someone other than their husband or wife, or forcing down their throats mouthful after mouthful of Sir Compton's finest food.

I do not think anyone noticed when I slipped away. I do not think they cared. Perhaps Mr Campbell noticed, but he was unlikely to give me away. Lady Bennie, seated further down the table, had claimed Neil's atten-tion, and Lord Strathconan simply grunted when I excused myself. Only the servants watched as I made for the door and walked straight out into the rain.

Yes, it was raining. The morning had been fine for

the wedding, but now a sea mist had blown in from the west and the hills had disappeared beneath the lowering clouds. Darkness was falling. I ran down to the strand and stood there, while the rain soaked my wedding gown and clung to my skin and beaded on my hair. I let the cold wind blow through me and felt the chill in my soul.

'Catriona?'

I turned. Neil was standing only a few feet behind me. He had come after me. I felt my heart lift with pleasure that he cared enough to follow me, and then plunge at the thought that maybe he was only there to force me to return to that interminable wedding breakfast.

'I'm not going back in there,' I said, before he could say another word. 'I'm not. I can't stand it.'

I ran off down the shingle, hearing the shells and stones crunch beneath my dainty little wedding slippers. I could hear Neil running after me. He was quicker than I was. Within two minutes he had grabbed me around the waist and pulled me hard against him.

'Wait!' He did not sound even slightly out of breath, whereas I was already panting.

I drummed my fists against his chest, horrified to find my self-control deserting me, and yet feeling powerless to resist my emotions now that I had finally let go.

'I wish I had never married you!' I cried. 'I *hate* all those horrible people, with their long noses to look down! If this is what my life is going to be like in the future then I wish I had drowned in the wreck of the *Cormorant!*'

Neil grabbed my wrists and held me away from him, to protect himself from my puny blows. 'Catriona, please don't say that—'

'It's true!' I said. I was losing my restraint completely. All the fears I had bottled up burst out with the force of a volcano. 'I only wanted to be with you,' I said, abandoning all discretion. 'I wanted to marry *you*, not your horrible family! I wanted it to be just the two of us—like it was on Taransay!'

'Sweetheart—' Neil said. He raised a hand and brushed a damp strand of hair away from my jaw.

'There is a servant watching us,' I said, looking over his shoulder to where a bashful footman in Sir

Compton's livery stood hopping from one foot to another in the rain. Lord Strathconan had evidently sent him to round us up like a pair of wayward sheep.

'I'll get rid of him,' Neil said. He looked at me. 'Stay there.'

I stood there, whilst the rain trickled down my cheeks and mingled with the tears that seemed to be forcing themselves out unbidden from the corners of my eyes. I did think about running off again, but I was cold and wet and dispirited and I knew Neil would only come after me.

'You have not seen us,' I heard Neil say. 'In fact you thought you saw a man and a woman taking the path towards Ghyll Head…'

There was a chink of coins and a muttered word of thanks from the footman. A moment later Neil had taken my hand again, and was pulling me along the beach in the opposite direction from the Manor.

'Where are we going?' I gasped, trying to keep up with him as he half dragged, half carried me over the shingle towards a tiny cottage on the edge of the shore.

'Somewhere we can be alone,' Neil said grimly.

I looked back at the lights of the Manor, winking in the dusk. 'They'll come after us.'

'They will have to break the door down to find us, and I do not think even my uncle would be so tactless,' Neil said. He pushed open the gate with his foot and bundled me up the short path to the door. 'When we made our original wedding plans I asked Mr Campbell if we could spend our first night together alone,' he added, opening the front door and drawing me inside. 'I had anticipated that we would be staying at the manse, and I thought that a night under that roof might dampen our…um…spirits. Mr Campbell suggested that we borrow this cottage. I understand it is usually used by travelling ministers?'

Under other circumstances the irony of the manse guest house being the venue for our first night together might have amused me. I might also have admired Neil's planning, for I knew what he meant—no doubt we would have spent our wedding night lying awake side by side like effigies in Mrs Campbell's narrow single beds, waiting for the daylight to come. But truth to tell this felt little better. I was tired and distressed and

I felt so lonely. I wanted my mother then; I wanted her warmth and her understanding and her uncritical affection. I wanted her to enfold me in her arms and I was shocked and horrified to feel that way.

Neil had gone over to the grate to coax the fire into life, whilst I stood and shivered in the centre of the room.

'Here,' he said, putting up a hand to the ties of my wedding bonnet, 'take this off. It is soaking.' The bow unravelled in his hand and the bonnet slid down to my shoulders and fell from there, unheeded, to the floor. I was glad it was gone. It had been making my head ache. I rubbed my brow irritably. My hair was too tightly pinned. I put my hand up to loosen the knot and realised that I was shaking. Everything seemed wrong suddenly—appallingly, terrifyingly wrong.

'I'm sorry,' Neil said, seeing my expression. 'I'm so sorry, Catriona. I did not realise that you felt so strongly about my uncle and his entourage.'

'How could you know?' I said, tired and bitter. 'We have not had chance to talk since you came back.'

'No,' Neil said. 'Everything happened so fast, and whenever I looked for you my aunts would tell me you were having a gown-fitting or were choosing your trousseau, or that it was bad luck for me to see you before the wedding.' He shook his head. 'I should have thought what it would be like for you, having them all descend on you like a plague of locusts when you were new to all this. I should have tried harder to get to you—climbed in through your bedroom window or something.'

I gave a little giggle, my spirits reviving slightly. 'I believe Sir Compton had stationed a gamekeeper below with a shotgun,' I said. 'Clearly no one has faith in my chastity.'

'More likely they doubt my honour—and with more cause,' Neil said dryly. 'Mr Campbell told me that you were bearing up well under the circumstances, but I should have pressed him for more information.'

'You asked him about me?' I queried. Mr Campbell had been the only person allowed to see me alone, and only then because he had insisted it was for my spiritual welfare in preparation for the wedding.

'Of course,' Neil said. 'The trouble is that he is so very discreet.'

'He told me—discreetly—that you had tried to dissuade Lord Strathconan from inviting so many guests,' I said.

'I did,' Neil said bitterly. 'I did not want our small wedding spoiled. My uncle and I quarrelled over it, as we do over so many things, until he—' He stopped.

'What?' I prompted.

He looked at me. His gaze was very sombre. 'Until he asked me if I was so ashamed of you that I wanted to hide you away,' he said. 'It was clever of him, because it angered me so much that I said I was as proud of you as I could be and he could invite the whole of Scotland to the wedding if he wished—which he promptly did.'

The cottage was silent. I could hear the muted roar of the sea outside, and see the moon dappling the shingle, but inside it was very quiet.

'You are proud of me?' I said softly. I felt the hard, unhappy knot in my stomach unravel slightly.

Neil touched the wet strands of hair that had been released from my bonnet. His fingers were warm against my cheek.

'I am more proud than I can say to have you as my wife,' he murmured. His hand fell to my shoulder. 'You should take off these wet clothes,' he added. 'You will catch a chill.'

Suddenly—as easily and as swiftly as that—I was shivering with a different kind of fever. Perhaps I was a little drunk on all the high emotion that had gone before. Perhaps I was simply relieved to know that he still cared for me and had *wanted* to marry me, was not acting solely out of honour and duty. Perhaps I simply wanted to blot out all my fears for the future and lose myself in him in this brief time that we had alone together.

Whatever the case, I wanted him desperately in that moment. I wanted him, and yet I felt abruptly and un-characteristically shy. Suddenly this night, which I had longed for with a most immodest excitement, seemed mysterious and terrifying.

'I'm frightened,' I blurted out.

Neil paused for a second. 'Don't be,' he said softly. 'Catriona, sweetheart, I'll not hurt you. I'd never hurt you.'

He was watching me. He must have seen the wild

jumble of my thoughts expressed on my face, for he put out a hand, caught my wrist and put an end to my doubts and fears by pulling me into his arms. His mouth covered mine.

I gasped, I think with relief more than anything else, but the instant I opened my lips Neil took advantage to take my mouth so thoroughly, so completely, that I forgot about being shy or fearful, and about everything else as well. My whole body responded to the touch of his lips. His tongue curled with mine in intimate seduction, slow and deceptively gentle. The heat flared and burned low in my stomach, and I pressed closer to him as his arms went around me and his mouth moved softly, tenderly over mine, yet with an absolute primal possessiveness that made me shake all the more. When he let me go I was gasping for breath, and he was breathing as hard as I was.

'Don't be frightened,' he said again, and his fingers moved to the front of my gown, unhooking the row of buttons there, moving lower and lower down the bodice.

His gaze was concentrated, and the intense, dark focus of his eyes made the flaring heat inside me build to a long, slow burn. A lock of hair had fallen across his brow and I put up my hand to brush it aside. He turned his lips against my fingers, but he did not take his eyes from his task until the buttons were undone down to my waist.

The gown crumpled to the floor and I was left in my shift and petticoats. Neil unpinned my hair and ran his fingers through it, loosening my curls, allowing them to slip through his fingers.

'When I combed your hair that time on the beach,' he said, 'I wanted to kiss every single curl.'

He put his hands on my bare shoulders, and then slid them down my arms until he was holding my wrists lightly. The hairs on my skin rose to his touch, every inch of me heating beneath his hands, though I felt cold and shivery at the same time as though I had a fever.

'I have something to confess to you too,' I said. 'You remember the time that I came upon you washing in the pool?'

He raised his gaze to mine. There was an expression in his eyes that had my heart thumping wildly.

'It was not the only time I watched you,' I said.

He smiled, that wicked flashing smile that made my heart turn over.

'Then I will also confess,' he said huskily, 'that the muslin curtain between us was utterly transparent in the firelight. I watched you every night, and I wanted you.'

I remembered undressing without inhibition, in the belief that I was hidden. The thought of what Neil had seen made me weak, but it was intolerably exciting at the same time. His soft, erotic words had conjured images of my nakedness and his response, and I closed my eyes. A second later Neil was kissing me again, and I kissed him back with all the heat and passion that was in me, winding my arms about his neck and arching against him. We slid to the floor on the thick rag rug that lay before the fire.

There was nothing but firelight and candlelight in the room, soft and golden. I pulled Neil's shirt away from his pantaloons so that I might burrow beneath the folds and touch his bare skin. I ran my palms over the broad planes of his shoulders and back, and heard him say something, rough and low, as he shrugged out of the shirt to enable me to touch him all the more. My inhibitions were gone now, and I wanted to explore every inch of the hard, muscled body I was exposing. I reached for him, but he pushed me gently back onto the rug, following me down, kissing me again, tempting, provocative, leading me to match him caress for caress.

At last he broke the kiss and I fell back, panting for breath. Neil was opening my chemise and leaning over to stroke my skin in one long caress from my neck down to my belly. My body ached for him, ached to be free of all clothes and all restraint. Except…

I would like to say that in this moment of extreme passion I was lost to everything except the demands of my body and the absolute need that I had for Neil. Unfortunately that would not be true. As the edge of my chemise parted I remembered that my chest was almost as flat as a washboard, and for a moment I felt as inadequate about my appearance as I had when confronted by Ellen's glowing beauty the first time I arrived at Glen Clair. I am not generally afflicted with lack of confidence in this way, but I almost stiffened and pulled away from Neil. Once again it was too late, however. His hand was resting inside my chemise, over my ribcage, just below the miniature curve of my breast, and now he brushed the material aside and lowered his dark head to take me in his mouth.

I cried out. The sensation was indescribably good and it pulsed through me, setting me tingling with heat and fire. My body rose to meet his, wanting something I could not quite understand; I reached feverishly for him, but he held me down so that he could prolong his caresses, his lips moving so slowly from my breast to my stomach and still lower, to graze the soft skin of my inner thigh. I did not know where the rest of my clothes had gone. I did not really care. I thought I would melt with the sheer pleasure he could give me.

'Catriona—*leannan, piseag...*' *Sweetheart, little cat...* His words were a whisper, a breath against the most secret part of me, a breath that made me shiver, the goosebumps rising all over my skin. He touched me *there* with his tongue and I shattered at once, my body clenching so tight and fast that I screamed. The power and force of the feeling stole my breath, and Neil kissed me slowly, thoroughly, taking my little cries and gasps into his mouth as the stars spun overhead and my body spiralled down to rest.

Eventually I opened my eyes wide and stared at him. 'What did you *do?*'

He laughed and smoothed the hair back from my face with tender fingers. 'I can show you again, if you like.'

'No!' I grabbed his forearms. His hands had started to move over me again, gently, almost stealthily, and I was shocked to feel my body responding to him. So soon…I wanted something, some fulfilment that had been denied me despite the blinding pleasure of that moment. This was all strange to me, and shocking in its newness, but there was also something deeply instinctive in it.

I am not a patient person—you will have realised that by now—so when I reached for Neil again in sheer desperation, and still he held me off, I think I ripped the remainder of his clothes from him with complete abandon. Yet even in my frantic state there was something about the first touch of his naked skin against mine that stopped me. The smoothness and yet the friction, the warmth of him, the sense of recognition, and yet the utter unfamiliarity, untried, unknown… I ran my hands over his body, desperate to know him, desperate to learn, but then after a moment I lay still, completely awed, my gaze locked with his.

'I did not know,' I whispered. 'I did not realise it would feel like this…'

'It can feel even better than this,' Neil said.

Slowly, carefully, he moved over me, placing his hands by my head, with the swollen tip of him resting just inside me. He was watching my face so intensely I could not have broken the contact had I wanted. His lips brushed mine.

'*Muirneag*—darling girl…' He eased himself within me, and I shifted to try to draw him in. I felt my body resist. I was frightened again now.

The thing that I remember most about that moment is my anxiety, for my heart battered my ribs so hard I was afraid it might burst.

It did hurt. Anyone who says differently is either very lucky, very forgetful, or they are lying.

'You said you wouldn't hurt me,' I said, almost accusingly, and Neil gave a rather shaky laugh. He looked very tense. I understand now just how much a strain such self-control was placing on him, although in that moment I had no idea. I think I made him suffer quite a lot in my innocence, which is perhaps fair.

'I had no choice, *ma cridhe,*' he said softly.

Beloved. That almost made up for the pain. I gave a little self-satisfied smile and moved slightly, to see if it still hurt.

Neil gasped. He looked as though he were counting, or doing some kind of complicated mathematical calculation, which struck me as odd at the time. There was a desperation in his eyes that was actually rather pleasing to see.

'Catriona,' he said, and his voice was hoarse. 'If it still hurts you—'

'It does not,' I said. I moved again, saw him close his eyes in anguish, and understood my own power at last.

Pushing matters a little further, I wriggled voluptuously and heard him bite off a word that was definitely an expletive rather than an endearment. Then I dug my nails into his back, and that was enough to banish his control as he moved and put an end to our waiting.

Even then he was careful not to hurt me. He moved within me in long, slow thrusts that after a while started to drive me mad with wanting. Yet when I urged him to quicken he would only prolong the pleasure, in those same unhurried, easy strokes, dipping his head to kiss me, or allowing his lips to drift across my breast until I was straining to him in an agony of need. Eventually I could bear it no more, and dug my fingers into his buttocks, pulling him more tightly inside so that he was as deep and hard within me as it was possible to be. Then at last he drove into me without restraint, and this time I slid with agonising slowness to the edge of bliss, and again slipped slowly, oh, so slowly over the brink, my eyes wide open, transfixed. Neil's fingers locked in mine, his release following my own and sweeping us both away.

When I opened my eyes I saw a look of absolute stunned astonishment on Neil's face. I will never forget it.

I frowned slightly. Did that mean it had been good, or bad, or indifferent? Normally I am not troubled with self-doubt, but on this occasion, with no means of comparison and no notion of how to go on other than by instinct, I was suddenly anxious.

'Is something wrong?' I asked. 'Did I…? Was it…?'

Neil seemed to waken from a trance.

'No,' he said. 'There's nothing wrong.' He blinked, still looking stunned. 'I've never…It was perfect.'

He rolled over and gathered me into his arms, tucking me snugly into the curve of his shoulder. The fire warmed us. I realised with a little jolt of disbelief that we had made love on the floor, on the hearthrug that I had helped Mrs Campbell and Mrs MacLeod to weave from spare rags. The thought of their faces if they had seen the use to which we had put their rug made me laugh.

'I thought we were supposed to do this in bed,' I said against the curve of his throat.

'We can do that soon, if you wish,' Neil said, and I shivered.

He carried me up the stairs to bed after that, and we did indeed do it again, several times, until we were both exhausted. Tucked up warm in the little cottage, ignoring the rain outside and the wedding guests at the

Manor and the world beyond, it was almost possible to imagine that we were back on Taransay.

But in the morning it was still raining, and there was a footman at the door with a note from Lord Strathconan, informing us that Neil's commanding officer had sent orders recalling him to Lochinver at once. *At once.* The Earl had underlined the words, as though he could not bear for us to have any more stolen time alone together.

Before he left Neil kissed me and held me tightly in front of everyone, and told me that he would come back soon. After all that had so recently passed between us it almost broke my heart to let him go.

'I hate to leave you, Cat,' he whispered. 'But I will write every day—'

'Come *on*, Sinclair!' Johnny Methven interrupted— rudely, I thought. He had been recalled as well, and was in a foul temper as he had apparently been anticipating some time in the Edinburgh bawdy houses instead.

Neil released me reluctantly with a final kiss. 'Wait for me in Edinburgh,' he said. 'I'll come as soon as I can…'

'Yours is the fate of a Navy wife in wartime,' Lady Strathconan said to me, trying to console, as we watched Neil ride away down the drive of the Manor. 'But do not repine. We shall go to Edinburgh and entertain ourselves there. We will have such fun! You will love it, Catriona. Just you see.'

She squeezed my hand and I knew she was trying to be kind; knew, moreover, than in my strange new life she really was my only ally. So for once I bit my tongue, and did not blurt out that the only thing that would make me happy would be to have more time with my husband, and that gown shops and dinners and fashionable diversions were no substitute for his presence.

Then, when they were almost through the gateway, I saw Johnny Methven lean over and clap Neil on the shoulder. Neil grinned in response to something that Methven said, and they kicked their horses to a gallop and were gone without a backward glance. It reminded me of the moment that Neil had left me and gone back to the wardroom that night on the ship. He had been turning back toward something welcome and familiar then. So it was now, for I had seen the expression on his face before he had been lost from my view. He had looked relieved.

Chapter Seventeen

In which I feel monstrously neglected by my husband.

We went to Edinburgh. I hated it.

Please do not misunderstand me. I love Edinburgh, and think it one of the most beautiful cities on earth, but the Edinburgh that I had visited with my father, with its libraries and lectures and learned debates, was a very different one from the city known to Lady Strathconan and Lady Methven. When I had visited with my papa we had stayed in the old town, with the scholars, scientists and philosophers who had been of his circle.

The tenements were crowded, the street smells strong and the hospitality was erratic, but the conversation was stimulating enough to help us all forget that we had missed our dinner. There were no formal visiting hours—guests would call late and talk well into the night, arguing philosophical or mathematical concepts over a bottle or two of the finest malt.

In contrast the Earl of Strathconan had a magnificent townhouse in Charlotte Square, newly built and designed by Robert Adam, no less. The new town was beautiful, spacious and elegant, and the smells and vivid life of the old city were banished. We did not visit there. When I suggested that there were friends of my father I would like to call upon I was politely discouraged. When I called upon them anyway, I was roundly condemned for my behaviour by Lady Methven. Her Ladyship kept a separate establishment in Queen's Street, where she lived with her glacially cold unmarried daughter Anne. Anne Methven had a disconcerting habit of watching me silently with her chilly gaze, and she never made the slightest attempt to befriend me, though we were close in age. No doubt she thought me beneath her touch.

At least the servants were friendly, all except Lady Strathconan's personal maid, Mackie, a thin-faced, thin-lipped woman who moved silently like a ghost about her mistress's bidding. My own maid was a cheerful country girl called Jessie, who had as little idea of how to be a lady's maid as I had of how to be a society lady. We muddled along together. I think all the servants, from the butler to the hall boy, were so surprised that I learned their names and actually spoke to them that they took me to their hearts immediately. I soon realised that Lord and Lady Strathconan never spoke to their staff except through intermediaries. This was entirely proper, of course, but it went against my nature to ignore the very people who made my life so materially comfortable, and Lady Strathconan was always chiding me for chatting to the housemaids.

Lady Strathconan's days consisted of walking in the Queen's Square Gardens, or browsing the new shops that were opening in Princes Street, or attending the assembly rooms to gossip and chat before the same people we had met there called upon us to gossip some more. I found it utterly tedious.

Naturally I was something of a novelty, the school-master's daughter who had caught the heir to the Earl of Strathconan. The word 'entrapped' was not used openly, of course, but once again, as with Lady Bennie back in Applecross, I caught the disapproval, the whiff of scandal. Every matron in Edinburgh picked over the *on dit* of my kidnapping as though it was a particularly tempting cut of meat, and whilst everyone agreed that I had been frightfully brave during my ordeal, I could see the speculation in every eye as all the matrons wondered privately what had happened between Neil and myself when we were marooned alone together. More than one lady allowed her gaze to dwell brazenly on my stomach, to see if I was showing signs of increasing.

As for the gentlemen, they were all that was charming and attentive, offering to take me driving or to escort me for a walk in the gardens, or to dance with me at the balls and assemblies. Chief amongst my admirers was a handsome but rather stupid army officer called Tolly Gulliver. He seemed to have no discernible job, for he spent all his time dancing attendance on me. I tolerated him, because he reminded me of a dog in his anxiety to please. I suppose that I should have been more careful of my good name, but I was miserable that Neil was not there and did not have the heart nor the energy to dismiss Tolly. His attentions meant nothing to me. They did not ease the pain of Neil's absence. They left me completely cold.

I missed Neil with a sense of loss that made me ache inside and brought the tears pricking the back of my throat. I pined. Naturally I did not stop eating—it takes more than being unhappy in love to make me starve myself—but it felt as though I were moving through a world that lacked colour and vitality, as though each day were in black and white tones and all the bright-ness had leached away.

After ten days of living Lady Strathconan's type of existence I was near screaming, especially as I had had no word from Neil, who, it seemed, was particularly bad at letter-writing despite his extravagant promises. After a month, I thought I would run mad.

Christmas came and went with neither sight nor sound of my husband, and not even the Hogmanay cele-brations could lift my spirits. The January days were long and dark. By now I knew that I was not increasing, and whilst a part of me was defiantly glad to prove the gossips wrong, another part of me was desperately upset that I was not to have a baby. I had nothing of Neil's except his relatives, and I did not want them.

Lady Strathconan tried to cheer me, but her words of consolation left me feeling gloomier rather than uplifted.

'You know what men are,' she would say brightly, when another day brought no word from Neil. 'They become immersed in their business for months on end, and so often forget we poor females left behind! I am sure that had he been assigned a ship we should have heard…' And then, having reminded me how little Neil must care for me, and the ever present danger of my never seeing him again, she would walk away.

Lady Methven was more blunt. 'A female is nothing more than a fool if she expects a man to care for her feelings,' she would say, and Miss Methven would nod her arctic agreement.

It was no wonder she was unmarried. If she had absorbed her mother's views on men then she could have nothing but contempt for them, and any man would freeze to death anyway if he attempted to climb into her bed.

When I finally did receive a letter, in the third week of January, it was not from Neil but from my cousin Ellen. She was settled in a cottage in the village of Morningside, a mere few miles down the road. The house belonged to Captain Langley's mother, and they were residing there whilst they awaited his next posting. She asked particularly if I would like to call.

I was vastly relieved. I had wanted more than anything to see Ellen again, but was acutely conscious that I had been the indirect cause of her father's death. Although it had been Ellen herself who had run away to raise the alarm, I was not sure what her reception of me might be, especially as I now owned Glen Clair, or would do when all the legal niceties were completed. My father, as I had once suspected, had made the property over to Uncle Ebeneezer for his lifetime only, on the understanding that he would hold it in trust for me.

On my marriage, of course, all my meagre fortune had become Neil's, but Lady Strathconan had told me that Neil and his uncle had argued over Glen Clair, with

Neil insisting it should remain mine as it was my dowry and should become my jointure, and his uncle calling him an indulgent fool. I was grateful for Neil's generosity in this, though sorry to be the cause of further discord with his uncle.

Anyway, I begged the use of the carriage from Lady Strathconan, and planned to visit Ellen the very afternoon that her letter arrived.

'Would you like to call with me, ma'am?' I asked. 'I know that Ellen is sincerely fond of you, and has always spoken of you with the greatest affection.'

Lady Strathconan had turned away from me, and now she shook her head. 'No, my dear,' she said, smiling gently at me. 'I think it would be nice for you to have time alone with your cousin. I will call another time.'

So it was that I met up with Ellen in the pretty little house in Morningside, where Captain Langley's mother resided. It had emerged from gossip that Captain Langley was very well connected, and as a younger son of a very rich family had been allowed to marry as he pleased. This was fortunate for Ellen, who did not have a feather to fly, and although I had the impression from

Mrs Langley that she wished her youngest had chosen an heiress, she was prepared to be indulgent, given Ellen's extreme prettiness and sweet nature. There was also the matter of Ellen's connection to the Earl of Strathconan, of course.

I was given a very warm welcome indeed, Mrs Langley's sharp brown gaze itemising my clothes and my bonnet and my jewels, and registering just the slightest degree of surprise at my appearance, probably because I had not had the patience to sit long enough for Jessie to arrange my hair quite properly. At any rate, she was extremely civil, poured tea for us, and withdrew tactfully after a twenty minutes' polite chitchat so that Ellen and I might talk properly.

As soon as she had left the room Ellen leaped up and embraced me very affectionately. She was dressed in a most becoming mourning gown of lilac edged with black, and looked pale but otherwise very well. Marriage clearly suited her.

'Catriona!' she cried. 'I have been longing to see you!'

We hugged each other hard, but then she let me go and hung back all of a sudden, the colour rushing into her face. 'I hope,' she added with constraint, 'that you are not angry with me, cousin?'

I was astounded. 'How could I be angry with you?' I asked. 'It was not your fault that your father sought to rob me of my inheritance. And I am truly sorry that he died, Ellen. I would never have wished that upon him, no matter what he did.'

'You are all generosity, cousin,' Ellen said, drooping like a cut flower. I thought it was a great pity that her husband was not there to admire how pretty she looked, for he would have fallen more in love with her by the minute. 'You are more kind than I deserve.'

'Rubbish,' I said, fearing she was about to give way to a fit of the vapours. 'It was none of it your fault.'

'No, but when Papa hit you and that dreadful sailor came in to the inn parlour and carried you away to the ship I did nothing to save you!' Ellen said, wringing her hands pitifully. 'And then there was Neil—I saw them knock him out and carry him off, too! Five to one, the fight was!'

'Five to one!' I said. It seemed Neil had not exaggerated after all.

'I was so shocked that I fainted dead away!' Ellen continued. 'When I came round we were in the gig and already jolting down the road back to Glen Clair. When I asked Papa what had happened he only growled at me and threatened to leave me at the side of the road if I persisted in questioning him. I was so distressed that I sat there and did nothing.'

'You did plenty,' I said, clasping her anxious hands in mine. She felt cold and tense, and she looked so distraught that I could not find it in my heart to be angry with her. Ellen was not like me. I would have screamed and bitten the kidnapper, and kicked his shins and made so tremendous a fuss that no one could have ignored me. But she was as delicate as Mrs Langley's bone china, and so fainting dead away had been her only real option.

'You did plenty to help,' I said again, comfortingly and only slightly untruthfully. 'You ran away to Captain Langley as soon as you could, and that was very courageous of you. You told the authorities what your father had done, which cannot have been easy for you either.'

Ellen seemed a little comforted by this, and she drew me down to sit beside her on the chintz sofa. Everything about the drawing room was chintzy and pretty, decorated in bright yellows and whites. It suited her complexion most perfectly.

'And, speaking of Captain Langley, I must congratulate you on your marriage,' I said, smiling. 'You do look very well on it.'

Ellen laughed and thanked me. She glanced at the clock. 'Robert will be home soon,' she murmured. 'We are to go to the ball at the castle tonight.'

'You move in the highest society,' I teased. 'You were wise to choose Captain Langley over Lieutenant Graham…'

'Oh…' Ellen smiled and blushed, looking even more pink and animated. 'There was never anyone for me but my own dear Robert! Lieutenant Graham was charming, but he was not the man to turn to in a crisis. He would never have exerted himself on my behalf as my dearest Robert did.'

I had to congratulate her on her perspicacity. Nine women out of ten would probably have run into Lieutenant Graham's arms, only to find that they were not strong enough to bear her weight.

'You are a dark horse, Ellen,' I said. 'I had no notion that it was Langley you preferred. And you had only met him twice!'

'Oh…' Ellen blushed deliciously. 'We wrote to one another after he had left Kinlochewe. Mrs Grant carried the letters for me, and posted them in the village. I kept it a secret from you, dearest Catriona—not because I did not trust you, but because I could not believe that anything would come of it. Had Papa found out—' She broke off. 'But when I needed help I knew there was nowhere else to turn but to my dearest Robert.' She bit her lip. 'Indeed, it was most immodest of me to throw myself on his mercy when we were barely acquainted, but I *knew* he had something of an admiration for me and might be persuaded to believe my tale. So I left the malt whisky bottle out for Papa one night, and when he was insensible with drink I crept out and up the glen and took the mail coach for Ruthven.' She shivered artistically. 'It was utterly terrifying.'

'I cannot thank you enough,' I said. 'You were very brave.'

She gave me a little smile of gratitude. 'I think I was. Robert says I was. He was horrified at what I had done.'

I could well believe it. Poor, conventional Captain Langley. No wonder he had hurried Ellen into a hasty marriage to formalise their relationship and cover up her lack of discretion. Still, he must love her very much, and it was greatly to his credit that he appreciated her worth.

'And your mama?' I said. 'How is her health these days?'

'Oh, Mama is excessively well now that she is away from Glen Clair and living with her sister in Inverness,' Ellen said. Her eyes twinkled. 'Of course she is in mourning, and cannot go out into society officially, but she plays cards and entertains the ladies of the town to tea, and they talk of fashion and play the piano, and all is so much better since she is back in society again.'

I laughed. It was good to see Ellen displaying a little backbone. I had been afraid that both she and Aunt Madeline would mourn Uncle Ebeneezer, despite the fact that he had ruled their lives harshly for so many years with his drunkenness and his petty cruelties. But I could see that both Ellen and her mother had been starved of joy for so long that now they had their freedom they were grabbing it with both hands.

Ellen checked the pot and ordered fresh tea.

'And you are Mrs Sinclair now,' she teased, 'one day to be Countess of Strathconan! How is Neil? I hope that you are both enjoying married life.'

I felt a sharp pain, as though I had tried to walk on a broken limb that had not quite healed.

'Neil is away at Lochinver,' I said, with constraint. 'I hope to see him return soon, but I am not certain...'

Ellen stirred the teapot. 'He seemed flatteringly anxious to marry you,' she said.

'Neil did the honourable thing,' I said lightly. 'Which was fortunate for me, since I could scarcely have come back from such an adventure with my reputation intact otherwise.'

Ellen lowered the tea strainer into the cup with a tiny chink. She looked at me thoughtfully with her blue, blue eyes. 'I am sure there is more to his feelings than honour,' she murmured. 'Neil always admired you, as I recall.'

The tears prickled my throat. Oh, yes, Neil admired

me. It was my tragedy that I wanted so much more from him than his admiration.

Ellen filled my teacup and passed it to me, and I stirred it fiercely, round and round, even though I had never taken sugar. The liquid splashed into the saucer, and from there on to the beautiful Indian rug.

'I'm sorry,' I said, as Ellen looked up in astonishment to see me so discomposed. 'It is simply that I feel so wretched and—' I stopped.

How to tell Ellen, so pink and excited and full of love for Robert Langley, that Neil did not care enough for me even to write? There was no other way than to spit it out baldly, and as I had never been one for prevarication I plunged straight in.

'Neil only married me out of duty,' I said. 'Oh, it is true that he desired me once, but that is scarcely a sound basis for marriage, and now that we are wed he has not been to see me in months! He left on the morning after our wedding and I have had no word from him since.' I glanced at her shocked face and carried straight on. 'Oh, Ellen, I love him so much! I loved him even when I was at Glen Clair—though I tried to dislike him when I thought he was a whisky smuggler and a criminal—and then when he saved my life in the shipwreck…' I ran out of breath, took a gulp of air and launched in again. 'But now I cannot bear to love him and know that he does not feel the same way about me! He would never have married me if he had had a free choice, and his relatives hate me and think me quite inappropriate to be the next Countess of Strathconan, and it is all a terrible disaster!'

I stopped abruptly. Ellen's eyes were as huge as saucers now, and she looked absolutely fascinated.

'Good gracious,' she said mildly. A little frown wrinkled the skin between her brows. 'But are you sure that Neil does not love you, Catriona? Men are not always very proficient in speaking of their feelings. They seem to find it difficult and even embarrassing. Men can be very strange.'

This was true, of course, and Ellen had evidently learned this already in her marriage, just as I had. We looked at one another and sighed again in unison.

'We both know,' I said, 'that Lord Strathconan expected his heir to make a great match.'

'To his cousin, Miss Anne Methven, so I hear,' Ellen said, nodding.

This was news to me, but when I thought about it I realised that it made perfect dynastic sense. No wonder Lady Methven detested me. Not only was I no heiress, and barely even a lady in her eyes, I had also cut out her daughter from her predestined role as Countess of Strathconan.

'But only think,' Ellen continued, 'that Neil has known Anne Methven all their lives. If he had wanted to marry her he would have done so long since.'

There was some logic in that. 'Very well,' I agreed reluctantly. 'Perhaps he did not wish to marry Anne. But that is the point, Ellen! Neil did not wish to marry Anne, and he did not wish to marry me—he did not wish to marry anyone. I am certain that that is why he stays away from me. Because he has realised that he does not wish to be married to me but does not have the heart to hurt me.'

'So,' Ellen said, fixing me with her bright gaze, 'what are you going to do about it?'

Chapter Eighteen

*In which Lady Strathconan shows her true colours
and Neil makes an unexpected entrance.*

Ellen was right, of course. I was not the sort of person
to sit around complaining of my fate. I had waited for
almost two long, solitary months with not a word from
Neil, and now it was time to take some action. By the
time that the carriage had rolled into the courtyard of
the house in Charlotte Square I was resolved to take the
mail coach for Lochinver and confront Neil there. I
knew that everyone would throw up their hands in

horror at my unmaidenly conduct in running off to the North West of Scotland alone on public transport, through snowdrifts and winter roads, but now that I was resolved on action I found I did not care a jot for their censure. For too long I had sat waiting and brooding, and it was not my way. If Neil's silence meant that he no longer wished to be married to me then I would force him to tell me that to my face.

Fine sentiments, perhaps, but deep down I was afraid. I did not want to see Neil's indifference to me or, worse, hear his words of repudiation. I remembered the expression on his face when he had ridden away from Applecross on the day after our wedding.

He had been glad.

I had seen it. And though I had tried to believe at the time that it was no more than the pleasure any man would take to be involved once more in the thick of the action, I knew I deceived myself. Neil had wanted to go away. There had not been enough at Applecross to make him want to stay.

I allowed the thought fully into my heart for the first time and it hurt. It hurt a lot. It was like the high spring tide racing across the flat sands at Applecross and drowning everything in its path. I felt bruised and lonely and foolish. I remembered overhearing Johnny Methven challenging Neil on his intention to marry me, and Neil telling him tersely that he knew what he was doing. Of course he had known—he had known that as a gentleman he had had to do the honourable thing.

Suddenly my pride that a Balfour was good enough to marry a Sinclair seemed childish and rather sad. I was out of my depth. I had loved Neil for his daring and his integrity and his courage, and for saving my life, and for a hundred and one other reasons that had blossomed during our time together on Taransay. And I loved him still, despite the fact that he had left me with no word for two long months. And though my pride had been childish my love for him was mature, and in its very maturity it was painful. I had ventured into marriage buoyed up by nothing more than a conviction that I was Neil's equal in every way, but of course I was not. We were unequal because I loved him and he did not love me. He had liked me, he had admired me, he had desired me, but he had not loved me, and perhaps he had now found that having a wife simply did not suit him. Perhaps he thought it easier to ignore me. Out of sight, out of mind.

Well, I was not the wife to sit by quietly and accept that fate.

I arrived back in Charlotte Square to be informed by Ramsay, the butler, that their ladyships were in the turquoise drawing room. There was no letter from Neil awaiting me on the silver tray. My spirits plummeted lower. I had absolutely no desire to join their ladyships and be the subject of Lady Strathconan's sympathy and Lady Methven's gimlet-eyed disapproval, but I supposed that I ought in courtesy to inform them that I had returned, before we all went to our rooms to prepare for whatever tedious entertainment the evening had to offer.

Ramsay had retreated discreetly behind the green baize door, and the house was quiet. There was no sound but for the chink of china in the drawing room, where Lady Methven and Lady Strathconan were obviously finishing tea. I realised that Ramsay had, in a moment of inexcusable carelessness, left the drawing room door ajar. I crossed the hall and raised my hand to push open the door. And then I heard Lady Methven's clear cut tones.

'This is a disaster, Emily! Why did Sinclair have to come back now, when our plans are only half formed? Now we will *never* be rid of that appalling chit!'

'Oh, yes, we will,' Lady Strathconan said, and I barely recognised her voice, for it was so hard and cold, and there was something genuinely terrifying in it that had fear edging down my spine. 'We *will* be rid of her, Margaret, and it will be this very night.'

They say that eavesdroppers never hear good of themselves, and certainly I had no one other than myself to blame for all that I heard after that, for I pressed my ear shamelessly to the door and listened for all that I was worth.

'Neither of them suspects anything, and the ground is already prepared,' Lady Strathconan was saying. 'It is merely a matter of bringing our plan forward.' She sounded excited, and I felt a curious tumbling, sick feeling inside as I realised that the woman I had started to think of as my friend was nothing of the sort. '*She* believes that Sinclair does not care and has not written for months,' Lady Strathconan continued. '*He* believes that she has not replied to any of his letters and has had her head turned by Tolly Gulliver.'

'It was clever of you to imply that she was out with Gulliver this afternoon,' Lady Methven conceded. Malicious amusement warmed her voice. 'Did you see Sinclair's face, Emily? To have come dashing back from the wilds of the Highlands in order to see his wife, only to hear she is in the arms of another man! No wonder he hurried off without waiting! He will be in a tremendous bad mood by the time we all arrive at the ball tonight.'

'Which is precisely how we want him to feel,' Lady Strathconan said with satisfaction. 'Since it will make him all the more inclined to believe in Catriona's infidelity.'

'There will not be much question of that when Sinclair hears of her indisposition tonight and hurries back, all concern, only to find Gulliver in her bed,' Lady Methven said.

I dug my nails into the palms of my hands very, very

hard, to prevent myself from bursting into the room and confronting the pair of them. My mind was stumbling over itself in an attempt to make sense of all I had heard.

So Neil had returned from Lochinver that very day and his aunts had turned him away, telling him I was out indulging in a dalliance with Tolly Gulliver rather than taking tea with my cousin Ellen. And now they planned to trap me in some compromising situation with Gulliver in order to persuade Neil that I was false. What a pair of old witches! Who would have thought that the high-in-the-instep Lady Methven and the sweet-as-apple-pie Lady Strathconan would act the part of procuress, like madams in a brothel? I realised that, whatever their reason for doing this, it had to be extraordinarily important to them. I had not flattered myself that either of them liked me very much, but this, I felt, went beyond mere dislike.

'Of course,' Lady Methven continued, 'divorce is unspeakably vulgar and will be a blot on the family name, but it cannot be avoided. At least the girl is not *enceinte,* which is more than could be hoped for after that embarrassingly coarse piece of behaviour when they ran off together from the wedding breakfast.' She sighed. 'I do wish that Sinclair were better able to control his physical urges. He is most intemperate.' Her voice rose, though whether because she was moving closer to me or through sheer outrage, I could not guess. 'And do you know, Emily, the morning after that vulgar fiasco at Applecross Catriona was still wearing the same gown? She looked as though she had been thoroughly—'

'Quite,' Lady Strathconan said hastily, cutting off the indubitably crude observation that Lady Methven was about to make. 'But as I say, Margaret, that is all to the good. Sinclair, fool that he is, is in love with the chit, but when he sees himself betrayed he will never want either to see or to speak with her again. It is perfect for our purposes.'

Neil in love with me?

I stood there in utter disbelief. Surely Lady Strathconan was mistaken. She had to be. And then she said, 'You should have seen his letters, Margaret.' She laughed. 'Actually, you should not, for they would have shocked you. But, believe me, they were most affecting.'

I think I almost gasped aloud, biting back my exclamation only at the last minute. I remembered that earlier on Lady Strathconan had made much of the fact that Neil thought I had not replied to his letters, and I thought that he had not sent any…I realised that he must have written, just as he had promised, and that Lady Strathconan had taken the letters and read them herself before destroying them.

My fury was so intense that I took an involuntary step back and collided with Jessie, my maid. How long she had been standing there was anyone's guess, but at least I knew she would not betray me. I raised a finger to my lips and she stared at me, round-eyed, as the door to the drawing room opened abruptly and both Lady Strathconan and Lady Methven shot out as though their skirts were on fire.

'Catriona, my dear!' Lady Strathconan said sweetly, her face wiped clean of all guile. 'I had not realised you were returned! When did you get back?'

It was then I think I *really* began to hate Lady Strathconan. Lady Methven had never made any pretence of disliking me. At least she had been honest and consistent. Lady Strathconan had betrayed my trust. Now she looked at me with soft, smiling eyes, and I wondered whether she had always been a conniving creature or whether she had changed since the days she had been governess to Ellen.

'Oh, I have been here but a moment, ma'am,' I said, matching her lie for lie. 'I was giving Jessie my instructions for this evening, and then I was going to come in to greet you both.'

Lady Strathconan looked at Jessie, who looked blankly back at her.

'I see,' Lady Strathconan said. 'Dismissed, Potts!'

Jessie looked at me.

'I will see you in my chamber in a moment, Jessie,' I said. 'Thank you.'

She nodded.

Lady Methven muttered something about being too familiar with the servants. I ignored her.

'And how did you find your cousin, Mrs Langley?' Lady Strathconan enquired, with a quelling look at her co-conspirator. No doubt she did not want Lady Methven upsetting me at such a delicate juncture in her plans. 'She is in good health, I trust?'

It was then that I think I saw into her soul, for her eyes were still smiling but behind their gentleness was a steely coldness that was deeply chilling. I knew then that it had not been because of my Aunt Madeline's indiscreet comments that Emily Strathconan had never visited Glen Clair after her marriage, but because the erstwhile governess had moved so far above her former employers that she never wanted to be reminded of where she had come from. I knew that she would never condescend to visit in Morningside because she did not want to remember the connection between herself and Ellen. And I knew that she did not wish *me* to be Countess of Strathconan in her place one day, because she was so fiercely ambitious and jealous of all she had achieved that she would never give up her prestige to a mere chit of a girl. I saw all those things in her eyes.

'Ellen is very well, I thank you, ma'am,' I said politely, 'and sends you her best regards.'

'How charming,' Lady Strathconan said, and I wondered how I could have thought her warmth anything but counterfeit before.

I waited to see if either she or Lady Methven would vouchsafe the important news to me that my husband had called whilst I was out. Naturally they did not. It did not suit their plan to do so. The anger that was already burning in me started to grow.

'I wondered,' I said, 'if there were any arrangements made for this evening, ma'am? I only ask because I fear that I feel a chill coming on, and would prefer to retire to my bed rather than go out.'

A look flashed between the two ladies. I pretended not to notice.

'I am sorry to hear you are indisposed,' Lady Strathconan said.

'Feeble,' Lady Methven snapped, though I do not know if she meant my excuse or my constitution.

'There is a ball at the castle tonight,' Lady Strathconan continued, with a glare at Lady Methven, 'but if you are unwell, dearest Catriona, it will be far, far better for you to stay here in bed.'

'Oh, indeed,' Lady Methven said, suddenly catching on. 'Far, far better.'

Well, of course I knew it would be 'far, far better' for

their plans. Although I had not heard the whole of what they intended, my guess was that they would both depart blamelessly for the ball, leaving me to my slumber, in which I would be aided by a sleeping draught. At some point a servant—my money was on the sour-faced Mackie—would usher in Tolly Gulliver, who was either being paid to be a part of this grubby conspiracy or was merely conceited enough to think I would welcome him to my bed. A short while later everyone would return home early from the ball, bringing Neil with them, full of concern for his ailing wife, who would then be found in bed with another man…. It was neat, it was simple, it was clever, and it would be the death knell for my marriage.

'I will have the footman bring up a hot brick for your bed, and I will prepare a tincture for your chill myself,' Lady Strathconan said, smiling. 'Poor, dear Catriona.'

Poor, dear Catriona indeed.

'Thank you, ma'am,' I said, with what I hoped was a proper gratitude, going along with her plans with the apparent meekness of a lamb to the slaughter.

* * *

Two hours later I heard the carriage clatter out of the cobbled courtyard on its way to the ball at the castle.

One long, tense hour after that, my bedroom door opened a crack and a flicker of candlelight appeared.

'In here, sir,' I heard Mackie whisper. 'Mrs Sinclair is waiting for you, sir.'

I heard a step, and a man's voice murmuring a word of thanks.

Mackie put the candle down on the nightstand. I lay as still as a trapped mouse, frightened even to breathe as she went out and closed the door softly behind her. There was a silence. Still I did not move. Nor did I open my eyes.

My heart was beating so hard now that I thought that the whole bed would be shaking with the force of it. This was proving far, far more difficult and more frightening than I had anticipated. My anger had carried me this far—anger, and a determination to expose the Ladies Methven and Strathconan for the evil, conniving conspirators that they were. But now I was terrified, and I was not reassured either by the cool handle of the knife in my grip or the knowledge that Jessie and Angus, the hall boy, were hiding in the wardrobe, waiting to burst out to save me as soon as I called them.

The bed gave slightly as someone sat down on it. I heard the chink of metal as the man undid his sword belt, and the thud of it as he threw it across the chair. I heard him shrugging himself out of his jacket, loosening his neckcloth, pulling his shirt over his head and finally un-buttoning his trousers. There was the slide of material on skin. Heaven help me—he was taking all his clothes off. I felt shocked and hot all over. I lay transfixed, as though I genuinely was awaiting ravishment. Then he threw back the covers and slid into the bed next to me.

He smelled of citrus and masculinity, and his skin was so warm against mine that I felt a treacherous desire to roll over into his arms.

I moved fast then, so that I was straddling his body with my knife at his throat.

'Touch me and you're dead,' I said.

'I thought that you did not approve of violence, Catriona,' Neil said, as his hand came up to catch my wrist and the knife fell from my grasp.

Chapter Nineteen

In which love conquers all.

'What are you doing here?' I demanded. 'I thought that you were at the ball, and that Tolly Gulliver would be the one creeping into my bed!'

Clearly this was not the most tactful thing to say on finding my husband in my bed rather than a conniving seducer, but then you are already aware that sometimes I have a talent for saying the wrong thing at quite the wrong time.

Neil raised one arrogant black brow. He was

leaning back, his hands behind his head, and he looked as though he was enjoying himself enormously.

'You were expecting Captain Gulliver?' he said.

'It is not what it seems,' I said hastily, as no doubt scores of errant wives had said before me.

'What it seems,' my husband said, 'is that you were not precisely welcoming him into your bed.' He turned to look at the knife, which he had safely stowed on the nightstand. 'Unless,' he added smoothly, 'you have developed a penchant for dangerous games with your lovers?'

The colour flared in my face. 'What would you care?' I countered unwisely. 'You left me alone for two whole months.'

'And now all the bucks in Edinburgh are dancing attendance on you?' Neil finished. Suddenly he rolled over and tumbled me beneath him. 'Oh, I care, Catriona,' he said roughly. His eyes were almost black with passion now. 'I care very much when the *on dit* is that my wife behaves more like a widow and flirts—and more—with Tolly Gulliver.'

'You have your aunts to thank for that gossip,' I said,

thoroughly incensed now. I did not like lying there beneath him. I felt too vulnerable. And yet in some ways I liked it very well indeed, and that annoyed me even more. 'They are the ones who have been spreading scandal and stealing your letters to me, planning to ruin me by drugging me and smuggling Captain Gulliver into my bed,' I said furiously. 'And now *you* have the audacity to turn up here and to blame *me!*' I looked around, struck by a sudden thought. 'Where *is* Captain Gulliver, anyway?'

'I detained him,' Neil said, not without satisfaction. 'We had a little chat.' He paused. 'No, that makes it sound too civilised. I asked him, with my sword at his throat, what his intentions were towards my wife. I had heard the rumours, you see.'

'Of course you had,' I said bitterly. 'I imagine your aunts made very sure of that.' I sighed. 'I suppose Captain Gulliver denied the whole business?'

'No,' Neil said. 'He sang like a nightingale. He told me that you had invited him to a secret assignation tonight. He said that you had been writing him love letters and encouraging his advances.'

'Why, the lying, deceitful, false-hearted, worthless scoundrel!' I said wrathfully.

I tried to sit up. Neil pushed me back against the pillows and settled his body more closely against mine. For all that I was fully clad beneath my voluminous nightgown, I felt as defenceless as though I were naked.

'He showed me the letters,' he said mildly.

I fell silent with shock.

'Neil,' I said desperately, 'this has all been set up to discredit me. Ask the servants if you do not believe me! They are hiding in the cupboard, ready to help me! Jessie has the very draught your aunt made up to make me sleep soundly tonight whilst Captain Gulliver was supposed to creep in. She overheard your aunts plotting, just as I did. And Ramsay can tell you what happened to all your letters and why they never reached me! And I *swear* I never wrote to Captain Gulliver, nor encouraged him in any way—' I stopped as Neil gave me his heart-shaking smile. At such close quarters it robbed me of thought, never mind speech.

'I know that you did not write those letters, Cat,' he said. 'They were riddled with spelling and grammatical errors. No schoolmaster's daughter could have written such a poor effort—unless English was not your subject, of course.'

I stared up at him. Could Lady Strathconan have made a mistake in her arrogance and pride and not written the letters herself? Had she thought such things beneath her and given the task to a servant? I had thought her too clever and too careful to make such errors, but she had also slipped up earlier that evening, when she had given Jessie the sleeping draught to deliver to me. She had come in later to see how I was, and I had made a fine pretence of feeling very drowsy, but by then her noxious potion was locked away as evidence.

'Neil—' I began again, hope sparking within me.

'Oh, my aunts were very convincing,' Neil continued. 'They planted just the right seeds of doubt in my mind. But they had not banked on my meeting your cousin Ellen early on at the ball tonight, and on her telling me how delightful it had been to see you this afternoon. That made me wonder why Lady Strathconan had been so insistent—in such a sorrowful way, of course—that you had spent the afternoon with Gulliver.' He raised his gaze to mine, and there was something in his eyes that made my heart turn over. 'But I would never have believed it of you anyway, Cat. No matter the evidence. Not in my heart of hearts. You are too honest to play me false. You might come to me and tell me to my face that you no longer wished to be married to me, but you would never deceive me.'

'Neil—' I said for a third time. I felt choked with emotion that he knew me so well, and that he had trusted me when everyone and everything had conspired to suggest I had betrayed him.

There was a confused sound of footsteps and voices on the landing outside the bedroom. Neil's hand closed on my arm in warning and I fell silent. He shifted a little, drawing me more closely into his arms in the most intimate of embraces.

'It sounds as though they have assembled half the household out there,' I whispered in Neil's ear.

'I rather think that that is the point,' Neil said grimly. 'They want everyone to be here to witness your apparent disgrace.'

'But Mackie showed you in,' I said suddenly. 'I

heard her! Surely she will tell them that it is you and not Captain Gulliver—'

'She's new,' Neil said. 'I've never met her before. I was at the appointed place at the appointed time and I told her I was Gulliver. She had no reason not to believe me.'

There was no time for more. Someone was already turning the door handle. In the middle of all the commotion I heard Lady Methven's imperious whisper.

'But where is Sinclair, Emily? He is supposed to be here!'

Lady Strathconan hushed her impatiently, and I felt Neil shake with laughter.

The room was suddenly full of candlelight and noise. I stuck my head out from under the covers, feigning shock and confusion, rubbing the sleep from my eyes.

'Lady Strathconan! Good gracious, ma'am— whatever is going on?'

Behind Lady Strathconan, Lady Methven was grinning like a gargoyle at the sight of another person in my bed, and the Earl of Strathconan himself—had he too been involved in the plot? I wondered—was puffing and muttering darkly at the back, showing quite an avid interest in proceedings for all that. I saw Mackie, tight-lipped with the virtuous pretence that she knew nothing about this, and Miss Anne Methven, with a vengeful gleam in her cold grey eyes. Jessie and Angus came tumbling out of the wardrobe to add to the general confusion. There were others there too, friends of Lady Strathconan, all the most sharp-tongued gossips in Edinburgh.

'My dear Catriona,' Lady Strathconan said, still sweet, still mild, but with her excited blue gaze riveted to the shape of a man beneath my blankets, 'we came to see if you had recovered from your indisposition, but we did not expect to see so *much*.'

She grabbed the covers and pulled them back with the flourish of a magician. Someone screamed. All the gossips in Edinburgh certainly saw a very great deal of Neil's handsome physique then. I do believe one or two of the susceptible ones fainted dead away. The others were talking about his attributes for years after.

'My dear Lady Strathconan,' Neil drawled, making no great hurry about covering himself, 'you have always shown the greatest of interest in my marital arrangements—indeed a rather unhealthy interest, if I may say so—but on this occasion I suggest that you and your minions—' he flicked a contemptuous look around the room '—retire and leave me to make love to my wife in peace.'

That cleared the room in the space of about ten seconds.

'Are you not going to confront them?' I demanded, as the last of the gossips was helped, shaking, from the room.

'Not now,' Neil said. 'Later.' He grabbed my nightgown and threw it aside. 'Good God, you are fully dressed!'

'Of course I am!' I said. 'You did not think I would run the risk of being undressed in bed with another man, did you?'

Neil laughed. 'You thought of everything, did you not, Cat? Lady Strathconan had no idea what she was taking on when she chose to cross swords with you.' He picked up the knife. 'Keep still. I need to cut your laces.'

'Neil, we must talk—' I began, but Neil shook his head and pulled me down into his arms.

'Not now,' he said, his lips an inch away from mine. 'Later.'

***

It was later—a week later, in fact—when we were walking in the gardens at Glen Clair together and finally we did talk properly. There had been much talking before that, of course. Before we had left Edinburgh, high words had been spoken between Neil and his uncle, which had led to a final rupture between them. Lord Strathconan could not break the entail and disinherit his heir, but he had cut off Neil's allowance. Now all we had was Neil's Navy pay, and whatever Glen Clair might bring in when it was set on its feet again.

But we were happy. We were ecstatically, deliriously happy to be alone together for a little while. Neil planned for me to accompany him to Lochinver when he returned there. All was perfect. Except that Neil had not told me that he loved me.

But I am getting ahead of myself.

Naturally Lady Strathconan and Lady Methven had denied any plot against me. The sleeping draught was put down to an unfortunate mix-up amongst the bottles in Lady Strathconan's cupboard. The words that Jessie and I had overheard were alleged to be all a misunderstanding. Tolly Gulliver was written off as a lovesick fool. Lady Strathconan's dramatic entrance into my chamber, accompanied by half of Edinburgh—the malicious half—was presented as no more than a touching concern to ask after my health. The missing letters, which Ramsay had told me had been delivered punctiliously to Lady Strathconan each day, along with all the rest of the mail for the household, were never found. When I discovered that Neil had sent a beautiful crimson and silver cloak as my Christmas present, and heard from the servants that it had been given away to the poor, I was almost tempted to run down to the Edinburgh stews to find it and take it back.

'Why did they do it?' I asked Neil now. 'I was not *that* unpresentable.'

Neil laughed. 'No, but you were not Anne Methven either.'

'Explain,' I said.

'I had forgotten,' Neil said, 'that there was a fund of money set up by our grandfather—Anne Methven's and mine—that could only be accessed when and if we married each other.'

I remembered what Ellen had said about it being an understood thing that Neil would one day wed his cousin. No wonder his marriage to me had thrown such a cat amongst the pigeons, and the family had decided I had to be disposed of as quickly as I had been wed.

'I suppose your family have been casting you and Anne in each other's way for ever?' I said, trying not to feel cross and jealous.

'They have,' Neil said. 'And the more they did it, the less I wished to marry Anne.' He sighed. 'It is unchivalrous of me to say it, but actually I never wanted to marry her at all. She is as cold as a snowy night on Sgurr Dhu, and less hospitable.'

I tried not to laugh. 'Poor Miss Methven,' I said. 'I think she wanted to marry you.'

'She wanted the money,' Neil said brutally. 'They all did—my uncle, his scheming wife, my aunt, her daughter…'

'Well, there is still time,' I said. 'If I were to meet with an unfortunate accident, or you were to change your mind about wishing to be wed to me—'

'You're clutching at straws,' Neil said. 'I'm not letting

you go now.' He linked his fingers through mine, warm and strong, and we walked on beside the lake. A peacock strutted across our path and gave its harsh cry.

'But you did not care about the money,' I said, 'or you would never have married me in the first place.'

He gave me a look that made the blood beat hot in my veins. 'No,' he said slowly, 'I did not want the money. I wanted you.'

The fresh snow crunched beneath out feet

'Did you ever wonder,' Neil said suddenly, glancing at me, 'what was in all those letters I sent you?'

I remembered then what Lady Strathconan had said about Neil being in love with me. I wanted to believe it. I ached to believe that he loved me as much as I loved him. But he had not told me so. Not when he had made love to me through the long, hot hours of our wedding night, not when we had been reunited so joyously in Edinburgh, nor even here and now, in the cold, clear Highland air.

'I suppose I did,' I said. My heart started to beat like a drum. 'Yes,' I said. 'Of course I wanted to know.'

He let go of my hand and walked a little away from

me. There was tension and wariness in his stance now. I saw it in his face and in the taut line of his shoulders. It reminded me of the distance that there had been between us on Taransay, when I had realised that he did not love me and did not want my love either.

'I have been very foolish,' Neil said, 'and I do not deserve you.'

For a moment I was terrified he was going to confirm all my fears and say that he could not love me, that I was too good for him, that he had betrayed me with Celeste McIntosh or one of her sisterhood, that he could never be faithful because it was not in his nature, that he could never feel for me as I felt for him. The pain blocked my throat and stole my breath. But then I saw the expression in his eyes, and for the first time there was vulnerability in his face, and a new awareness that somehow made him look older.

'When the *Cormorant* was wrecked and I thought you would die,' Neil said, his voice shaking, 'I knew then that I loved you, Catriona, but I could not accept it. I had never felt that way before.' He moved his shoulders uncomfortably, as though the weight of the emotion was still too grave to bear. 'I am not practised in love,' he said roughly. 'I do not know how to love someone. Not really. I never had the experience.'

He looked at me, and for once I was silent. I remembered the confidences we had shared on those long dark evenings on Taransay; the tales of his loveless childhood. I held my tongue.

'I thought about what it would be like to lose you, and the feelings so terrified me that I could not face them,' Neil continued. 'I thought that if I backed away, if I withheld something of myself from you, then all would be well. I had done it before with women.' He grimaced. 'It does not seem right to talk to you of them, as though it cheapens what we have—'

'Never mind that,' I said, as impatient as always. 'Get to the point.' Hope was rising in me like mercury in a barometer. I never could hold my peace for long.

But Neil was not to be hurried now that he had decided to speak.

'Women always wanted something from me,' he said, 'and I always held back from giving it to them. I thought that I could do the same with you.' He looked at me.

'But I could not. When we spoke each night by the fire in our little white cottage I ached to make love to you. You know that. But I ached to *love* you as well, and as we grew closer so it became more and more difficult for me to keep my feelings at bay. I told myself that what I felt for you was lust, and when I faced the need to marry you to save your reputation I told myself—and everyone else—that I was only doing it out of honour. I was stupid and cruel and arrogant in my attempts to protect myself.'

I did not contradict him. I had suffered quite a lot on account of my love for him, and it seemed fair that he should suffer a little too before I told him how much I loved him.

'Then we were married and I made love to you at last,' Neil said. 'It was all that I had ever secretly dreamed of, but so much more—so much that it tore down those barriers I had erected in my heart and I knew I would never be able to keep you out or pretend again. Yet still I was not ready to accept it, and I was glad when my orders arrived to take me away. You saw that, didn't you?' He looked at me. 'You saw in my face that I was glad to be leaving, and you thought it was because I did not care for you. But it was not. It was because I loved you too much, not too little, but I was too young and immature to be able to confess that.' He came back to me and drew me close to him. 'Well, I confess it now, Catriona. I confess it with all my heart. And if you love me too—'

I stood up on tiptoe then, and stopped his words with a kiss. It would have been pleasant to make him confess his love for me over again a few times more, but I am a generous person, and could not stand to see his unhappiness any more. Besides, I wished to kiss him, and for him to kiss me back, which he did with very satisfactory ardour.

'I do love you,' I whispered against his lips. 'I have loved you for a very long time, even when I believed that you did not want my love.'

He caught my hand and we ran towards the house. He swung me up into his arms to carry me over the threshold, then did not put me down until we had reached the top of the stairs and the privacy of the little room that had been mine from the first time I had come to Glen

Clair. He tossed me into the middle of the bed and followed me down, and the poor bed creaked in protest.

'Be careful,' I said, as his fingers started to unfasten the buttons of my bodice, 'for I do not think this bedframe can take too much strain.'

'I will be as gentle as I can,' he promised.

His fingers were shaking, and his breath hitched in his throat as I reached up to kiss him again, and then we were tearing each other's clothes off, both gasping as we lay hot skin against hot skin. He pressed his face to my hair and called me his darling, and told me he loved me again and again, as he took me with a fierce passion that did, I am afraid, break my poor little wooden bed.

'Perhaps,' I said later, as we lay on the floor in a tumble of blankets. 'I can stay here in future when you go back to the sea.' I propped myself up on one elbow and ran my hand down Neil's bare chest. 'And you may visit me when you can, as though I am your mistress, for that is what you wanted of me when you first met me.'

He laughed and trapped my fingers within his. 'From

the moment I first saw you I wanted you,' he said. 'But now I want you as my wife and my mistress and my love, Catriona. And I want you to be with me wherever I go.'

After I had kissed him, to demonstrate my approval of his words, we lay in dreamy entanglement, my head on his shoulder, my hair spread across his chest as he played with the strands.

'Of course,' I said slyly, looking up at him, 'I understand that really you only wanted to marry me to get your hands on Glen Clair, because you knew that it could turn a tidy profit if it were not so neglected…'

He rolled me over beneath him and trapped my squirming body with his own, hard on mine. 'I am restoring Glen Clair because I love it and I love you,' he said. He took my face in his hands and held me still for his kiss. 'No matter where we travel, he said, 'this will be home for us, and for our children, and for our children's children.'

And so it was.

* * * * *

Read all about it...

MORE ABOUT THIS BOOK

2   The story behind *Kidnapped*

4   Nicola Cornick's Scottish Diary

MORE ABOUT THE AUTHOR

8   Author biography

10   A day in the life

WE RECOMMEND

13   If you enjoyed *Kidnapped* we know you'll love…

Read all about it...

EXTRACT FROM AN INTERVIEW ABOUT *KIDNAPPED* FROM THE RISKY REGENCIES BLOG

Kidnapped is inspired by all the places I love to visit in Wester Ross in the Highlands of Scotland. The village of Applecross, which is Catriona Balfour's home at the start of the book, is a very special place, accessed by only two roads, one of which is a high mountain pass with views across the sea to the Outer Hebrides. The Gaelic name for the Applecross Peninsula is 'a Chomraich', which means 'The Sanctuary.' The site of the old abbey at Applecross, built in AD 673 by the Irish saint Maelrubha, still has one of the most peaceful and inspiring atmospheres that I have ever experienced.

Further along the coast is Sheildaig, a village that was built originally to raise and train sailors to fight in the Napoleonic Wars. Grants were given for boats and £2,700 was spent building the three main streets, which these days are neat and whitewashed and very pretty. From there the road turns inland between the high mountains of Torridon and this is the route that Catriona takes in my story as she travels to her new home in Glen Clair. The old house at Glen Clair is another place inspired by a real location – the Coulin Estate. In a spectacularly beautiful setting in the mountains, Coulin is somewhere we return to year after year. It was in the ownership of the MacKenzie family of Gairloch from the sixteenth century and in the Regency period the tenants suffered eviction in order to make way for sheep farming. This was of course the fate of many Highland families during the eighteenth and nineteenth centuries. These "Highland Clearances" forced many families to the coast, the Scottish Lowlands and abroad to

"... In a spectacularly beautiful setting in the mountains, Coulin is somewhere we return to year after year..."

Read all about it...

countries including Australia and Canada.

At Glen Clair my heroine Catriona becomes embroiled in the illegal whisky distilling business! There were many illegal stills hidden in the mountains, in caves that were away from the prying eyes of the excise men and in remote glens. The euphemistically named "teahouse" at Coulin really did provide illegal refreshment for drovers crossing the mountains and it is still there, though these days it is used as a mountain bothy rather than a place offering alcoholic beverages! Just as smuggling was condoned or even encouraged by many of the gentry in England, so many of the Scots would turn a blind eye to what was going on. Ministers of the church were even known to hide the whisky in coffins to deceive the excise men!

For more from Nicola, visit http://riskyregencies. blogspot.com or http://www.nicolacornick.co.uk

Further Reading:

The Scottish Nation 1700–2000 by T M Devine

A Maritime History of Scotland by Eric J Graham

Morningside by Charles J Smith

A Tour of Scotland 1769 by Thomas Pennant

A Description of the Western Isles of Scotland by Donald Monro

NICOLA'S SCOTTISH DIARY

Saturday – Two days after leaving home we are on the Road to the Isles. It is a beautiful sunny day. The mountains look sharp and dark against the clear blue of the sky. The sunshine is the pale silver of late summer. We stop in Fort William, where a band of kilted pipers are playing in the open air.

Monty the Labrador, who has sulked during the long drive north, becomes very excited as we drive over the top of the hills and down the track to the little cottage by the loch. He discovers his inner puppy and runs around madly, jumping in and out of the river.

The first night is very stormy. The wind roars in the Scots pines and the rain lashes the roof, but it is snug inside.

" . . . Monty the Labrador . . . discovers his inner puppy and runs around madly, jumping in and out of the river . . . "

Sunday – Our first day, and it is straight on with the full wet-weather gear to walk the dog. In the process I discover that my waterproof coat and trousers aren't waterproof at all. Let's hope the weather improves. Weather watching can be a full-time activity here. The cloud formations change every minute. One moment they are obscuring the tops of the mountains and the next the sun is streaming through the gaps like a spotlight.

Despite the rain we decide to walk around the loch in the afternoon. It is seriously wet – great drifts of mist are blowing across the water and drenching us. Monty looks very sleek and is as soft as a mountain-spring-washed dog can be. The water is thundering down the heathery hillsides and into the loch. Every so often the clouds lift to give a hint of sun and a sparkle on the water before the rain comes across again like a grey curtain.

Read all about it...

Eventually the rain stops and the sun comes out. So do the midges. Fortunately we have remembered to bring the repellent spray. Never has there been so effective and hideously smelly a concoction. The midges fly towards us and then veer violently away. Success!

Monday – We walk to the lookout seat on Lake Clair this afternoon. The water in the ford is too high to walk across, so we take our boots off and wade. It was very refreshing (cold). It isn't warm enough to swim in the loch today, but tomorrow is supposed to be a lovely day.

The red deer arrive at twilight. Several of them come into the garden and crop the lawn. There is a fine young stag and some beautiful fawns. We wake in the night to find the moon pouring down and one of the deer right outside our window. It is magical. They are still there at dawn.

"... We wake in the night to find the moon pouring down and one of the deer right outside our window...."

Tuesday – It is a beautiful day. I take a dip in the river. The water is peaty brown, incredibly clear and icy cold. After about a minute I hop out again, unable to breathe!

In the afternoon we climb a mountain called Sgurr Dubh, which is pronounced Skoo Doo. There is an excellent path for some of the way and once it is finished we struggle on to the top. We are coming up to the final ridge when six deer pop their heads up for a look at us. They seem more curious than nervous and stare at us for a long time, no doubt wondering what on earth we are doing there, before running off up the hillside. Running. Uphill. Finally I drag myself to the top. It is a lovely grassy peak and the views are tremendous.

Wednesday – After such an active day yesterday we decide to take it easy today and sit reading in the sunshine and walking by the loch.

Thursday – It is another lovely sunny day today. We go to Diabeig and walk around the bay. We find a lovely pebbly beach that we have all to ourselves and eat our lunch under a rowan tree. Have afternoon tea on the strand at the end of the walk back and sit in the sunshine. I even paddle in the sea! Wonderful day.

Friday – This morning we see a golden eagle, our first of the holiday. It glides over the cottage, huge, powerful, the sun dazzling on the gold of its head. Today we decided to climb another mountain. There are some stunning views on the way up and from the top you can see the whole of the Letterewe wilderness stretching away with no roads, no people, no civilisation. A very windy, wet and stormy night follows.

Saturday – This afternoon we went to Victoria Falls. Not the more famous waterfall of that name but the one named after Queen Victoria's visit to the area in 1877. She stayed at the Loch Maree Hotel, which is still there today. She commented in her diary how beautiful the scenery was but that nobody much lived here. We have our afternoon tea by Loch Maree, which has apparently been voted one of the three most beautiful lochs in Scotland. How do you choose?

Sunday – We climb Beinn Eighe. According to Wainwright, this is a mountain for heroes. There are spectacular views from the top. It is amazing to be as high or higher than everything else round about, and incredibly beautiful. This is the highest mountain I have ever climbed and it feels like a great achievement as well as providing stunning views. The weather has been wonderful all this week. Hot and sunny – can this really be Scotland? The holiday jigsaws remain untouched!

Read all about it...

Monday – Today we go to Gairloch and to the beach at Red Point. In the harbour we see porpoises, seals and otters! It was another fantastic sunny day and we paddle in the sea and look at the view across to Skye and the Outer Hebrides. It is getting colder at night now. The skies are very clear and the Milky Way very beautiful. Each morning there is a mist over the loch and then the sun comes up and it vanishes slowly. Today is a cloudless blue sky – just right for eagles and for swimming in the river.

Tuesday – We drive over the 2053 mountain pass called the Bealach na Ba, Pass of the Cattle, a famous, twisting road, and eat fish and chips at Applecross, looking over to Skye. We see an otter and a basking shark in the harbour. What a fabulous ten days and a wonderful holiday!

Read all about it...

AUTHOR BIOGRAPHY

Nicola was born in Yorkshire and spent the first eighteen years of her life there. She credits these early years with having a formative effect on her writer's imagination in several ways. Firstly she went to school in an historic house – Gateways High School, the eighteenth-century dower house that once belonged to the Earls of Harewood. In such auspicious surroundings her love of history and writing flourished, encouraged by some wonderful teachers. She also spent hours walking on the moors that inspired the Brontës and devoured a diet of costume dramas and historical novels. It was also during this time that she developed a love of choral music and sang with various choirs that toured the UK and Europe.

When she was eighteen Nicola went to London University, where she studied Medieval History and met her future husband. It was also at this time that Nicola began her first book, which, fourteen years later, was to be published as *True Colours*.

After graduation, Nicola returned to Yorkshire and took a post working at Leeds University organising student scholarships. Over the next fifteen years she was to develop her career in university administration, and worked in various educational institutions, organising examinations and degree ceremonies, arranging open days and managing a team of staff providing pastoral support to students. She worked for the Department for Education in the South West for three years, organising the provision of funding for short courses for adult learners. This job necessitated a move to Somerset, where her home was a seventeenth-century cottage haunted by the ghost of a cavalier.

It was during this time that Nicola and her husband travelled widely and her fondest memories include lying in the snow to watch the Northern Lights in Norway, taking a balloon over an African game reserve, swimming in hot spa springs in Iceland and swinging through the rainforest canopy in Costa Rica.

Nicola has written twenty-six books for Harlequin Mills & Boon and has been a finalist for several prestigious romance awards, including a double nomination for both the Romantic Novelists' Association Romance Prize and the Romance Writers' of America RITA® Award. She lectures in creative writing and in history.

In 2006 Nicola was awarded a Master's degree with distinction in Public History at Ruskin College, Oxford for her dissertation on hero myths and celebrity. She is currently researching the history of the National Trust property Ashdown House, in Oxfordshire, where she works as a guide. Her other interests are wildlife and conservation, music and reading.

Read all about it...

A DAY IN THE LIFE

The cats – Bob and Petra – wake me up at 6.00am demanding that I let them into the bedroom. I know that if I ignore them they'll rip the carpet to shreds so it's easier to stumble out of bed, still with my eyes closed, and open the door. Once we're all in the bedroom it's a four-way fight for the duvet between Bob, Petra, my husband and me. I lose. I am just drifting off to sleep again on my remaining square centimetre of bed when the alarm goes off. I push my husband several times until he gets up to make our morning tea, at which point the cats move onto his side of the bed, the dog comes up to join them and I shiver under my tiny bit of duvet.

If it's my turn to take the dog out for a walk I will go out early. I love walking on the hills whilst the sun is rising and the dew is still fresh on the grass. My best writing ideas come to me when I am out in the open air. Out on the Downs, walking along the Ridgeway, I can actually *feel* the layers of history beneath my feet and the presence of it all around me. There is something so refreshing and inspirational for me in being outside. Sometimes when I am in the house I feel too confined. If I am stuck on a point of plot or uncertain which direction my characters are going to take, I'll put on my walking boots and set off for the hills. Our dog gets plenty of walks! Sometimes I think he'd rather lie on the couch, fast asleep, but he never refuses to come with me.

When I get back at about 9.00am I'll make a cup of tea and settle down to my writing. My office has big windows looking out over our garden and the fields beyond. This is a problem because the view is so wonderful and frequently distracts me. In the summer I have the long windows open so that it is almost working outside. I write directly onto the computer, although I make notes in longhand in lots of big notebooks. Sometimes the writing is quick and easy, flowing so smoothly that I can't bear to stop and resent any interruption or other demand on my time. At other times it feels leaden and seems to take forever just to get the words down on the page. But it's important to persist because I can improve on bad writing whereas I can't improve on a blank page. I always find a cup of tea in hand helps too! Occasionally I will look at the clock and realise that for fifteen years I worked nine to five in an office and although I miss the people I worked with, I would far rather be an author. Then I feel very fortunate.

If it's my day to work for the National Trust at Ashdown House I will go out after lunch and spend several hours there guiding visitors around the house and gardens. I love Ashdown with a deep passion and enjoy sharing it with other people and showing them what a fascinating place it is. It's a seventeenth-century hunting lodge with an extremely romantic history and I am busy researching the estate at the moment in order to write a book about it one day. Working in an historic house is another huge inspiration for me. Sometimes I just stand on the stairs and inhale the fabric of history that is all around me. To me, history isn't just something that's in the past. It's tangible in the present, all around us, influencing what we do and how we think. I love to try and capture that feeling in my writing and make my historical stories come alive.

My husband usually cooks dinner for us. He enjoys cooking and is great at it so there's no point in me slaving away in the kitchen to produce a vastly inferior meal. I always do the washing up, though! In the evening I'll often go

"...My best writing ideas come to me when I am out in the open air..."

"... To me, history isn't just something that's in the past. It's tangible in the present, all around us, influencing what we do and how we think. ..."

back to my writing again, re-read what I wrote that morning, decide it isn't too bad and add a few more pages before bedtime. If I'm not writing, then I'll be reading, either for pleasure or for research. I love historical non-fiction, but I always have to read with a paper and pen at my elbow so that I can jot down story ideas that come to me. Occasionally we'll go out to the theatre or cinema, but my husband says I am the worst sort of person to see a film with because I will always be analysing the plot and the structure as I go along and will make whispered comments that put him off the story. It's hard not to do that as a writer. The books and films that I admire the most are the ones that are so good I forget to analyse and just sit back and enjoy.

At about 8.00pm I will have my final cup of tea of the day and then I take the dog out for his bedtime stroll around the fields behind our house. It's very peaceful and I will take in the view and unwind after the day. Sometimes we will see a barn owl hunting over the fields, or watch the moon rise over the hills and the stars come out. I need my eight hours sleep a night, so by ten o'clock I am usually curled up in bed with a good book – what could be better?

Read all about it...

If you enjoyed *Kidnapped*, we know you'll love these great reads.

From the sparkling ballrooms of Regency London to the wealthy glamour of the country house – let Stephanie Laurens be your guide!

Tangled Reins

Miss Dorothea Darent is making her debut in London society. She may not be hunting a husband, but the rakish Marquis of Hazelmere has her in his sights!

Fair Juno

The scandalous Earl of Merton never expected to be captured by an innocent – but now he must find the lady he knows to be his destiny.

Four in Hand

Society was stunned when the Duke of Twyford introduced four beautiful debutantes to the *ton*. But one by one, the most confirmed bachelors fell at the feet of the Twinning sisters. And the Duke knew that he couldn't long escape his fate – marriage to Miss Caroline Twinning!

Impetuous Innocent

Miss Georgiana Hartley thought her only hope lay in a suitable position as a lady's companion or a governess, until she met Viscount Alton. He only meant to oversee Georgiana's launch into the *ton* – until the viscount realised that he wanted Georgiana for his own!

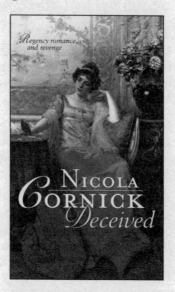

He could marry her –
or ruin her!

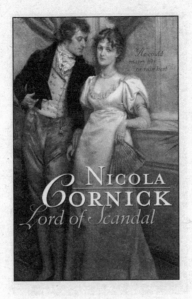

London, 1814

Scandalous and seductive, Hawksmoor is a notorious
fortune hunter. Now he has tasted the woman
of his dreams, Catherine Fenton, and he will
do anything to make her his.

Though heiress to a fortune, Catherine is trapped
in a gilded cage and bound to a man she detests. She
senses there is more to Ben, Lord Hawksmoor, behind
the glittering façade. She believes he can rescue her –
but has she found herself a hero, or made a pact
with the devil himself?

M&B

To unmask her secrets, he will have to unlock her heart!

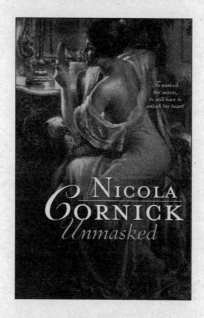

Wickedly handsome Nick Falconer has been
sent to stop a gang of highwaywomen.
But the woman he suspects of leading them
is intoxicatingly beautiful and Nick sets
out to seduce her.

Mari Osbourne's secrets are deeper and
darker than Nick could ever imagine.
Will trusting the one man she wants lead
Mari to the hangman's noose?

www.millsandboon.co.uk